BLINK AND WE'LL MISS IT

GINNY KOCHIS

For the real Dr. Hilary Towers.
This book would not exist without you.

attempt number seven. why do i do this to myself?

Lowell-Howard Precollege Writers Program

Prompt: The Keith College Lowell-Howard Fellowship celebrates writers across a wide variety of disciplines and genres. To that end, please provide a **new** composition on any topic within your preferred genre. Do not submit previously written work. Word Limit: Between two thousand and ten thousand words

Title?

The Neuse River was wide, so wide I had to squint to see the shore directly opposite. It was a real shore, broad with sand like brown sugar. "She has tides, you know," my grandmother said, holding my hand at the top of the steep hill leading down to the water, where crests of white foam pounded against the shoreline. The Neuse was a roaring vessel wrapped in cliffs and tall pines on its way to the Atlantic Ocean.

It reminded me of my mother, to be honest.

I'd tried to explain to her boss at the gallery that Mom's talent could swallow her whole. That I could take care of myself; that I'd been taking care of both of us for just about forever.

Ana was not convinced.

inviting questions probably a bad idea

She called the police and Mom's emergency contact, a woman I'd never heard of named Lil. And while I'd woken up that morning the only child of an orphaned single mother, I went to bed the granddaughter of Luther and Dora Bell Griffin. This was the first time my mother lied to me.

I had grandparents. Who knew? ⟶ *just focus on the grands?*

Luther and Dora Bell Griffin earned temporary custody and moved me to Minnesott Beach. It was a tiny little town on the banks of the Neuse River, where I was now standing, feeling alone.

Dora Bell squeezed my hand and led me up the hill from the river, back to a three-story house. I scarfed down a sticky-sweet pecan roll and listened, cheeks full, to my grandfather. "DB and I have an appointment in New Bern. Nathan Cartwright—"

focus on Nathan's character

"Mr. Nathan," my grandmother said, interrupting.

"Mr. Nathan, our groundskeeper, will be here if you need something."

Secretly, I was glad about this. Mr. Nathan had a kind smile and blue eyes. Yesterday, he'd helped me from the car and introduced me to the barn cats. He even shared the *push-in, then turn* secret to opening the sticky back door.

I hadn't seen Mr. Nathan yet that morning, so I headed for the upstairs porch. I could see pretty far if I craned my neck, trailing my eyes up the street past beach cottages, permanent homes, and a trio of condo buildings plopped along the waterfront. The ferry was just beyond, the closest river crossing for vehicles. Driving a car onto a boat and taking that across the water seemed way more exciting than a bridge.

A flash of white caught my peripheral vision. I turned my head to the left. There was a house there, an old farmhouse, maybe? Morning sun fell across the yard and the old woman standing in it, pinning laundry to a clothesline. She stilled, then turned in my direction.

The hair on my arms stood up.

cliche?

I fell back against the wall of the house, curiosity burning. She'd looked at me like she knew I was there. My imagination took off. Was she a witch? A pirate?

Suddenly, I wanted to know.

I ran down the stairs and through the back door, across the lawn to where the boathouse stood open. A rusty bike leaned against the wall.

"You sure you're okay taking off on that thing?" It was Mr. Nathan. Startled, I gave a sharp nod.

He pulled a blue and yellow can from a cabinet behind me, spraying its contents on the rusted metal. "Little WD-40 ought to do the trick," he said, then reached for the kickstand. It squealed but slid right up.

dramatic much?

The wind tore through my hair as I streamed up the main street, not a single car in sight. I breezed past the ferry dock and bumped my way across the road, coasting through the front yard of the farmhouse. Magnolia branches swayed in the breeze off the river, mirroring the linens on the line. The woman wasn't there, but the sound of her voice carried through the open doorway, a sullen alto harmonizing with the wind.

The world tilted. Colors shifted and changed. Twilight replaced the once-vibrant sun, and the front porch where I stood was gone, pitching me forward into the darkness. I ended up on my hands and knees in the grass.

unintentional repetition – grass

A small creek burbled ahead of me. A young couple sat nearby on the grass. They leaned into each other and laughed, a sound barely distinguishable from the creek's current.

"Lila Mae Griffin. I wondered how long you'd be."

The world snapped back into place. Back to the sun, back to the farmhouse steps and the old woman I'd seen hanging laundry, standing next to me now at the bottom of the steps. Woozy, I grabbed the porch railing for support and tried to breathe through the wave of nausea.

What the heck had just happened, and who was this woman? Why was she smiling at me?

"I know your Mama," she said, leaning closer. "Nice to meet you. My name's Lil."

Lil. "Ana called you," I said. "She called you when Mom didn't come home."

"She did," Lil nodded. "And I called Luther, your grandfather. Of course, the cranky pants hasn't given me so much as an update." Her eyes softened and she lifted a hand toward me. "I'm sorry about what happened. Is your mama doing okay?"

Heat climbed my neck. It had nothing to do with the sunshine. She knew my Mom wasn't okay. *choppy*

"I have to go," I said, grabbing hold of the bike with shaky fingers.

I didn't look back.
I didn't know it was the beginning.
I didn't know it would all be my fault.

Reasons to trash this:
too personal
throws mom under the bus
makes me look like a weirdo
No structure, No point

ONE

Yesterday, at around three in the morning, I found my mother unresponsive on her bathroom floor. I'm a hero, they say, because I saved her from a lithium overdose.

I'm not a hero. This is all my fault.

"It's a good thing I looked up when I did, Mae," Ms. Robins says. "I never would have seen you walk out."

"That was kind of the point," I grouse, and she barks a laugh that in another life, I would have appreciated. But I don't live in a life like that.

I live in a world where Ms. Natalie Robins is my social worker, where she's assigned to me because my mother's a nut. We met three days ago after Mom's run-in with the Virginia Beach police department. Ms. Robins is less professional, more human-looking today than she has been previously, ditching the starchy pantsuits and heels for a pair of wide-leg pants and driving moccasins.

"Tired?" she asks, and I nod because I'm supposed to.

Also because it's the truth. Ms. Robins drove me up to the hospital at eight this morning, where I spent the next several hours at my sleeping mother's bedside cataloging the clues I ignored. I didn't wake Mom up. What would I have said to her, anyway?

I'm sorry I didn't notice?

Making friends again was the worst idea I've ever had?

My frustration with my mother hasn't waned because she's in the hospital. I'm just as resentful as I was before the overdose, when I drove her to it with my harsh, unfeeling words. So I just sat in her room and made constellations with the dots on the ceiling tiles. Then I stood and walked out, hiding my eyes from the gaze of the charge nurse. I slipped from the lobby like a ghost.

Not a talented ghost, apparently, since Ms. Robins caught me in the hall. Now she's driving me home in her white, county-owned sedan while I keep mental track of the street signs.

I'm up to twenty-six so far.

"I know the past few days have been difficult," Ms. Robins murmurs, "but we should talk about what's next."

I sink lower in my seat. "She'll come home when she gets better. That's what always happens." And we'll fall back into our Richmond routine.

Ms. Robins is quiet for a moment, her hands on the steering wheel at ten and two. "When you were at the hospital, Mae, did you speak with Dr. Fleischer?"

"His patient's in the hospital because of me, so no."

Ms. Robins sighs. "You love your mother, Mae. That

much is clear, and it's beautiful. But you're the child here, not the parent."

I haven't been a child since preschool, but she doesn't need to hear me say that. I focus on the practical. "I turn eighteen in six months."

Ms. Robins does that thing adults do when they're irritated but trying to hide it, breathing out long and low through pursed lips. Her index finger goes up, and I bet if we weren't driving she'd be wagging it at me. "In *six months*, yes. Until then, you are a minor whose custodial parent ingested a lethal amount of lithium, for which she does not currently maintain a prescription, *after* quitting her prescribed medication, *after* hiding that from you and her doctors, *after* carting you off on a manic episode where the two of you lived out of your car. And *do not* get me started about the run-in she had with the Virginia Beach Police Department."

I jam my feet into the floorboard, desperate for purchase. "I defused the situation."

She takes a corner too fast and I smirk.

"You are incredibly stubborn." The smirk slides off my face. "You know this thing with your mom's not a blip? This is a big deal. An *overdose*."

I know. I really do. But it's also a disaster of my own making, something I have to fix on my own. The weight is back, that crushing sense of foreboding I've felt since Malik's party last Friday. "I could have stopped it if I'd been paying attention," I whisper.

"You are not responsible for your mother's choices." Frustrated, Ms. Robins slams on the brake. The intersection's clear but she doesn't move, trapping us in a thick, stony silence. Unfit parent means foster care or a group home. If I can't convince Ms. Robins otherwise, I'm staring down a loaded gun.

Ms. Robins moves the car forward, finally. "What about the Lowell-Howard Fellowship?"

I dig my nails into thighs, the physical pain preferable to the ache of losing my dream school. "How do you know about that?"

My tone is sharp but it doesn't phase her. "I know because it's important to you," she says.

"It's not important to me," I say, pulling my arms tight around my middle.

At least it's not important to me now.

Ms. Robins pulls the car in front of my bungalow, a cozy, one-story cottage in Richmond's Carytown neighborhood. A navy blue pickup sits in the drive, the big, burly kind that could haul tanks if necessary. The plate's numbers and letters are red, stamped across a blue image of the Wright Brother's biplane.

North Carolina.

First in Flight.

I burst from the car and trip up the sidewalk, so angry I can hardly breathe. That monstrosity's Nathan's truck. I knew he was in town. I heard his voice in the house right before I found my mother. If he's here, still, there's only one reason. I call over my shoulder. "I'm not going to Minnesott, Ms. Robins."

Her hand smacks against the storm door just as I reach it. "You don't have a choice," she pants.

"State guidelines disagree."

"They are *guidelines*," she bites out. "The upper limit is seventy-two hours without adult supervision."

"Come check on me," I beg. "Twice a week and we'll be golden."

"Mae. You have to *live* with an adult."

"Come check on me," I beg. "Twice a week and we'll be golden."

"Mae. You have to *live* with an adult."

I resist the urge to tear my hair out and stomp my foot like a child instead. "I *do* live with an adult. An adult who needs me."

An adult who I let down.

Heat pricks at my eyes. I won't cry on my front doorstep. Ms. Robins softens her tone. "Taking care of your mother is not your job."

"Lady's right, you know."

Ms. Robins and I both startle. Tall and sun-drenched, Nathan slips through the backyard gate. Even if his truck weren't here, I'd know it was him from the voice and that ratty Neuse River Bait and Tackle cap he's worn forever. He smiles at me, eyes crinkling at the corners. He's aged like my mother has. "You get into that Fellowship yet?" he asks, and I bristle at the familiarity.

I want to punch him and throw my arms around his neck.

Ms. Robins holds out a hand to Nathan. "Mr. Cartwright?"

He nods and tips the bill of his cap. "Nice to meet you,"

he drawls. "Call me Nathan. Mr. Luther asked me to come fetch Mae."

Ms. Robins smiles in a rare show of approval. No one's immune to Minnesott Beach charms. "I'll need your driver's license and the notarized letter from Luther Griffin, please," she says, still smiling as Nathan pulls his ID from a weathered canvas wallet.

"Nathan," I snap.

He jerks like I've stung him. "You were here, two nights ago," I say. "I heard you talking to Mom. Right before I found her."

Nathan gives a slow shake of his head, brows furrowed. "No, kid. I just got here. Drove straight up this morning."

"Hold on a minute, Mae." Ms. Robins's voice is unyielding. "The police questioned you at length. *I* questioned you at length. Not once did you mention additional people at the residence."

My gaze stays fixed on Nathan. "Guess it just didn't come up."

Ms. Robins huffs, exasperated. "Mr. Cartwright, have you been inside this home at any point during the last week?"

Wide-eyed, Nathan shakes his head. "No, ma'am. But I understand wanting to verify and I'm happy to help you." Nathan pulls out his phone and hands it to her, open to my grandfather's contact information. "Mr. Luther can vouch for me. I've been in Pamlico all week."

Ms. Robins takes the phone from him just as mine rings in my bag. "You don't have to call," I say, stepping aside with shaking fingers. I have to swipe three times to answer my phone. "Pa," I say, then cough to cover up the way my voice trembled.

"Lila Mae," he says, his tone business-like as ever. "You 'bout packed and ready to go?"

"No, sir." My gut churns. "Nathan…"

"Young lady, Nathan what?"

"Sorry," I breathe. Pa's not super patient. I pace in a tiny circle. "I was going to say Nathan is here."

"Made good time," he says. "Left the house 'round eight o'clock this morning."

It's warm in the sun, but a sudden, unwelcome chill skates up my arms to my shoulders, lodging itself at the back of my neck. I know what I heard. I heard Nathan talking to my mother. And if he wasn't in the house—

My mind drops to a summer afternoon, to a new place without my mother. To the moment reality first shifted on a dime. If Nathan wasn't in the house, there is only one, uncomfortable explanation.

Dear God, don't let it be that.

"Lila Mae?"

"Yeah," I breathe.

"You mean yes, sir?" There's humor in his voice, but I don't respond. Pa continues, unbothered, apparently, by my silence. "We'll see you in a few hours."

And because no one says no to Luther Griffin, I turn and do what I'm told.

TWO

"Four days, Mae," Mom shouts against the wind and the gull cries. "Four days, and it's our best sunrise yet!"

Heaving a huge sigh, I hike up the hem of my skirt and steel myself against the blue-green surf of the Atlantic. Memorial Day weekend might mark the unofficial start of summer, but this is Virginia. Late May means the water is still cold.

"It's beautiful," she says, tilting her head as I wade up beside her. "Aren't you glad we took this trip?"

Glad? We've spent five nights in the car and bathed in the ocean. "Yeah," I say, careful to keep my voice even. "Definitely. It's been fun."

Waves catch my mother's skirt and swirl it. "How are you not freezing, Mom?" She's soaking wet, and even in the cast of the sun her skin is bluish. I take her hand in mine and rub it a little because her palm and fingers are cold.

Mom laughs and pulls her hand away. Hypothermia's

hilarious, I guess."It's the ocean," she shrugs. "I feel at home here."

The sad thing is, I know it's true.

I've always thought of my mother like the ocean, rolling in and out of my life like the tide. She's been physically there, dragging me across state lines and back again in search of a home for us, for her art, and for her disorder, but she hasn't always been *present*. Not when she's manic, which happens a lot.

She'll paint for days, not eating or bathing. Surviving, though, because I take care of her. And then comes the crash of waves, the strong dark eddies that drag along behind her. Until I pull her up gasping for air. She'll be Dewitt Griffin for a few weeks, loving single mom, sought-after artist, while I float on the swells secure in her presence and wait for the tide to go out.

It's all I can think about now, the years we spent like nomads, until that last summer before middle school. And it's not lost on me that we're on a manic quest, standing on the shores of the Atlantic. Each swell brings another rush of water, tugging the sand from beneath our feet.

"I have school today, you know." I blurt it out without thinking. I tense, wishing I could take it back. But she doesn't get upset. She just smiles.

"Girls' trip, Mae! It's been years since we've done one. That's what I told them when I called your absence in."

"We've never done one." She doesn't hear me, not over the roar of the park ranger's Jeep. This stretch of beach is closed, and even manic, she knows that. She grabs my hand

and tugs, nearly wrenching my arm from the socket. And then we run, up the dunes and dripping sweat and salt water when we finally reach the car.

I gulp air and lean against the window, wheezing. "Thanks for calling the school," I pant, but I know she's lying. Well, not lying, per se. More…wishful thinking? Her rational brain knows she should have done it. Her lizard brain won't let her follow through.

But I'll play along if it gets me back to Richmond. "I need WiFi. Maybe we could hit a coffee shop?" And be inside. And take a break. And let me figure out how to get home tonight instead of who knows when. Next weekend? A tight, burning sensation climbs its way up the back of my throat.

"No time." Her voice rattles in my head as she rips the driver's side door open. Eyes wide, she vibrates with energy, words falling from her mouth at top speed. "I'm booked at three different spots," she says, rambling on so fast about where and why that my brain hurts. I open the contacts on my phone and scroll through, hovering above a name I haven't tapped in ages. A gust of wind crosses the dunes, tossing my hair and bringing with it the thick scent of the ocean. I click my phone off and slide it back in my pocket.

I don't want to call Pa. Not yet.

FROM THE OUTSIDE, my mother as a manic is a tremendously beautiful creature. Her cheeks are typically flushed, her dark brown waves pulled into an artfully messy topknot, a few stray strands falling across her eyes. There's a fire in her gaze, and when she looks at you, it's breathtaking and terrifying. Like staring into the depths of a deep green pool and wondering what's underneath.

She's pulled in several different crowds today at bars and parks and shops. Our supposed last stop is Sea Glass Gallery on the ocean front. She pulls the easel from her bag when we arrive and sets it up on the sidewalk. I had to help her break it down at her last gig. She nearly tore the thing in half.

"Welcome, everyone. Welcome!" Mom says with a vibrant smile. The crowd gathered is an eclectic mix. It's big, too, and I'm still trying to figure out why no one's gone into the gallery for a check in. Most places hand out tickets for my mother's scheduled events.

Mom's midway through her introduction when my phone dings with a text.

Jane: Where are you, girl? People are talking

Me: No one misses me. Unless by people you mean you

Jane: It's me. I'm people. I'm not talking, exactly, but I am curious. Did you skip?

Yeah, right. Like I ever do anything to bring attention to myself or get in trouble.

Me: We're in Sandbridge. Visiting friends

The little dots go up and down and stop a few times before I get the reply I expected.

Jane: You have friends in Sandbridge?

Me: I don't. They're my mom's

It's mostly true. We spent a night with Mom's friend, Gemma Broaden. She owns an A-frame on the beach. That's when I thought we'd be okay, when I told Gemma I was still on board for the Fellowship she runs at Keith College. I lost that hope somewhere between rubbing the seatbelt imprint from my cheek and squeezing ocean water from my dirty underwear. I can't even think about attending a residential writing program when Mom's chasing a manic high.

Sharp voices tug at the edge of my attention and I turn my head to look. A patrol car's pulled up at the curb, a state trooper standing cross-armed beside it. She's focused on a goateed man in a summer-weight suit, jacket sleeves stretching as he flails his arms. "I have no idea who this woman is," he shouts, pointing at my mother. Realization sinks like a stone.

"This woman showed up and started some sort of...*demonstration.*" Suit guy's veins bulge in his neck. "She didn't consult me, and I never would have granted permission." He points at my mom, finger wild with rage. "Escort her off the property, please. I won't press charges if she goes willingly."

Excellent. Mom didn't bother to ask the owner if she could set up a class.

I start back toward the group riding a swell of irritation. I'm watching her cracks widen like chips in window glass. Mom hisses through her teeth. "Do you know who I am? You have my work in your little shop. I don't need your permission to present to patrons. I'm bringing you business, you piece of sh—"

"Ma'am, you'll need to step away from Mr. Gardner." The officer takes hold of Mom's arm.

"Mom!" I'm finally even with her. "Hey, Mom!"

Mom smiles wide as the anger slides off. "Everyone, meet my daughter, Lila Mae Griffin. Come on, Lima Bean, tell them what I do."

I choke, because stable Dewitt and manic Dewitt are very, very different. I turn to the officer and spot her name plate: Lt. Gutierrez. "Lieutenant Gutierrez, hi. If you'll give me a minute we'll be out of here, no problem."

"Mae, no." It's a whisper. "Mae, you have to tell them it's my job."

Mom's protests grow louder as the crowd disperses, onlookers backing away wide-eyed. At least two have their phones out and I groan, imagining the headlines:

Renowned Artist's Tantrum Goes Viral.

"Officer, she's scaring away my customers," whines Suit Guy.

Like he even had any before we showed up.

Mom hisses at him, and Lt. Gutierrez lunges for my mother. Panic tightens my throat. I fumble for my phone. Tap my contact list with trembling fingers. Scroll through the whole thing twice. Finally my finger lands on Luther Griffin, my grandfather. He picks up on the third ring. He listens, then I listen, and I put my fingers in my mouth and whistle. Everybody stops, even Lt. Gutierrez. I hold the phone out, arm trembling.

"Mom, it's for you."

———

I PULL the car in the garage around midnight. Tears stream down my mother's face. I don't know what Pa said to her, I just know she hasn't stopped crying since we left the waterfront. The pink warning slip sits on the dash, a glowing reminder that we were lucky.

Lucky my grandfather's a persuasive goat.

Mom opens her door and falls to the concrete. I abandon our bags and walk around to her side. I help her stand, and in the glow from the street lamp, I can see she's bruised and bleeding. We maneuver through the door and down the hallway. I have to support her on the way to her room.

Mom flops down on the bed and I die a little, the blood from her scraped knees seeping into the quilt. One more thing to wash. One more mess to clean up before this is over. I head into the bathroom, not sure if I picked up bandaids the last time I went to the store.

Fortunately, I find two decent size bandages and set about tending to her wounds. My phone lights up on the bed beside me. I silence it. I'd much rather be alone than have this life exposed to the world the way it was this weekend, starting with that party at Malik's.

I pull a nightshirt over mom's camisole and help her brush her teeth. When I lead her back to bed and try to pull up the covers, her arms curl around my neck.

"I'm sorry. I can't. God, Mae. I'm so sorry."

Her heart races under my cheek. Tears prick at the corner of my eyes. I'm tired. Hurting. Wishing for the time before, the old Richmond.

"It's okay, Mom," I say, because that's my job.

I lay in her arms until her breathing slows and the rhythm of her heart drops to a steady beat. I slide off the bed and tuck the covers over her, then cross the room to close the shades. The bags I've yet to unpack start mocking me from the corner. And while I'm not in the woods or even near the woods, lines from Robert Frost beat their way into my psyche.

> The woods are lovely, dark, and deep,
> But I have promises to keep,
> And miles to go before I sleep,
> And miles to go before I sleep.

You and me both, Mr. Frost.

THREE

Jane's waiting for me as I climb the steps from student parking, her hip cocked against the painted brick wall. She kind of blends in, the kelly green of her dress an exact match to the surface behind her. All she needs is a little post-production editing, *et voilà* — Paris. Maybe I should offer her a croissant.

"What's with the giggle, Mae Griffin?" She winks at me. "Getting high in the parking lot?"

I reach the heavy metal door and slam the metal bar much harder than necessary.

"Hey," she says, her tone earnest. "I was just kidding."

She's always kidding. "I know."

Jane grips my bicep and escorts me into the hallway. It's packed, humming with the collective excitement of two thousand kids nearly done for the school year. Jane's face lights up, her concern for me wiped away by the energy. I'd much rather hide from the chaos than willingly take part.

I manage to put myself mostly together by the time we get

to the junior hall. Jane stops, whirling around so that her blonde hair whips me in the face and I blink, eyes watering. "It's Evan Pollard, Mae. Act normal. Open your locker. Pretend you didn't see him. Be one hundred percent cool."

I roll my eyes because one, I *didn't* see him, and two, Jane's perception of "acting normal" is far different from mine. "He's looking at you," she whisper-yells. "Look his way, but be sneaky."

"Are we really doing this? We don't need to do this."

"He likes you, Mae. Come on."

Sure enough, Evan's eyes are on me. I didn't answer his text last night. Wasn't a good time, considering I was peeling clothes off my mom and sudsing her hair while she sobbed in the shower.

"Go talk to him. You've been ignoring him since the party at Malik's."

"I'm not ignoring him. I've been busy." Talking with police officers. Pulling my skinny-dipping mother from the Atlantic when she fancied a swim at a family beach.

Jane searches my face like she's looking for something, then frowns and takes a deep breath. "Things are…off…with your mom. I get it." She doesn't get it. "But Evan likes you. Josh told me last night. Josh said Evan asked you out."

"He did," I say, my voice cool and even. Jane tosses her hands in the air.

"Then what's the big deal? He's hot. And that mouth…" We both look his way. "I bet he's a great kisser." My cheeks burn despite the chill from the air conditioning. I've got less than five seconds before Jane—

"Oh. My. Gosh."

Okay. I had less than three seconds.

"Mae. Did you kiss him? You kissed him. At the party."

"I did not."

I did. In Malik's basement while my mother was having a breakdown a block and a half away. Not a shining moment, and exceptionally mortifying when Evan walked me home and Mom met us at the door wielding a number five brush and sporting head-to-toe Prussian blue as an accompaniment to her underwear.

Stellar first meeting, let me tell you. I'm surprised Evan still wants to talk to me at all.

Jane stifles a squeal. I slam my locker. Evan's still standing there. Still tall, still honey-blonde and sun-kissed like he spends his spare time surfing.

It's Richmond. He doesn't.

But there are no butterflies there, no feeling of excitement.

I'm surrounded but utterly alone.

———

AT LUNCH, Jane finds me in the courtyard where I'm lying on a bench in the sun. I'm just about to drift off — eight hours of sleep in four days is kind of killer — when I hear her. "Mae, what's going on?"

I sit up straight and lean my elbows on the table. "I was about to take a nap."

"I mean with your mom." She's not going to relent. I can

see it in her eyes, in the you-elected-me-class-president set of her shoulders.

Which lie will I use today?

I settle on the simplest one. A girls' trip. "Every so often my mom and I take a trip…." A child squeals across the way, the sounds of her joy floating down from a neighboring playground. A young woman — a mom, I'm guessing — swoops up the toddler as she cackles with glee.

My heart aches. Last week, Mom and I were dancing in the kitchen to *Love Shack*.

Last night, I had to drag her into the house while she sobbed against my shoulder.

I kind of hate that playground kid.

Jane follows my gaze to the playground. She scoots next to me, rapping the table once to get my attention. "You are so closed off."

My laugh is empty. "Thanks for that."

"I'm not trying to be mean." Jane colors. "You're my friend, and you know how much effort it took for that to happen. It's our junior year and I'm still one of, like, three people you actually talk to. The other two are teachers so they don't count."

She's right. I don't talk to anyone really. It's just easier that way. "I talk to Evan."

"You *text* Evan. And if sneaking off into a dark corner at a party is considered talking, then maybe I'll allow it if it means you're interacting with someone. Someone other than me."

"I can't help it if I'm shy."

"You're not shy. You're difficult."

"And yet you still want to be my friend."

"Because you're lonely, you goof. And you're actually pretty cool when you're not clammed up and hiding." She scoots closer to me and slides her arm through my elbow, squeezing gently. "Something's bothering you, and I'm pretty sure it has to do with your mom. You're prickly but I love you, and I'm here if you want to talk about it."

I'm so tired. "My mom has moments where she needs a little help."

————

I DON'T NOTICE the white sedan at first when I pull mom's car into the drive. My hands drip books and papers and my broken water bottle, my concentration focused on not falling up our front steps. But the water bottle slips and rolls headlong down the driveway, stopping at the edge of the yard. That's when I see it, an institutional-looking Ford with the red county seal stamped on the side. It looks out of place on our tree-lined street where we know all our neighbors and their various vehicles. I lean over and spit a metallic taste from my mouth.

Water bottle in hand and my books still on the porch steps, I turn the knob to the house and step inside. I hear voices from the living room; my mother's a little strained, our visitor's decidedly formal. I turn the corner and stop in my tracks.

A woman I've never seen before sits on the overstuffed arm chair near the coffee table. She's dressed in a burgundy pantsuit, her dark hair pulled back in a knot. Her skin is clear, not a blemish or wrinkle on her olive complexion. A pair of wire-rimmed, circular glasses and a clipboard sit in front of her on the table. "You must be Mae," the woman says, her voice smooth and reassuring. "I'm Natalie Robins. Social worker with Henrico County Child and Family Services. I've already chatted with your mom. She's given me permission to speak with you. Is there someplace we can chat in private?"

Betrayal, sharp and heavy, cleaves its way through my spine. During sixth-period math with Mr. Riley, Jane got an office request. I raised an eyebrow at her and she waved it away, mouthing something about college stuff. Now that I'm standing in my living room with child protective services, it's pretty clear Jane lied.

I breathe in through my nose and out again, my eyes flitting to my mom.

"Mae, I know this is unexpected." Ms. Robins says. "I only need twenty minutes."

I bite down on my cheek and swallow the taste of copper. "Alright," I say in a voice I don't recognize. "What do you want to know?"

I walk Ms. Robins to the door thirty minutes later. She presses a business card in my hand. "I understand this was a blip, and for the most part, things have been going well for you and your mother. But given the back-to-back reports from the Sandbridge police department and your school counselor, along with your mother's history and diagnosis, I felt it would be prudent for me to check in."

"It *was* a blip. You don't need to come back here." I say it like it's a truth I can believe.

"Yes, well…" Ms. Robins gives a tight smile and walks to her car, pausing before she unlocks it. "I'll see you again next week."

I don't know how long I stand there after Ms. Robins leaves. I watch the younger kids get off the bus. I wave at Mrs. Welty as she walks her dog, Eudora. No one asks me what's wrong. I'm just a normal-looking kid on her front porch, representing her normal-looking family. All is well, from the outside, anyway.

Until Jane pulls her car in front of my house.

"Mae! Wait!" Jane's voice rings out behind me. My front door's jammed, or maybe I just can't turn the knob. "Mae!" Again. "Mae!!!" Louder. A hand closes around my wrist and tugs me backward. I rip my arm away from Jane's grasp.

"I have nothing to say to you," I snarl.

"Come on, Mae. Let me explain!"

"I trusted you. I trusted you with my secret and you opened your stupid mouth!"

Jane wrings her hands. "We were worried!"

My throat closes. "Who's *we?*"

"I just…crap. Darcy and Morgan. They swore they wouldn't tell anyone and they didn't — they said I should tell Ms. Saltman."

"The school counselor who helped you with college stuff?"

Jane flinches. She steps tentatively onto the porch. "Don't even *think* about coming near me," I growl. She freezes.

"I was trying to help you," she says, her voice pleading. "I was trying to help your mom."

I finally get the knob to move and I push the front door open. "*I'm* her help, Jane," I say. "You were nice to me. I appreciate that. But honestly?" I'm halfway through the threshold when I throw my last words over my shoulder. "Our friendship was a huge mistake."

———

I MAKE DINNER AN HOUR LATER, still shaking from the events of the day. Mom isn't eating much; she's just sitting across from me, cutting her food into tiny pieces and shoving them around her plate.

"What did you tell Ms. Robins?" It's the first thing she's said since we sat down.

"That we had a girls' weekend," I say.

"And the police report? How did you explain... um...that?"

I sigh. "I said it was a misunderstanding between you and the gallery. There was a voicemail, right? A missed email? Something?" I draw out the words, my skin tight with desperate anticipation.

She presses a hand against her forehead. "Mae, I—"

"Mom. Please tell me you thought you had permission."

"I don't need permission."

"To hold an art class on private property? I'm pretty sure you do."

"I *don't!*" she shouts and slams her hands against the table, sending her silverware flying. "I have never needed permission to be an artist. I've had to fight for it every day of my life." She lowers her voice and leans in, nearly hissing. "I don't need permission to be myself."

"I wasn't aware *being yourself* included living out of a car for four days and facing potential assault charges."

"Watch how you speak to me," she snaps.

"Why, Mom? Why should I? I left everything I loved for you. This—" I motion around me at the house, the table, "was supposed to be a fresh start for both of us. I left the only family I've ever known, and ditched the only real friends I've ever had, for you, Mom. *I chose you.* Don't tell me to watch my mouth. Don't lecture me about whether or not you need permission. I've let go of so much to have a real mother, and you *ruined* it." Seething, I stand and gather the dishes. "I have to clean the kitchen now."

"Mae, love. I'm so sorry. I—"

"I don't want to hear it, Mom. Just...fix yourself. Take your meds. *Do something* to help me fix this mess we've both created." I dump the dishes in the sink and turn on the water, grateful the sound of it drowns out her tears.

FOUR

PRESENT DAY

"We got an hour left, kiddo. Still don't want to talk to me?"

Sunlight streams in through the window, dancing shadows across my legs. We're off the highway now, onto two-lane backroads past farms and fields and family graveyards. We left Richmond around one; the display on Nathan's watch reads two fifty-nine (and forty-five seconds).

Forty-six seconds.

Forty-seven seconds.

"Alright, then," he says. "Suit yourself."

I stare out the window at the scenery: swampland and tall Carolina pines. I try not to look at the Spanish moss, a collection of long, beard-like tendrils hanging in clumps from the trees. The moss here is alive and vibrant, a grayish-green that plays well with the palette of the swamp. It's not brittle and dry like the handful Mom tried to transplant to our live oak in Richmond. That lasted three days, I think, before it shriveled up into black clumps and disintegrated.

How prophetic of you, Mr. Moss.

Nathan must get tired of my prickly silence — he fills me in on all the changes since I left. The trash cans have gone from green to blue. The Church of Christ and the Methodist Church had a dispute over Miss Mary's chess pie at the Spring pig-picking. My grandfather's company, Griffin Industries, hired about a dozen recent grads from the community college. And the kegs at The Silos quit working, so everybody got free beer.

"Sheriff Kelly had to haul away a ton of the kids from the high school. Asked me to come down and help work security for Rob Kugler. He owns The Silos now. Anyway, Sheriff asked me to come down since I know some of the kids through the vo-tech program and…" he pauses, unsaid words hanging between us.

He knows some of the kids through me.

The truck bumps across the kind of two-lane bridge you find in the country, this one stretching across a wild creek. Emerald green moss, exposed roots, and the dark reflection of the water call up a memory I'd all but forgotten. "You took me fishing at a creek like that once."

"She speaks," he says, voice full of humor. I roll my eyes and he laughs. "You mean Alligator Gut. You were a tiny thing for eleven. Think you'd been in town maybe a week."

I shrug. "Maybe. I didn't know the creek had a name."

"You were twitchy. One mention of an alligator and you would have hightailed it out of there, all the way up to the house."

I'm not a wimp. I wasn't then, either, and he knows that. I

fire back at him. "The move was a little overwhelming." My grandparent's house, Pinecliff, is huge. And I missed my mother like I'd just come up for air and she was oxygen. It wasn't easy.

Nathan spares me a glance, the kind that says he knows what I'm thinking. His voice goes a little soft. "I'm just teasing," he says. He drums his fingers along the steering wheel. "You're still the spitting image of Dewitt."

I check my reflection in the passenger side mirror, distorted through the window glass. Same heart-shaped face as my mom, same eyes the gray-green of the ocean. Our hair color is different — hers a jet black, mine more strawberry-blond than anything — but I *do* look like my mother, at least physically. I can't think about her mental health.

"How's Pinecliff?" I need to change the subject.

"Same as ever, I s'pose. Did manage to talk your Pa into doing some upgrades to the boathouse. Put in a vegetable garden. Stuff like that."

"Impressive," I say. "Pa's stubborn."

"Well, when you work for a man long enough…"

"It's been twenty years?"

"Closer to twenty-five, actually. Been a while since you and Dewitt last made your way down here."

I lift a shoulder, well aware the next words from my mouth are wishful thinking. "Living in Richmond's been good for my mom."

———

THE LAST LEG of the drive passes quickly. My stomach swoops when we cross the county line. Pine forests give way to crop-heavy fields, the occasional farmhouse or one-story ranch nestled among them. Relief and resentment bubble up, relief that I'm here, in a place that's as beautiful to me as it is nerve-wracking. Resentment that once again, my life's been uprooted because of my mother.

Because of the mistakes I made.

"You remember Daughtry's." Nathan nods to a white clap-board building, boxed-shaped with big front windows and a set of rusty vintage gas pumps outside. I rub the ache in my chest and try not to think about the hours I spent there. Miss Mary's pecan rolls. The sweet burn of a melting Fireball candy. Lazy afternoons with Mason and the Sutton twins, licking away ice cream as our cones melted in our hands.

"Still got the Jeep?" I ask him. It was open-air. A stick shift. He'd take us off-roading in the swamps. I loved it.

"Sold it," he says.

"What?"

"You weren't around." He shrugs. "I got a solid offer. It still needed work after all those years I spent restoring it. It sat in that overgrown lot by Daughtry's a long time before I tracked down the owner and offered to take it off his hands. I had too much to do. Got tired of working on it." He pauses for a moment, and I can't tell if he's reminiscing or treading care-fully. "A kid I know had the money. Also had the interest and the time."

Something's going on here but I don't push it. I just stifle my disappointment as he gradually slows the truck. The state highway dead ends, and you can turn right into Minnesott Beach or left toward some incorporated houses. In front of us stretches the Neuse, connected to the opposite side by two hulking River Class ferries. Driving your car onto a boat and crossing the river is way more exciting than a bridge.

We sit there in the middle of the intersection. There's nobody else around. Nathan lowers the window and briny air fills the cabin. I fight an inconvenient urge to spring from the truck and run to the water and let the waves crash over me. Feel the sand beneath my toes. The day is clear, the sun is high, and there's not a single cloud on the horizon. I'm not supposed to be happy about being here. I shove my hands under my legs and sigh.

Nathan rolls up the window and pushes forward to the right. The road narrows from two lanes to one, a mix of water-front cottages and traditional residences spread out on either side of it. We reach a bend in the road, choppy river to the left, the rest of the town to the right of us. Nathan goes straight and we lurch a little before bumping down Pinecliff's oyster shell drive.

"Driveway's still a menace," I mutter, rubbing the scar on my knee. It's a ragged oval right below my kneecap, courtesy of a bike accident on these broken, crushed shells.

"Hey. This is environmentally sound. And I seem to remember you ignored the basic safety rules when riding a bike on a variegated substrate."

"In English?"

He flattens his lips at me. "You're supposed to slow down on gravel or sand."

Pinecliff shines like a beacon in the middle of a quiet wood. The shutters are red, the siding a white so pure I know it's been recently painted. "The house looks amazing."

The tips of Nathan's ears turn red.

Over a hundred years old and three stories tall with two porches, the house requires an excessive amount of care. Anything that doesn't move grows a brownish-green scum from the brackish salt air and pine tar. That includes the separate garage, the boathouse, and anything else on the wide, grassy lawns that spread out in all directions. It's a lot of cleaning and painting and mowing and repairing. Nathan's done it by himself for years.

"Welcome home," Nathan says. "I'll grab your luggage." He exits the cab while I swallow my nerves. I loved this place once, before my mind started playing tricks on me.

Before I bugged out and burned the bridges I'd built.

"Nathan?" My grandmother Dora Bell, or Deebie, as I call her, stands in the doorway, every bit an older version of my mom. Same high cheekbones, same sleek dark hair framing a heart-shaped face with freckles. There's more than a few streaks of gray in Deebie's hair, though, and the fine lines around her eyes have gotten deeper. She looks older than I remember. It makes me a little sad.

"Lou!" Deebie calls out, cupping her hands around her mouth for volume. When there's no answer she impatiently taps her foot. I can't hear what she says, but she looks irritated when she holds her smart watch at arm's length and taps a message out, one-fingered.

"He's around here somewhere, I reckon," Nathan says to her as he ambles around the side of the truck.

Nathan reaches for my door handle and smiles at my grandmother. "Fetched your granddaughter, though for a while there I thought she might be mute."

I bang the side of the door with my fist and he jumps, winking at me. Deebie straightens her sleeveless blouse and floats down the porch steps, elegant as always. "Oh, for Pete's sake, Nathan. I need to get some sugar. You leave that girl alone."

"Hi, Deebie," I say, pushing the door open with shaking fingers. Her arms come around my waist and squeeze hard.

"You have grown, young lady." She stands back and gives my traveling clothes a look, nose scrunching. "Well, goodness. Looks like we need a shopping trip."

"I'm in leggings and an oversized sweatshirt, perfect attire for four hours on the road. My clothes are fine, Deebie. Save your money."

She waves a dismissive hand that sets her charm bracelet jingling. "You don't get to be Shrimp Fest Queen three years in a row without a sense of fashion. Shopping's my love language."

"Yes. Please. Go shopping." A man's voice sounds from behind me. "Better my granddaughter than me."

Pa's in his puttering clothes as he comes around the corner, a standard uniform of cargo shorts and a paint-splattered tee. This one's a vintage model from the ferry system, the navy-blue cotton hanging from him. Deebie wrinkles her nose. "I heard that. About the shopping. You smell like a pig-picking gone awry."

"Nonsense." He pulls me into an embrace, and while he does smell, the odor's not entirely unpleasant. It's sunshine and river water mixed with an honest day's sweat.

"I thought you weren't working the fields anymore," I tell him.

"Eh, well. I do from time to time. An old man's got to keep himself active. Keep the joints moving."

"You're not that old, Mr. Luther." Nathan piles my bags at the bottom of the porch steps. "I haven't hit forty yet."

Pa laughs and slaps Nathan on the shoulder. "How is my granddaughter, he asks?"

"Your Mae here was an excellent travel companion."

He's being sarcastic. I shoot him a dirty look.

Nathan laughs. "If you don't mind, Mr. Luther, I'll take these bags up to Mae's room."

Pa gives him a tight nod. "You want her in the white room, DB?"

"I do. And Nathan while you're up there? Could you pop into the blue room and check the window seals for me? Rosie said it smelled a little musty the last time she came to clean."

Nathan's head bobs in assent but his smile falters. The blue room used to be my mom's. There's some unresolved thing, I guess, between Nathan and my mother. They hung out together when they were kids.

I grit my teeth against the whirl of activity as my grand-parents usher me into the house. They don't say a word about Mom. I'm clutching a sweating glass of water and biting the inside of my cheek when Nathan reappears, the happy-go-lucky smile back where it should be.

"Windows look good, Miss DB, at least from the inside. I'll get the ladder and take a look at the outer casement tomorrow morning."

"Thank you," Deebie says. She glances at her watch. "You're almost done for the day. Why don't you show Mae what you've been working on in the boathouse?"

Umm. "Boathouse?"

Nathan grins and claps his hands together. "The boathouse. I cleaned up that old bike."

FIVE

I decide to take the bike up to Daughtry's, which in hindsight is a monumental mistake. Not because of the bike itself — Nathan gave it a new chain, a new seat, and a shiny silver paint job — but because of the weather. Minnesott Beach humidity is brutal. I'm about as victimized by it as you can get.

My goal was to get in, get out, and enjoy my pecan roll in *I'm not a Griffin* obscurity, but I don't know if that's going to happen now. The sweat bleeding through my clothes will do enough to announce my arrival.

I'd feel less awkward if I had a bugle and seventeen angry goats.

Daughtry's front window shines in the sunlight: *Gas and Groceries since 1928.* Add a few more "g's" — guilt, grudge, gossip — and they'd have Minnesott Beach in a nutshell. I suspect this is why no one asks me about these things.

Arctic air blasts my skin when I push through the doorway. The chill's absolutely worth it for the smell. Waves of caramelized sugar, cinnamon, and vanilla dance around the store, up the aisle, and straight to my nose — a gift from heaven. Miss Mary's sign: *Pecan Rolls — Hot n' Reddy* is just visible on the back wall over the tall shelves of groceries. I keep my eyes on the ground and edge forward, seeking cover in the dairy case.

Except there's a long line, darn it. Irritation pricks the back of my skull. Maybe the rules have changed, but there's supposed to be a strict no-fraternization policy. When the pecan rolls are *Hot n' Reddy*, you get in, you get your goods, and you get out.

Today, though? There's talking. Laughter I recognize. Shifting across the aisle to the cereal, I peek out from behind a towering display of artificial flavors and colors.

And that's when my stomach drops.

They're here, the Sutton twins and Mason. They're here and I look like I've been dragged behind a truck. I knew I would see them eventually, but in my head I wasn't red-faced and dripping. I was going to be calm. Cool. And I'll lean further into the cliche with collected. I was supposed to look good and happy and like I didn't just go five rounds with a bear in a sauna.

My plans have been shot to hell.

Evangeline—Van—Sutton is tall, way taller than I remember. Though we *are* older now, so there's that. She's in high-waisted cut-off shorts and an oversized tee tied at the waistband. Lips pursed, her auburn waves fall down her back as she leans against Miss Mary's counter. A manicured hand rests against her cheek.

"Boys," Van says. The word's quiet but commanding. Asserting her authority while avoiding a scene. I scoot to the right. Ezra's twirling a set of keys on a sailing team lanyard, a weathered cap with the Pamlico High School logo obscuring most of his face. Mason's sandy blond hair is askew and falling across his forehead as he whispers something in Miss Mary's ear. She laughs, the dimples in her ebony cheeks deeper than I've ever seen them. "Miss Mary," Van says, and the sound of her voice makes my throat tight, "these boys will stop at nothing to swindle an extra pecan roll from you. They want to fight over which one of them is your favorite." She turns to the boys, arms crossed and hip out for emphasis. "And y'all already know I'm her favorite, so…."

Miss Mary laughs again. Is this an alternate universe? Four years ago we couldn't get the woman to crack a smile. Roughly eighty years old and tougher than a cast iron pot, I don't recall Miss Mary as a bastion of frivolity. But she turns to the boys, wizened eyes full of laughter. "You act tough on the outside, Ezra, but underneath you're a pecan roll. Mason, on the other hand…" she smirks, wipes her hand on a faded dishrag. "You've got too much charm for your own good."

Mason gasps and takes a step back from the counter, hand resting on his heart. "Miss Mary, you wound me! I'm a cherub."

Ezra smirks and mutters something I can't hear but is patently hilarious, considering the four of them *and* half the line of hungry patrons laugh until they're almost out of breath.

I clench my fists. All I want is a pecan roll. No facing the friends I lost. No getting within six feet of the boy I may have loved and definitely hurt, on purpose. I take two steps forward.

Dang it.

My stomach growls. It's unnaturally loud.

The whole line turns to face me. Van's mouth drops open as Mason's eyes go wide. There's a tic in Ezra's jaw, a thinning of his lips as he steps backward.

And in a series of unfortunate events the likes of which I will never forgive myself, I run for the counter, vault it, and slap a five dollar bill next to the register. Adrenaline high, I grab a still-warm roll from a baking sheet and run straight out the kitchen's back door.

Humidity punches me in the stomach as soon as I breach the walls. Clutching the sticky confection in my hand, I collapse against the building, mortified and giddy. I have sugar all over my mouth.

My phone buzzes in my pocket.

Nathan: Hey. You at Daughtry's right now?

Me: Sorry. Who's this?

He sends an eyeroll emoji.

Nathan: Don't pull this nonsense with me.

I'm embarrassed *and* in trouble. Perfect combination.

Nathan: You take off on the bike and I get half a dozen text messages. Some new girl's jumping the line for rolls. Ain't a whole lot of new girls in Minnesott, Lima Bean. Pretty much leaves us with you

I bristle at the use of my old nickname.

Me: I'd been standing in line for ten minutes

Nathan: Heard it was closer to four

Mae: I was on pecan roll time. Like dog years, only more urgent

Nathan: Mae

Mae: Nathan

It was the Suttons' fault. Not mine.

My phone rings in my hand. "You talked to the Suttons?" I ignore the note of hope in his voice.

"What do you think?"

He huffs, then mutters something unintelligible.

"Nathan, you're going to have to speak up."

"Look, kid. You've got no idea how long you're staying here. Could be one week, could be four. Sure, I'll put you to work. You can hang out with your grandparents. But I just think…"

Don't say it…

"You need to smooth things over."

He said it.

"Not a grand idea."

There's silence on the line and it lengthens, so drawn out that I ask, "Hello?"

"I'm here," Nathan says. He sounds old. Weary. "Those kids miss you."

I think back to the looks on their faces, the utter shock and disgust after seeing me. "Didn't seem like it from over here."

Nathan groans. "You didn't even talk to them." I bet he's pinching the bridge of his nose right now. "Second chances are rare, Mae. Don't waste the one in front of you." There's

silence on the line, and I can't help but think about my mother
— all the second chances I've given her.

I drop my head against the wall and set my phone on the
ground beside me, sighing when a breeze ruffles my hair.
Nathan's right in one sense: I could be here a while. Ms.
Robins said at least three weeks. But I'm the one who left,
then pushed them away so I could heighten the carnage. Just
the simple thought of reaching out to them fills my stomach
with a buzzing dread.

A car door slams on the other side of the building. It's
quiet out here apart from that. With only one car in the lot —
a vintage Jeep someone's restored and painted turquoise, of
all colors — I drink the silence in, reveling in this small bit of
peace so welcome since my life went off the rails last Friday.

So, of course, that's when the world breaks apart.

The vintage Jeep. It *was* beautiful and shiny. I look up
again to find it rusted out. Tall grass fills what was once a
gravel lot, the height of it reaching up above the tires. Weeds
and wildflowers grow up through the hood and the floorboard.

Before he bought it, this was the state of Nathan's Jeep.

I breathe deep to steady my heart rate. Nathan's voice in
my house, and now this. It makes sense, I guess, since I'm
back in blink territory, dropping back in time at the whim of
the universe in the town where it started. At Lil's farmhouse
on the front steps.

I walk over to the Jeep, remembering. Nathan bought this
before I knew about Minnesott, a couple of years before Mom
went inpatient for the first time. I've only seen pictures of it
like this, photos Nathan had pinned above his workbench in

the boathouse. Whoever bought it from Nathan must have parked it here. I'm seeing it in the past, the way it used to look in this lot next to Daughtry's. One foot on the wheel well, I pull myself up and stretch forward, reaching for a wildflower just beyond my grasp.

"That'll be twenty bucks. Cash only."

I lose my balance and fall face-first against the hood of the Jeep.

Three things happen at once.

One, I realize Ezra's here, stupid arms crossed, scowling darkly.

Two, searing heat cuts through my t-shirt and crackles my exposed skin.

And three, I discover the heat level of pristine, turquoise metal. Also known as surface-of-the-sun hot.

I yelp, jerking backward in an unflattering fashion. The heat has scrambled my brain. And the bike ride, and the lack of sleep, and the fact that for the second time in four days, I've slipped back into a blink. I should just lay here for a while. Let the heat take me. A Lila Mae Griffin flambé.

Strong arms slide beneath me and deposit me feet-first on the ground. "I don't need a new hood ornament," he says and steps back, dusting the front of his shirt like I've tainted him.

"I'm not auditioning." I sink to the ground. Dizzy, loose-limbed, and awkward, I rest my forehead against my bent knees. Go away, Ezra. Go away and leave me to my whacked-out life of humiliation.

"I'm trying to," he says.

I freeze. "I did not say that out loud."

"You did, actually," Ezra says. "And you're in my way, so move it."

"I'm *next* to the Jeep," I insist. "Not on top. Not behind it."

"I know my prepositions, thanks," he says. "You're leaning against my tire."

"It's a freaking Jeep, Sutton. Get in on the other side."

His feet shuffle back and forth. "I'll do that. I'll be sure to crush your fingers in a minute, too."

I gasp and look up. "You will not. You—" Ezra points. I've put my hands on the ground right beneath the tire. "Fine." I push myself up off the ground.

I don't know if it's the heat or my embarrassment, but I immediately sway forward. Ezra's scowl twists into concern. We're the closest we've been in years when he reaches out to steady me. His eyes are the same vibrant green. I'd forgotten the way his eyes fit his face, two points of light above a jawline you could shred cheese with. And those cheekbones — heck. You'll prick your finger if you're not careful. With a bone structure like that in the Sutton family genetics, no wonder Pa says they destroy everything they touch.

I narrow my eyes. "Take your hands off me, Sutton."

His face goes slack. "Fine."

"She's a line jumper, E. Not a felon." Van drips the words from her mouth. My humiliation's complete when Mason skids to a stop after rounding the corner.

"So, like, Miss Mary says these new things are a cross between a cronut and a pecan roll, but I think they're more like—woah."

Nobody moves, not even Mason to take a bite of his half-eaten pastry.

As usual, Van's the force that propels us out.

"Oh, for Pete's sake," she drawls. "This is ridiculous. Mae, good to see you again. E, I've got filing to do in Dad's office. We done here?"

Ezra's sharp gaze burns a hole through my heart. I can't stand it. He opens his mouth and I flinch. Leaning back at my reaction, he sighs and climbs into the driver's seat.

"Griffin," Mason says, "You here for the summer?"

I hope not. "I don't know."

Mason gives Evangeline a leg up, then swings himself in after her. "Well, if you are," he continues, "feel free to grace us with your presence."

Ezra starts the engine and they're gone.

SIX

Here's the thing about Minnesott: generational roots run deep. If you're born here you stay here, and then your children stay here, and then your children's children stay here forever and ever, Amen, for all eternity. You can lose your land, your farm, your business, or your morals, but don't you dare lose that family tree.

It's not that my mom didn't get the memo. She just ripped it down and tore it up. Dewitt Griffin left at eighteen. She hitched a couple rides to Washington, D.C., and as the town gossips love to report, had a *liaison* with some guy who picked her up at the state border.

Nine months later, I was born.

My existence is pretty scandalous by Minnesott standards, hence my initial plan to lie low. But that stunt I pulled for a pecan roll blew my cover. The blink afterward blew my peace. I've been hiding, avoiding people — the twins and Mason —waiting for my mother to come home.

"You're hiding again," Nathan says as he appears from around the corner and heads toward his giant truck. "It's not worth it, kid." He drops a box in the back and looks up, his smug grin at high volume. If I had a pinecone, I'd throw it at his head.

"I'm not hiding, Nathan. Just sitting here. Out in the open. On the porch."

He shakes his head. "I got a sixth sense about these things, remember? You've got that Griffin *look*."

What, the look of a woman contemplating violence? "This is my normal face."

"It's the one you ladies get when you're ready to smack somebody. I learned to spot it on your mama first."

"You probably deserved it, Cartwright."

He leans against the truck, the mischief in his eyes twinkling out beyond the brim of his hat. "You know what? I probably did."

I bite my lip so I don't smile. Mom's being discharged today, a mere two weeks after her overdose. I'm nervous, both ready to see her and not. Perceptive as ever, Nathan opens the door to his truck and climbs in, an elbow draped over the window. "Tell your mama I said hello."

"Tell her yourself," I nudge him. But Nathan doesn't respond right away. Instead, he smacks the outside of the door twice before gunning the engine.

"Let's make it a double date. Bring Ezra. I hear you've got a thing for his car."

———

PA'S BUICK arrives half an hour later. Mom is the first one out. Rosy-cheeked and missing her under-eye circles, she looks healthy and rested. But the closer she gets, the more I see the tightness around her eyes and the tension in her shoulders. The ride home must not have gone well.

"Mae." My voice on her lips is a whisper, but it might as well be a storm. Every cell in my body's agitated, like I'm a bottled bit of sand and river and someone's shaken me up.

Mom arrives with two hardback suitcases. I tug both inside and upstairs. Raised voices float from the porch, and when I come back to the foyer my hands are tingling. Pa and my mother are arguing. Of-freaking-course they are.

"So you expect me to uproot her? Take her from her home, her friends, her school?" Mom's leaning against the porch railing, the skin on her knuckles taut with anger. Pa looms over her, flushed.

"You've done that already. Or haven't you noticed?"

"Lou." Deebie uses her debutante's voice. She grabs hold of his arm, a gentle tug as firm as it is tender. "Let's give Dee a minute to get situated. We just got back to the house."

"A house she plans to leave before she's even thought about what this might do to our granddaughter?"

"That's exactly what I *am* doing." The floorboards squeak under her feet. "I want to get things back to the way things were before."

"Before you dragged her down the coast and made her bathe in the ocean?" Pa asks her. "Or before you tried to kill yourself?"

Deebie gasps. "Luther Griffin!"

"It was an accidental overdose," Mom hisses. "I was trying to fix things and I got confused. The choices I made were wrong, and if I take her back home now, I can make it right. Better."

Pa turns toward the door and flings it open. "You've said that a million times over, Dewitt." He steps through the door and his eyes widen, shocked, I guess, to see me here. He opens his mouth like he's going to say something but he turns back to my mother. "Don't take her back to Richmond. Make the right choice, Dewitt."

The right choice, apparently, is to stumble through the doorway and fly up the stairs to her room. Deebie pulls me close, close enough for me to see a single tear dance through her eyelashes. "I think I need a cup of tea."

Forty minutes and three awkward sips of chamomile later, I'm fidgeting at my mom's bedroom door. "Mom?" I move through with a tentative step to find mom on her bed, her right arm across her face, her chest rising in an easy rhythm. I sit on the edge of the bed and rest a hand on her knee. "Hey, Mom. How you feeling?"

"Peachy," she says, peeking at me. "Your grandfather's a total gem." Mom's voice wears a frustrated tone, but underneath it, I hear resignation. Like she was supposed to run a marathon but tapped out at mile five. "You don't need my snark, Bean. I'm sorry. The drive wore me out."

My smile's forced, a mask, really. "Come to the shore with me. We can talk."

Mom rolls onto her stomach. "Not right now," she says. "Bed's comfortable."

"You sure you don't want to come?" I don't know how much I should push her.

"'M'sure," she slurs.

Mom's breathing slows and grows even. I lay a blanket across her legs. I stand and press a kiss to her forehead, whispering, "I love you. I'll check in when I get back."

———

DEEBIE'S at the front door with snacks and other sundries, including a repurposed pickle jar. She shakes the jar, jostling the fossilized shark teeth so they rattle. "Find me a big one, Mae. For a project."

A project. Deebie's never crafted a single potholder in her life.

This has to be a ploy to keep me busy. I drop the jar into my satchel and nestle it close. Mom needs time. My grandmother needs a giant fossil. I guess this works for all three of us, considering I need time to write out my feelings and feel the sand between my toes.

It's a short walk across the sideyard to the river, through scrub grass and a line of trees. I'm so busy picking through sand spurs and pine needles, I don't hear Mason and the twins until I'm practically on top of them: Van in a sling-back chair pulled into the shallows; Ezra and Mason on the pier.

Shrimp on a biscuit. Van's in my favorite spot. I shift

gears and trudge to the right, shoving back the inconvenient longing I feel as I move closer to the oyster-rock jetty.

Darn used-to-be friends who make me sad and take my beach spot.

Darn Army Corps of Engineers who built a jetty that cuts my feet.

I manage to cross without incident, still muttering as I drop my satchel in the sand. I tug off my threadbare tee and stand in my swimsuit, relishing the cool breeze against my skin. Hair stuck to the back of my neck, I tie it out of the way and into a topknot as my eyes drag along the shoreline. High winds today mean the waves are rolling. Decent conditions for writing, but not great for a shark tooth search.

"It's not the best day for that," a voice says. Ezra.

"Why are you even here?" I mean, I know why he's here. He lives here. And he's butting in on my tooth-hunting because he thinks it's his business. But why is he *here*, here, at my side with his prominent nose, angled jaw, and high, chiseled cheekbones, smelling of salt and sand and ocean?

Good golly this boy has gotten hot.

My cheeks register that thought before my brain does. My stomach clenches when I feel them overheat. Embarrassed and mad at myself — no ogling! — I drop my eyes to the tanned skin of his forearms. He's got a collection of black bands — Van's hair ties, because she always loses them— stacked on his left wrist.

"I'm taking a walk," he says, pulling me from my observations.

"Why this way?"

He shrugs. "Why not?"

"Because this is my spot." I put my hands on my hips and scowl at him. "You stole the other one."

"You don't own the beach, Griffin."

I don't, and neither does my family. We own the land directly behind me, the stretch you walk through to get here. The shore itself is public property. "I *know* I don't, but I'm looking for fossils."

"Which won't be productive today."

"I didn't ask your opinion, so..." Moses, he's infuriating.

"No, you didn't ask." He smirks, his eyes sweeping over my form before settling back on my face again. "But since you and my Jeep are...well acquainted..." he raises an eyebrow, "I figured I might try and help you out."

He's standing close, the heat of his skin too close for comfort. I take two steps back. "I don't need your help," I spit. "We got those paleontology badges from the Aquarium, remember?"

"When we were eleven and twelve..." he says slowly, eyes dancing. I want to shrivel up and die when he salutes. "See you around, then, Professor Griffin. Let me know if you want another photo shoot with my car."

I make a face at his back and mutter, *"See you around, Professor Griffin."*

Whatever. I clutch the jar to my chest and pick my way down the shoreline, practically vibrating with annoyance. But I power through, too agitated to write, too stubborn to stop until I suddenly realize I'm lightheaded. I stand and falter to the left as stars dance in my vision. Something's...off. My arms and legs are made of sand, heavy and hot and shifting. I let out a shaky breath and look back over the rocks, spotting the Sutton twins and Mason where I left them.

Until the world tips and I fall forward, my surroundings twisted and gone.

SEVEN

Pressure squeezes my lungs. My eyelids. I close them tighter and count to ten. Given the incident with the Jeep, I knew it was only a matter of time before I had another one.

Another stupid blink.

The breeze is gone, the only movement the occasional raindrop. I twist behind me to find Mason and the twins gone, too. I know I'm still on the shore, but I don't know *when* I'm on the shore. What time period. It's one of the many reasons I hate blinking. Aside from making me question my sanity, it's incredibly disorienting.

I wait. Bite back a wave of nausea. Shove my hands and knees tight in the sand. I don't want to be here, but it's like being a Griffin or Dewitt's daughter. I don't get a choice.

Movement catches my peripheral vision. Startled, I sit back on my heels. A girl in her late teens, early twenties, maybe, kneels in the sand at the edge of the water. Eddies swirl the shift dress she's wearing as she pins up her strawberry blonde curls. A lithe but muscular guy stands waist-deep in the river, watching her. "Effa. Quit messing with your hair."

"I have a sense of style, Patrick," she teases. "Don't you know anything at all?"

He moves closer, playfully splashing water in her direction. "You've cared about fashion since when?"

"Since always." She stands with a shrug and winks at him. "I *am* a Griffin, after all."

She's a *Griffin*? I've never heard her name before. And I should have, considering Pa made sure I know the family tree backward and forward.

According to Griffin family history, *Effa Griffin* doesn't exist.

Rain begins to fall in earnest. Effa pushes back toward the shore. Patrick reaches for her hand and pulls her toward him, studying her face like she's an island and he's a drowning man.

"Come to Asheville with me," he begs her. "You know you have a gift."

"Don't you mean a curse?" Effa laughs, but it's a dry sound. Mirthless.

"Your father's being unfair. His opinion shouldn't matter."

"I can't ignore the fact that he's hurting." She backs away from him, sinking down to her shoulders in the water. "It's my mother. He's afraid I'll end up like her."

A hush falls over the river, thick shame rising at the back of my throat. I should look away, stop eavesdropping on a private moment. But I can't tear my eyes away, not when

Effa's existence challenges everything I thought I knew. I have to talk to Pa. I have to ask him about her.

"Effa! Effa Griffin! Where are you?"

A gruff, male voice carries through the pine trees. Patrick and Effa leap apart. "Go," Effa says, pushing Patrick into deeper water.

"We're not done talking about this," Patrick vows.

"I promise we'll talk. If my father sees you—"

Patrick's eyes roll as he holds his arms out beside him. "He'll shoot me dead on sight."

"Don't be ridiculous," she says. "You know I have to tread carefully if there's even the slightest chance."

Patrick splashes forward, eyes sparking. "So you're saying there *is* a chance."

"Effa!" the man yells again, "If you are down at the river, so help me, I will—" A wind gust cuts off the rest.

"Go, Patrick. Go now." Effa turns and trudges toward the shoreline. Grinning, Patrick sinks beneath the water without a splash.

I turn my eyes toward the line of pine trees. He's standing there, the yelling man. A rain hat obscures his face, but his arms are crossed, his stance livid.

"I'm coming, Pop," Effa calls. "Hold your horses."

I'm tugged backward through a tunnel, thrust back onto the dry afternoon sand. I blink, the sun in my eyes and a steady drip-drip-drip on my forehead. Van leans over me as I lie in the sand, her wet hair shedding river water. "I don't remember you being this clumsy," she says.

Clumsy. Right. If only. My head spins when I try to sit up.

Van curses and breaks my fall, muttering something about catering to invalids. "Where's your water? And forget about clumsy. Since when are you this sensitive to the heat?"

I don't answer. My mouth doesn't want to work. She heaves an irritated sigh, then yanks me up to standing. "You're dehydrated. I got water in my bag."

It takes a fair bit of maneuvering to get over the jetty, but we make it with Van bearing most of my weight. I'm not physically ill. I'm just…disoriented. Like my DNA's been shuffled around.

Van deposits me on their beach blanket and thrusts a water bottle in my hand. "E!" she shouts. "Do me a favor and get Mae's bags across the jetty." It's not long before his shadow falls over me for a minute, long enough for a whispered sibling chat.

The water's cool. I needed it. With each sip, I re-orient myself. Mason's standing in the shallows, arms crossed, head tilted. I'm not wanted here. I stand.

"Thanks," I say. "For the water. And for the help with…" I motion across the jetty, "that."

"It's fine," Van says, the look on her face unreadable. She takes my bag from Ezra when he walks up.

"Here," I say. "I got it."

Van just shakes her head. She grabs my arm, tucking her own in the crook of my elbow. "I'll be back in a minute, y'all," she says, her eyes on Ezra and Mason. "I'm taking the invalid princess home."

————

"LILA MAE WENT down to the river earlier." Deebie smiles at me. I flinch and fumble my fork, the loud thunk of metal reverberating against the dining room table. "I sent her down there to find a fossil for me," Deebie continues. "Lila Mae, how did it go?"

Mom doesn't look up from her sketchpad or acknowledge me or her untouched food. Pa's brow furrows at me, then goes back to giving my mother the stink eye. Deebie's smile falters a little until she clears her throat.

I die a little inside. Force a smile. "It was good," I say.

"Good?" Pa asks, his attention back on me.

"It was…splendiferous."

Please. Just kill me now.

Deebie beams at me, grateful. "*Splendiferous* is quite a word. You must have found something very special."

If she means my ex-best friends, a new blink, and an ancestral family mystery, then sure. But I can't say that, so I mutter the first thing I think of. "I found some driftwood. I left it on the porch."

Deebie's smile freezes in confusion. Finding driftwood's about as exciting as finding a blade of grass in the yard. Pa leans back in his chair, eyes narrowed in suspicion. "I saw you walk up from the shore with the Sutton girl. I didn't realize you were speaking to her."

I didn't either, actually. "I fell," I say. "Got a little woozy. Van saw and helped me up."

Deebie reaches over and pats my elbow. "Did you drink the water I sent? Hydration's important, you know. Heat's dangerous down here. Sneaks up on you."

I didn't drink *her* water, but I did drink someone's. I nod, the dutiful granddaughter. "That's what Van said."

"I know you were close to those kids some years ago," Pa interrupts us, "but I'll be honest with you, Lila Mae. You made the right decision when you moved to Richmond. I was glad when you cut them loose."

"Lou—" Deebie's disapproving tone doesn't phase my grandfather.

"What, DB? It's true. I held my tongue when Lila Mae lived with us—"

Mom's intake of breath is sharp. Pa angles a bird-like stare at my mother. "I can't help if you're uncomfortable with the history of your parenting."

Where is this side of my grandfather coming from?

Pa turns back to my grandmother. "I know Mason Copley and the Suttons. They're trouble. I've said it for years. I've yet to see anything that might change my opinion. That Copley boy ain't got the sense God gave a rabbit. And the Suttons ruin everything they touch."

I drop my eyes to the floor, embarrassed. In my case, those three didn't ruin anything. I'm the one who cut them off. I didn't say goodbye. Didn't answer their calls or return their text messages. I left the going-away gift they gave me on the Sutton's front porch *after* I'd opened it, all because I couldn't stand the reminder of how much they meant to me.

Now I'm back in their orbit, an ache of regret in my chest. I was trying to start a new life, one I could live untouched by the fallout of mom's illness and my blinking. I should have known better than to drop the people who loved me for a pipe dream life with my mom.

"It's fine, Pa," I say, tired of the fighting. "You don't have anything to worry about. Van was just being nice. She wasn't trying to repair things." But I do wonder if maybe I should.

Deebie's eyes throw daggers at my grandfather. "Van's a lovely girl. I've got some stationery in my room. You should write a note. Tell her thank you. Griffin women have a reputation to uphold, you know."

My mother snorts. "So *that's* what we're calling it."

Deebie turns to her, "What are you talking about?"

Pa curls his lip. "She's antagonizing you, DB. Don't pander to it.." The vein in his neck bulges as he leans toward my mother. "I don't care how old you are — you are still my daughter. And as my daughter, you will show respect in this house."

"Respect is *earned*," Mom says, eyes flashing. "My whole life, you've been afraid of me. My mental illness is a liability to you – a mental health stereotype."

Deebie clears her throat. "We best save this conversation for—"

"You're taking your childhood completely out of context," Pa sputters.

"Because I'm delusional, right?"

Mom stands abruptly from her chair, the clatter of the wood startling my grandmother. "You want to know our reputation, Mae? Griffin women are the weirdos locked up in the attic. *That's* how people know us. Courtesy of your grandfather, that is."

Pa's out of his chair now, too, menacing as he learns toward my mother. "The behavior you're exhibiting is exactly why my granddaughter should stay away from the Sutton twins."

"Luther! For heaven's sake." Deebie tugs on his arm. He shrugs her off and snaps at her. "If we'd held this line with Dewitt—"

"*What line?*" Mom hisses. "You didn't care that I hung out with Gill and Rosie. You still think Nathan hung the moon."

"Gill Sutton was absolutely on my radar, but his evil was the lesser of the two. You spent entirely too much time with that...that...eccentric woman up at the farmhouse."

Woman at the farmhouse?

Wait a second. Is he talking about Lil?

Mom closes her eyes and rubs her temples with her fingers. "Why are you hung up on that? Lil supported me. She encouraged my art and let me be myself without worrying if I was embarrassing you. You said you wanted to help, but what you wanted was to make me your definition of normal. Lil's presence was a gift."

My heart twinges. When I was younger, Lil was a gift to me, too. Pa knows we were close, and he must sense my train of thought because he turns to me with a stern warning. "Don't you even *think* about going to see her."

Mom bristles. "Lil's harmless."

Pa's face shifts from purple to blue. "Then why did you lie — consistently — about the time you spent with her?"

"Because I was a kid!" Mom's hands are in the air, flailing

wildly. "You were always focused on what people might think. You made it pretty clear you thought Lil was a bad influence."

"I was protecting your reputation."

Mom scoffs. "I was just an embarrassment, *Daddy*. All you cared about was your own."

Deebie sniffs into her napkin. I reach out and squeeze her hand in mine. "It's fine!" I yelp. "Just stop. Stop fighting. I'll write a thank you note to Van. I won't contact them after that, Pa. I promise." I turn to my mom and hold her glare, determined to somehow settle this. "You are not an embarrassment, Mom."

My mother crosses her arms, her laugh ringing loud and clear and out into the foyer. I stand and start collecting the dishes. "Dinner was good, Deebie. Thanks."

EIGHT

Lil Rooney's farmhouse overlooks the river on the other side of the ferry terminal. It sits on an acre or two of land, the front porch facing the river. With its backyard creek and trees and thick brush for hiding, the backyard's a perfect hideaway. Van, Ezra, Mason, and I spent lazy summer afternoons in the shade of the forest, wading in the water and climbing trees.

I see Lil right as I dismount the bike, her silver braid draped across her right shoulder. She sits on the front porch, her soft, weathered skin a rosy hue in the last rays of the day's sunlight. It's teetering on eight o'clock.

"Finally," Lil says like she's been expecting me. I bite an automatic apology on my tongue. I cruised the neighborhood for a while first, trying to make up my mind as to whether or not I should go see her. I'm not sure I need to apologize for my mixed-up feelings, though.

Lil waves me up onto the porch as I engage the kickstand. The knotted pine stairs groan in protest as I follow Lil into the house. Her braid swings in time with her hips, a rhythm as earthy as it is distinctive. The house smells of farmland and river and dust.

"Excuse the mess," she says, waving at the quarter inch of film on the furniture. "I moved out to the trailer last fall." She points to the yard through a wavy, centuries-old window. "Stairs have gotten to be a bit much."

I peer through the glass at the trailer in the sideyard. It's olive green, the color saturated in the evening light. Lil hums behind me and flicks the light switch, immediately flooding the room with a warm glow.

"Lord, have mercy, you take after your mother."

My gut twists. "My mom and I are nothing alike."

"Of course not, shug." She winks. "You're total opposites." Kindness crinkles the corner of her eyes, but my uncertainty still bubbles to the surface. I step back, suddenly sure I shouldn't have come to see her.

"Miss Lil. It's late. I should go."

"'Course not." She plants her hands on her hips. "You just got here."

"I wasn't planning on coming inside."

"I don't plan for the sun to rise but it does every single morning. Some things are just inevitable, shug."

Lil pulls out a chair from the dining room table. "Here. You. Sit." It's the MeeMaw voice, the one all southern kids obey from the moment of conception. When a MeeMaw says jump, you comply.

Lil drops a beat-up, seventies-era shoebox on the table and dumps the contents out with a huff. "Good gravy does this box need organizing. I like to never find what I'm looking for." Lil combs through the mess, stopping every so often to giggle over a photo. Eventually, she turns to me with a triumphant glow. "What a nice-looking pair they were."

There's a photograph in her hands. My heart stops. "This is—"

"Nathan Cartwright. The girl next to him is—"

"My mom."

They're on the front steps of the farmhouse, young and sun-kissed and salt-caked from the surf. Mom's in board shorts and a bikini top, her back up against Nathan's bare torso. Nate's arms circle her waist, his mouth a breath away from her shoulder. The potent intimacy makes my breath catch. I swallow the lump in my throat.

"Nathan has always been handsome," Lil muses. "Girls loved him something fierce. But that boy? From the first day they met, he was smitten with your mother. Never looked at another girl. Hasn't since."

"When was this photo taken?" I sound like I've swallowed a frog.

"Nineteen years ago? Your mama was seventeen, here, in any case. Nathan's a year older, so he was a senior. Eighteen. Van's mama, Rosie, took the photo." Lil's voice takes on a wistful quality. "Those kids were like you and that trio. Spent a lot of time over here."

Fireflies and late nights and creek swimming — memories I've tried to keep away rush back. It's one more similarity I haven't wanted to accept: my mother and I both cut ties with people we cared about. Apparently, we both wanted a definable break.

"Things change, Miss Lil. It's inevitable."

"Tossing my words back at me, I see."

I shrug, doing my best to look aloof and uninterested. I point at the photo. "Why are you showing me this?"

Lil holds up a hand and ticks the reasons off her fingers. "You're here unannounced, and I pride myself on being a thoughtful hostess. It's after eight. I didn't have anything planned. So," she gestures to the box in front of us, "exploring old memories seemed like a good idea."

Deebie's disappointed frown pops into my head, unprompted: "*You know better than to visit after eight, Lila Mae, especially when your host is elderly.*" I set the photo of mom and Nathan back on the table. "I shouldn't have come over," I say, standing. "I'm going to head out."

"Oh, for heaven's sake. I'm old, not on my deathbed. Don't leave on my account. Especially since we haven't talked about why you're here, which is a valuable conversation."

There's something in her voice, a note of insight. K*nowing.* "There's nothing. I just came to say hi."

"No," she drawls, those dark eyes of hers looking through me. "No, there's definitely something else."

Lil stands now, too, and shuffles toward me in her house shoes, the rubber soles squeaking lightly across the floor. Call it a hunch, but I don't have to tell her about the blinking or seeing Effa.

I don't have to tell her because she knows.

"Mae, we need to talk about what's happening."

I sidestep in the direction of the foyer. "Actually, we don't."

"Don't you want to know the truth?"

"I'm good, thanks."

Lil's hands go to her lips, her smile flattening. "You're right eager to avoid that gift."

No one knows about the blinks. I've been careful to keep them a secret since the first one I had on Lil's porch. I even scrapped the first essay I wrote for the Fellowship application: it felt good to write about it, but it was something I couldn't share. Somehow, though, Lil knows, and my stomach sinks at the realization. My voice is small when I answer her. "What happens to me isn't a gift."

Lil's demeanor softens like maybe she understands. But then it changes again, a focused determination settling on her features. "Well, then," she says, huffing a little. "If bribery's all I've got..."

Lil takes three purposeful strides toward the breakfront, a wide, standing chest with upper shelves and lower drawers. The wood squeaks in protest as she tugs a sticky compartment. "If this ain't the orneriest thing I've ever had the pleasure of meeting," she mutters, then grunts as she pries it open. After a moment of rummaging, she stands and holds a vintage camcorder in her hands.

The light in the room grows a little hazy. I grab the table for support. "Where...where did you get that?" That was supposed to be mine. I was supposed to take it.

"Ezra brought it to me."

Which means he must have found it when I left the box at his front door.

"That camera doesn't belong to you," I say to her.

"No, but I've been holding on to it."

"I want it back." Not to watch what's on it, no. I just don't want it on display, a visible sign of my own failures.

"Promise me something?" Lil asks me.

I shake my head, lips pursed in defiance. "No, Miss Lil. Not a chance."

I lunge for the camcorder. For a woman in her seventies, Lil is surprisingly quick. She clutches the device to her chest and holds a finger up to scold me. "Your mother and her friends were very special to me," she says, a little breathless. "It killed me when your mama left. I don't put stock in regrets, not the way most of the world thinks of them. But if I had to do it over again, I would have handled your mama differently. Now you're here, and—"

"I am *not* my mother."

"Lima Bean," she huffs, exasperated, "I *know*. But Minnesott's a small town built on salt and sand and secrets." Her hands are trembling. "If you would just let me talk."

I cringe. I'm being awful. "I'm sorry, Miss Lil. Go ahead."

She nods, taking a deep breath like she's gearing up for something major. "The Suttons are going to lose the shop."

All the air in my lungs rushes out of me. The twins' parents own Sutton Seafood and Engine Repair. It's a local one-stop shop: get your boat fixed, grab your bait, and get a bottle of wine and fresh fish for dinner. Losing the shop wouldn't just devastate them. It would be a blow to the entire community.

"That's impossible," I breathe, not wanting to believe it. "They've been in business for, like, a hundred years."

"History's a funny thing, sugar. Sometimes the past doesn't matter, and sometimes it matters too much." Lil sets the camera down and takes a step back, away from the table. "Ever wonder why your grandfather hates the Suttons?"

I stiffen. "That's his business, not mine."

"And yet you're here, talking to me about the situation. Not your grandfather. If you're willing, you can help the Suttons. *And* your Pa."

I scoff. "That's impossible. My family just had a major blowup at dinner and the Sutton twins hate my guts."

The steel softens in Lil's gaze, and the touch of her hand feels like a million tiny whispers. "Everybody's bogged down, shug. Tied up in their secrets. But you have a window to all that. You slip into the past the way the rest of the world slips on a bar of soap. You have a purpose."

My stupid voice shakes when I answer her. "I don't know what you're talking about."

"Oh, I think you do. I need you to trust me." She takes both of my hands in hers. "You have a gift. You need to use it." Lil lets go, pressing the camcorder in my hands.

NINE

The air's salty and warm when I leave the farmhouse, the post-sunset darkness a velvety black. I turn right instead of left, away from Pinecliff. Away from the river, the water, and the shore. I pedal aimlessly, biding my time by skirting the glow of each street lamp. It's just me, the night, and my memories. I've got the streets to myself.

I try not to look at the camcorder in the basket, but its presence is hard to ignore. We'd been out of school for about three weeks when we found it — long enough to rub the shine from our endless summer thrill. Miss Deborah, Mason's mom, had just started working in town at the Piggly Wiggly across the street from the new Goodwill.

Mason's dad Eric was a drug addict. He also cheated on Mason's mom. He finally walked out on them that past spring, leaving Miss Deborah holding the bills and Mason holding the fort for both of them. Mason was sad, and we were sad, and the constant pall over our days only added to our seventh- and eighth-grade boredom. We helped Mason's mom and kept our friend company with property maintenance ignored by Eric, the deadbeat dad.

It was a weeding and mowing respite that set everything in motion. Miss Deborah pulled in the yard. "Well hey, y'all," she said. "The flower beds look amazing. Now come unload this stuff from the car."

Her trunk held groceries *and* treasures. Miss Deborah had been to the Goodwill. We unloaded the food, then oohed over other people's castoffs: salt and pepper shakers shaped like mushrooms. A pair of fuzzy slippers shaped like cats. The coolest find, we thought, was a ceramic cookie jar that screamed every time you opened it.

"She got all that for ten bucks," Mason said, and his eyes looked alive for the first time since his dad left. "We should go check it out."

We took the bikes to the Goodwill that evening, sweaty and red-faced from the heat. I shivered in the air conditioning until Ezra tossed me his hoodie. "You don't want it?" I asked, a secret part of me all fluttery.

"Nah," his teeth chattered around a crooked smile. "I'll warm up in a minute. I'm good."

For the better part of an hour, the four of us scoured the crowded shelves and racks. Van found a vintage cherry-print halter top, the beginning of her rockabilly obsession. I spent a single quarter on a tiny ceramic frog.

"That's it?" Van asked like I'd bought a stale potato chip.

"What do you mean, 'that's it?' He's cute."

Van pulled a pair of T-strap Mary Janes from the shoe

rack. "You could snag these beauties for the grand price of fifteen dollars, and instead, you get a ceramic frog."

I shrugged. She rolled her eyes at me. Ezra sidled up between us. "I like frogs."

"You, too?" Van cried.

"Frogs are polite," he said at my ear, and that weird, wobbly feeling came back with a vengeance.

"Polite frogs." Her words were heavy with skepticism. "Amphibians don't have manners. They're slimy and roll around in the dirt."

Mason walked up, his blonde hair askew and his hands clutching something boxy. "Frogs don't roll. They jump. But who cares about frogs, because I'm about to blow your mind with this awesomeness I discovered."

"A camcorder," Van said, voice flat and uninterested. "We're scoping ancient tech from the nineties now?"

I elbowed Van in the side. *Be nice to him.* She didn't apologize, but at least she had the decency to look chagrined. Seeking a subject change, I assumed, she held up her phone and tapped the weather app, showing it to us. "Storm's coming. We should get going unless we want to bike in the rain."

"Not yet." Mason's head shook. "Miss Doris says this baby's operational." He pressed a button on the side to deploy the viewfinder. Grinning, he pointed the camera at Ezra and peered through the eyepiece. "Work it, E. Give me that brooding Sutton smolder."

Ezra made a rude gesture instead.

"I think it's cool," I said, and held my hand out to try it. It was heavy but pretty easy to hold. I trained the camera on Van, her demeanor instantly changing. She turned to the side, popped her heel, and framed her face with her bright red fingernails. "I'm ready for my close-up now, Ms. Griffin."

Laughing, we bought the camera. Pooled our money and biked as fast as we could to avoid the rain. Mason still mourned his dad, but the camera's creativity breathed life into him and renewed energy into our summer. For the next two years, that thing came on every single one of our adventures, each one of us taking a turn as filmmakers. We held a million memories in our hands.

Memories I push away as I end up back at the ferry, fighting tears and biting the inside of my cheek. I pull off on the side of the road, knocking the crossbar of the bike with my foot and cringing as the metal hits the pavement. The camcorder bounces out into the street, coming to a rest on the road in front of me. I should stomp it into a thousand pieces.

I'm just so…mad. At my mom, at myself, at Lil, and the trio. To begin with, I should have made sure Mom was taking her meds. But I didn't, and now I'm here, losing my mind and making Lil think I'm some sort of superhero, while I fail miserably at keeping to myself.

I don't care about the town's secrets.

I don't care about the Suttons.

I don't care. I don't care. I don't care.

"Lila Mae Griffin — that you?" A jacked truck pulls out from the parking lot, stopping next to me with its windows down. In the passenger seat is Bexley Bennett, one of the girls I used to know in school.

"Hey, Bex," I say, willing myself to look as sane as possible while I'm tear-stained and on the side of the road in the dark.

"Brent, I told you it was Mae Griffin." Bex's words are muffled as she turns back inside the truck. But her blonde head reappears a moment later, arms waving. "Well hell, girl. It's good to see you!"

"Nice to see you, too," I lie.

"What are you doing in town? It's been a while. Brent, how long's it been since Dewitt Griffin up and left for that artist job in —"

"No," I shout, my voice louder than I meant it. I clear my throat and take it down a notch. "No, you're right. It's been a while. Years, really." And really, y'all can drive away at any time.

But they aren't driving away, and now it's not just Bex but Brent Hadley, Travis Holler, and Molly Evers leaning out of the cab.

"Lila Mae Griffin! Holy hell!"

Bex smacks Travis in the shoulder. "Be nice, you big galoot. Mae, it's so good to see you. The Suttons and Mason really missed you. Y'all were so tight. Have you seen them yet?"

"I've seen them."

Molly's gaze hones in on the bike. "Do you need a ride?"

"No, thank you." I shake my head.

Bex smiles and sits back in the truck cab. "Alright, then. Brent's having a field party at some point this summer. You should definitely come!"

The tail end of Bex's voice gets lost under the truck's acceleration. I pick up the bike and then the camera, tossing the latter back into the basket on the front. I push off toward home, the breeze kicking up the closer I get to Pinecliff. A hint of woodsmoke blends with the salt air. There are voices, too, and laughter, and as I round the bend by the stand of live oaks, I know where it's coming from.

Van, Ezra, and Mason are on the beach. They've lit a fire.

Longing stirs in my soul.

I shouldn't. I know I shouldn't, but I dismount the bike and lean it against a tree. Mason's riffing on his guitar, and in the light of the moon I see Van at his feet with a longneck. Ezra's there, too, leaning back on the sand with his eyes turned toward the heavens. A sudden ache fills the hole in my heart.

At the ferry, Bex asked if I had seen them. Oh, I've seen them alright. I see them now, the same as they were before I met them: unbothered that I'm not around.

Something cracks inside my chest, a desperate yearning. There are probably fifty or so feet separating me from the trio, but at this point, it might as well be miles. I can't turn off the tug I feel.

It's not hard to see myself at fourteen, running down the hill breathless with laughter and tripping over my feet. What would happen if I walked down there now, no preamble, no announcement? Just Mae showing up like she did in middle school. I've got my fingers through the camcorder handle when the hairs on my neck stand up.

Ezra. I'm not sure how because I'm in the shadows, but he

sees me, that much is clear. He doesn't move or call out. He just watches me, arms crossed, jaw lifted like he's daring me to walk down there. We hold a silent stand-off in the dark.

He's changed so much, from the span of his chest to the width of his shoulders, and yet, I still see the boy I used to know. Because I know this stance. I know the look in his eyes, the real truth behind his body language.

He's angry at me, and he's sad.

I look away first. I have to. I feel his eyes on me as I pedal away. At the edge of the drive, I look back at the shore to find three sets of eyes trained on me.

I loved those people and I hurt them.

I don't want to hurt them again.

TEN

"You're out late."

Mom's voice floats down from the back porch glider. I park the bike and glance at my phone. It's been an hour since I left Lil's. An hour of boarding up fears and rebuilding the walls my visit with her upended. "Lost track of the time," I say, though I'm not sure it matters. This is more conversation than scolding, knowing my mom. She moves the glider back and forth, the slow, steady squeak of the metal oddly soothing. She holds an empty wine glass in her fingers. A wine glass she's not supposed to have.

"Please tell me you've been out causing trouble," she says to me.

"Please tell me you're not drinking on your new meds."

Mom straightens her back, legs falling from the seat as her feet hit the ground with emphasis. "Meds or not, I'm still your mother. Maybe don't dodge my questions, yeah?"

Guilt pricks at my spine and I soften my shoulders. "I rode to Baird's Creek and looked at the stars."

It's not a lie. I couldn't go home, not after that staring contest with Ezra. So I rode to the end of Minnesott proper and sat by the creek's edge to watch the universe float by.

Mom ducks her head, watching the pinpricks of light beyond the porch roof. "It's a good night for star gazing," she says.

"I'm tired," I yawn and tug the camera bag's strap up my shoulder. "I think I'm going to head in."

"What's that?" She points at the bag, and I shrug like I'm not holding a great artifact of my failed relationships.

"Just an old camera," I say. "Thought it might give me something to do."

I move toward the door, but she pats the seat beside her. "Don't go in yet. Sit with me."

She looks so worn, like the weight of it all is pressing down on her shoulders. I sit down because I don't want to be a jerk.

"Mae, about dinner —"

"It's fine, Mom."

"Actually, it's not. My dad can make rules, but he's not *your* parent. You shouldn't have to avoid the twins and Mason because your grandfather's got his boxers in a bunch."

This is…not what I expected. I thought for sure she'd bring up the whole *Griffin women are crazy* thing. But okay. If this is where she wants to start things.

"You provoked him. Of course, they were in a bunch."

Mom stills, her knuckles white around the wine glass. "You want to talk about what I said to him."

I wait, tapping my foot to the rhythm of the locusts. The silence between us stretches out. She made a pretty big claim about the women in our family. If I'm sitting here in the dark on this ancient metal glider, then yeah, I want to know.

My feet move from tapping to bouncing. I cross my ankles and take a deep breath. "For so long, Mom, it was you and me and your bipolar disorder. No cousins, no aunts or uncles. No dad. Then I met Deebie and Pa–"

"Can we not talk about the circumstances?"

"You mean you don't want to relive an epic manic episode?" I bump her shoulder with mine, a wordless, *I'm teasing.* "Anyway, when they brought me, Pa took me in his office and let me dig through every family record."

"So you know the family line and the lack of direct female descendants."

"Yes. But what you implied about the way people see Griffin *women…*" I look down at my hands, my fingers shaking, Effa's voice ringing in my ears. "What am I missing here?"

Mom's grimace gives way to a chuckle. "Apparently, child, not much." She rests her elbows on her knees and stares into the empty wineglass. I take it from her and set it on the ground.

"I was talking about me," she says. "Exaggerating. I wanted a reaction from him. He's a control freak, Mae, and he can't stand when people don't do what he's asked of them. I wanted him to leave you alone."

The ache in Mom's voice sends me reeling. This goes way deeper than I thought. I reach out and take her hand, trying to reconcile the Pa I thought I knew with the man my mother grew up with. "You picked a fight so I wouldn't have to follow his rules?"

Mom blinks a few times and drags a knuckle under her lashes, exhaling a watery huff. "Some of his rules are good, like I agree with the idea of a curfew. And I don't think you should swim in the river alone. But he's not the custodial parent. I am. And those kids are good people. I've known their parents since *I* was a kid."

I let out a long huff of air and lean forward. "Seems like that's part of Pa's deal."

"You're not part of that equation, though. That's between me and Dad, not my dad and his granddaughter." She shakes her head and laughs a little. "You're so focused on taking care of me, you'll look for any excuse to push people away."

My jaw goes slack, her words reverberating through my body. Mom's rueful smile tugs at my heart. "I'm mentally ill, Lima Bean, not oblivious. I pay a lot more attention than you think."

For the second time tonight, my world shifts on its axis. I disentangle myself from the glider and stand. "Your disorder, Mom. It's complicated. It's not something you can handle by yourself."

"I can."

"That's what you always say. You start new drugs and life is perfect. Then it isn't, and we're falling apart. I'm chasing you around town and dragging you home at three in the morning. Calling you in sick when you can't leave your bed."

Mom stands and walks toward me carefully like I'm an injured animal she doesn't want to spook. "Things with me haven't been easy. I am so sorry about that. You have a life to live, and I can't stress enough that my disorder is *my* responsibility. I don't want the cycle, Mae. Not now, not ever." She leans in close and folds her arms around me, surrounding me in linen and lavender. "We're not going back to Richmond, Bean. We'll spend the summer here, and in the fall, you'll head to Charleston. Start your Fellowship. It's time for you to stop feeling like you have to be my caretaker. We both deserve more than that."

———

I'M AWAKENED the next morning by a buzzing on my nightstand. Frowning, I sit up and stare at my phone.

Unknown number one: Daylight's burning, losers. Get your butts out of bed

Unknown number two: I think you mean good morning, beautiful

Unknown number three: He meant option one. Sorry

Unknown number two: Whatever. I'm not talking to you

Unknown number three: Glad to hear it. Quit knocking on my bedroom door

Unknown number two: You ate all the Pop-Tarts, dork

Unknown number three: I thought you weren't talking to me

Unknown number two: WHAT AM I SUPPOSED TO EAT

Unknown number three: I don't know. Real food?

I wasn't sure, at first, who belonged to these numbers, but it's clear the longer I watch the thread. I'm about ninety percent sure this is a group text with the twins and Mason.

Unknown number one: Hey - no shade on the Pop-Tarts. My mama scanned that box

I close my eyes and consider throwing my phone out the window. Yep. I was definitely right.

Me: Wrong number. Quit texting me

Unknown number one: Griffin. Wondered how long you'd lurk

Unknown number three: Take me off the chat

Unknown number three: Why do I put up with you people

Unknown number two: Well, roughly eighteen years ago, our mama and daddy shared a very special night and nvklaksng

Looks like Ezra just took Van's phone.

Ezra: I took Van's phone. Don't bug me for the next thirty minutes

Mason: We're supposed to leave at nine

Ezra: Take me off the chat and let me get the boat ready

Van: galksgkjhdsakjhgdas

*Van: @#$%**********LKJSFDKLJ*

Mason: If all this gibberish means y'all are fighting over confiscated technology, I have to say my money's on Van

The longing for what we used to be returns with a vengeance. I need to shut it down.

Me: Is there something you want before I block all three of you?

Mason: The adults think you should hang with us

The adults. Like, my mother?

Me: You got my number how?

Van: You fight dirty, E, but I am victorious. I have my phone back and my brother has a fist-shaped bruise

Our source asked us not to tell, just to reach out and get you to hang with us

I was right—it was my mother.

Mason: Yeah, Cartwright swore us to secrecy

I flop face first on my bed, betrayed and a little ragey. Cheese and crackers. Nathan, too?

Me: Whatever. I'm not interested

Ezra: I'm turning off my phone

Van: E, don't be a jerk. Mae, be ready in thirty minutes

My eyes catch the camcorder right as I'm about to type a giant *NO*. Even if it wasn't completely self-motivated, *they* reached out to *me*. They could have gone on with their lives and forgotten about it. If his text messages on the thread are any indication, Ezra certainly has.

And then there's my mom, who last night was so vulnerable. She's been open like that with me before. But it's always been a disorder thing, the depths of her heart churned up in a depressive episode.

I feel a little unmoored.

I decide not to answer and make my way to the kitchen, thankful it's empty except for me. I dig around in search of food, completely lost to the grumbles in my stomach. I jump out of my skin when someone speaks behind me. "Got any plans for today?"

"Dang it," I curse, banging my head on the shelf that holds the oatmeal. It's my mother. "Did they teach ninja skills at your hospital?"

Mom scowls at me, her face softening as I rub the back of my head and grimace. "Sorry," she says, reaching around to do her own inspection. I breathe through the closeness of it, soaking in her nurturing.

"Ehh, you look fine," she says. "Are your pupils funky?" She reaches for my eyes and I flinch.

"Eyes are fine, thanks. Just, maybe announce yourself a little less...abruptly?"

"Got it." She takes a step back and leans against the kitchen table. "Still haven't said whether you've got plans."

The smirk on her face is so obvious. "You're an evil mastermind," I say. She holds her hands out like *who, me?* a mask of innocence across her features. "I thought I was an artist."

"Subtlety is a virtue, Mom."

I abandon the oatmeal from the pantry and take a pecan roll from the counter instead. Mom's eyes track my moves, and I'm midway through my first bite when she starts talking. "I think it's patience, actually, that's the virtue. But did my *subtle* efforts work?"

I give her a look. *What do you think?* She pulls a prescription bottle from her purse. "See this? I'm taking my medication." She shakes one out and downs it with a glass of water. "I told you I'm doing fine."

And actually, she kind of looks it. Her hair falls in glossy waves along the neckline of her yellow dress. She holds my gaze. Her breathing is deep and peaceful. There's no rapid speech, and she's not lethargic or weepy. If I took this moment in isolation I could believe her. But we're not in isolation, so…

"Mom, look. Please stop meddling. And tell Nathan to knock it off."

"Knock what off?"

The man in question has a voice that spreads like sunshine, filling up the corners of the room. Mom heads for the dishwasher and starts unloading what I'm pretty sure are dirty dishes. Nathan's gaze is everywhere but on her.

"Lima Bean. Am I in trouble?" Nathan asks me.

"Quit giving out my number and we'll be fine."

"What if they ask nicely? Like Mason did yesterday evening?"

Seriously? "What if I shoot coffee up your nose?"

Nathan hides a smile behind his travel mug as my grandmother floats in the room. "Well." Her eyes light up. "If it isn't my three favorite people all together in the kitchen! What an interesting surprise."

"Were you in on this, too?" I eye her coolly.

"In on what, dear?" She looks as innocent as a day-old lamb.

"Giving my number out to random people," I say, glaring at her.

Deebie sniffs and grabs a packet of Toast-Chee crackers

from the cabinet. "I haven't the slightest idea what you're talking about."

Right. And I'm the Queen of England. These three are the absolute worst. "Well, I have zero plans for today," I say, then look at Deebie. "You're taking Mom to her appointment?"

Deebie nods at me. "I am happily escorting my daughter to New Bern, yes."

Ever the maven of manners, Deebie spreads her crackers on a plate. She bites one in half, then dabs her mouth with a napkin. She waits 'till she's done chewing to speak.

"Nathan, since my granddaughter insists on being antisocial, I trust you'll have plenty to keep her occupied?"

Nathan nods. "Yes ma'am." He tips his hat, then looks at me with determination. "You," he points at me. "Boathouse in forty-five minutes."

Mom takes my arm and guides me into the hallway. Nathan laughs at the rude gesture I make behind my back. Mom and I reach the front door, and while Deebie fiddles with her keys, Mom leans in close and whispers. "Please think about what I said. I don't need babysitting."

"I'll think about it."

I won't.

ELEVEN

I'd rather pout in the sun than mope in the air conditioning, so I walk to the river for a bit. I don't go far, sliding down the hill to the pier, watching the vibration of my steps disturb the stillness of the water. It'd be a good day to take the kayak out.

I slip off my shoes and settle down carefully, my legs dangling off the edge of the pier. I lay back against the wood and close my eyes, letting the sun warm my skin and the water cool my ankles. Try to burn away the anxiety I feel.

A month ago I lived in Richmond. I had friends and a social life. Something I hadn't planned to have again, a mistake two years in the making. Because I kept my guard up even as my mother took her meds and went to work and slept on a regular schedule. Mom needed me. I didn't want to let her down.

Until I did. It was a gradual thing, the way my focus shifted. Last fall, I was too busy to count her pills. Conversations about therapy stopped in December and weeks went by before I realized she'd quit going. But she was putting away her paints at night and going to sleep and getting up and driving to the gallery in the morning. Life was mostly normal.

Mostly kept my delusions alive.

A cloud passes overhead and I shiver, whether from the temperature or my stupidity, I can't say. I *wanted* so much, and Mom was doing so well that maybe, I thought, I could have it. Actually meet people, lower my walls enough so a few select people could get to know Mae Griffin, curated.

A few select people like Evan.

It was the Friday of Memorial Day weekend, the sun and warmth making summer's entrance clear. Malik Dayton's house was the place to be that night, and with all the flirting we'd done over text, Evan's invite text was a logical progression.

What makes you think the crowd will pass the vibe check? I teased him. His response made my skin buzz in anticipation and excitement:

It won't if I'm not with you

I made the short walk from school, giddy. Mom was there when I opened the front door, her paints spread across the floor in between loose sheets of canvas. Dread filled my chest. This was problematic. Lungs constricted, I managed to squeak out, "Mom?"

My voice must have been an electric current. Mom jumped like she'd touched a live wire. "Lima Bean—woah!" She held a hand to her chest and laughed. "I didn't realize you'd come in. Sorry I—" she broke off, hands fluttering about while she shuffled paints and brushes. She mumbled something I couldn't quite make out. She looked at me, a little disquieted. "Umm, how was school today?"

My instincts took over immediately. Her porcelain skin held no flush in her cheeks. Her words were calm. She was a little fidgety, yeah, but her hair was up in a neat ponytail. "School was good," I said, my muscles tensing. "How, um, how was your day?"

If she were manic, I knew this would be the tipping point. A million words and moments would spill out. But she just shrugged and said, "Pretty good. Mona asked me to think about a few new pieces I'm having trouble with. A little art block, I guess?"

Hands on her hips, she surveyed the mess around her. "I thought if I laid the canvas out it might help. Like if I could see it here...." She trailed off, then walked to where I stood and put her hands on my shoulders. "Whatever. This is boring art stuff. And *you* have a party tonight."

I almost lied and told her it was canceled, or that I wasn't feeling well. But the scene was just barely off, like I could tilt my head a degree and it would shift back into focus. So she had a ton of canvas and planned to tack it all over the living room. For a full-time artist, that wasn't entirely odd.

I went to Malik's. I held a flat beer in a red cup and leaned against Evan in the hallway, my senses fuzzy from his scent. I let him kiss me long and hard until I lost track of time, more drunk on him than anything. He walked me home at Four a.m., hours after curfew, my knees still weak and my heart in my throat, and every nerve ending I had on fire.

The lights were on in my living room. Every other house on the street was dark.

"That's…a lot of light," Evan said like he was annoyed about it.

"So you want me to fall on my butt…"

"No," his voice was coy, and I swear I could hear him smirking. He dropped my hand and slipped his arms around my waist. "I was hoping I'd get to kiss you again. Without an audience."

I giggled and slipped away from him. "Come on," I said, and led him to the shadows of the oak. I leaned back against the tree and brought my chin up in silent offering. He moved in, the space between us a fraction of a distance.

That's when my mother yelped.

Evan jumped back. I froze and squeezed my eyes shut and prayed there was a burglar in the house. I wanted it to be anything - anything other than Mom ranting in the living room.

"What's going on with your mom?"

My mom, of course, was manic, wearing her short silk bathrobe and covered head to toe in paint. She was flinging it around the room, great swathes of color arcing across the walls, the furniture, and the windows. A splat of blue hit the glass and dripped down, apparently just the right spot for her to drag her fingers through it. I choked a swell of acid down my throat.

"Hey, um. I had a great night and everything," I mumbled to Evan. "I'm going to…" freak out, fall apart "go inside."

"Are you sure that's safe?" Evan's eyes were comically

wide. How I wished this whole thing were funny. "She looks a little crazy."

She is crazy, I remember thinking. *She's crazy and so is my life.*

"It's fine. She's fine. I'll see you later?"

The front door flew open "Mae! I need your help." Mom was standing at the door, her robe barely covering all the parts that needed covering.

I was four hours late for curfew and she didn't mention it at all.

"Evan, just go." I tried to shove him toward the sidewalk but he stood rooted to the spot, transfixed.

"What going on, Mae?" he asked. "Is she, like, losing it?"

Yes! I thought. *She's always losing it!* I shoved him harder. This time, he stumbled back toward the street.

"It's a new technique I'm trying with the canvas," Mom called out. "But I need more hands, and - oh! You have a friend with you. He can help." But no one could help, and that night (morning?) was the beginning of our five-day road trip up and down the Virginia coastline, all in the name of art.

It was all my fault. I let myself get distracted and believe my mom was okay. I'm not falling for that again, not here in Minnesott, not in Charleston at the Lowell-Howard Fellowship. I let people in and this is where it got me: exhausted, angry, and fighting my own brand of crazy, alone at the end of the pier.

An outboard motor hums in the distance, the drone quiet enough to lull me into sleep. Except the sound grows, and before I can react, the guttural *glug glug glug* of a bilge materializes next to me. I bolt upright to a seated position and blink hard in the bright sunlight.

"Lila Mae Griffin. Fancy meeting you here."

It's the trio. In a freaking boat.

It's a late model Boston Whaler, the white hull sleek and shiny in the sun. Blue cushions line the seats in the stern; white faux leather wraps the top of the bow's observation seating. The captain's chair and controls stand tall in the vessel's middle, a blue canvas shade stretched over the top.

"This is my family's dock, Mason."

"Your's, mine, our's...it's communal property." He shrugs.

"It's not, actually."

"Nobody cares, Mae."

They do, though, specifically my grandfather. Mason should know that by now.

Van's head peeks out from behind Mason, her wild waves pinned up in a bun. She's wearing an oversized pink tee from the Piggly Wiggly, the words *Mason Copley* printed on the pocket. I wonder if he's working there.

Van cocks a hip and lowers her sunglasses."Come on, Mae. Get in."

"You're resorting to kidnapping?" I ask her.

"If this were a kidnapping, I'd be much less polite."

"You're not being polite now." I deadpan.

"Guess it's a good thing you aren't being kidnapped, then." She smiles.

"You haven't even told me where I'm supposed to go." I'm whining.

Ezra's standing at the helm, scowling. "I told you — I'm not the only one who thinks this idea sucks."

Van gives a dismissive wave and turns back to me. "Ignore him. If you don't want to come, fine. But I have to at least be able to say I made an effort or I'll be grounded."

"Made an effort?"

Van steps over the rail and hops down, shoving her phone at me. There are about a million text messages from my mom and her parents, each one suggesting they pick me up.

"Sorry." I'm not. "I've got work today."

"You're telling me you got a job."

"Not really, no. I'm just helping Nathan."

"Interesting," Van says, turning her gaze back to the shoreline. "Are you sure about that?"

I follow her gaze and see Nathan, waving at the top of the hill. Van's phone pings in my hand. She unlocks it.

MR. NATHAN: Change of plans - got to head into New Bern. Mae should go with you

"He's so dead," I spit. "What a liar."

"Fits right in with the Griffins, then." Ezra salutes, then sits back in the chair and props a tanned foot up on the steering column.

"Ezra," Van warns.

"I'm just being honest."

He holds his hands up but won't look me in the eye.

Maybe that's what spurs me—Ezra's blatant disregard. I hand the phone back to Van and board the boat, unwilling to be intimidated. Ezra's not a Griffin fan? So be it. I'm not going to make it easy on him.

TWELVE

Wilkinson's Point is a half-mile-long sandbar accessible when the tide is low. You can walk to it, but only if you like barbed wire and trespassing. Since the beach and the sandbar are public property, most people visit by boat.

In the twenty minutes since we got here, Van and I have cultivated a tentative peace. We hauled the cooler up the beach and chose a spot along the curve of the sandbar. Behind us, the river flows wide and long and blue on its way out to the ocean. In front of us stretches a brackish cove and the beach just beyond it, then Lil's farmhouse up the hill. Ezra and Mason are to the left of us, tossing a football. Both of them are shirtless—not that I'm watching, or anything.

Okay, yeah. I'm watching. And I'm pretty sure they're watching us, too.

"What's up with you and Mason?" I ask Evangeline, realizing my mistake as soon as she looks at me.

"You've lost the right to ask that." Her eyes narrow. I mumble a quiet apology.

Dried pine needles litter the beach in front of us. I grab three of them from the sand. We used to braid these things, making bracelets and rings or the occasional banner for a sand castle. Van drops her eyes to my hands.

"Whatever." She shifts, her features softening. "The answer's nothing. *Mason* is my best friend."

And you're not, is the implication. My heart sticks in my throat.

I could lay it out right now, my reasoning, how my choice earned me two years of a typical life. I don't regret what I did, but Van's words still tug at my conscience. If I were braver, I would take her hand and say I'm sorry, that it wasn't about any of them. That it was about what I needed then, and what I thought I had to do to move forward.

I don't regret it.

At least I don't think I do.

Van's whispered curse captures my attention. She's ogling Mason, eyeing his bare torso as he leaps into the air for a catch.

"He's your *best friend*," I smirk.

"And I can acknowledge rare beauty when I see it."

My laugh is the squeak of a rusty gate hinge. I clap a hand over my awkward mouth.

Van eyes me, lips pursed. "You allergic to laughter now?"

"No." My cheeks heat. "It's just been a while."

She raises an eyebrow. "Been a while since what?"

"Since I, uh, laughed. Like that. Loudly."

She peers at me over the top of her sunglasses. "What kind of sad, sorry world were you in?"

"You don't know anything about my life." I bristle.

"If you remember, that wasn't my choice."

Van fiddles with her chair, her back straightening as though preparing a presentation. "You've been back three weeks," she says. "This is our longest conversation since you got here. We were inseparable. And when you chose to go with your mom to Richmond, I was sad you were leaving, yeah. But you didn't just leave. You cut us out completely. And then you come back and act like the last thing you want is to be anywhere near us—"

"I'm here, aren't I?"

She throws her hands up in exasperation. "Because our parents made us drag you out by force!"

Van leans back in her chair as though the air's gone out of her. "Look. I know life with your mom is hard. But I know *you*, probably better than anybody on this planet. And the Mae I knew *before* wouldn't be freaked out by the sound of her own laughter. She'd relish it." Van stands and dusts the sand from her legs, picking up her empty seltzer. "I have to pee. Tossing this and going swimming for a bit."

I watch her walk away and throw the can into the boat's garbage, then enter the water and disappear behind the boat. "Polluter!" Mason calls, not breaking his and Ezra's rhythm with the football. Van's voice floats above the smack of the boat on the water. "Mind your business, perv."

"Mae," Mason calls. "Football?"

"No thanks." I stand and stretch my legs.

"You just going to stand there, then?" he asks, his tone clear he thinks I've lost it. Mason's never been one to sit still.

"Looks like it," I say, and a sharp pang fills my chest at the disgust Ezra aims at me.

"She doesn't want to be here, Mase." He moves closer to me, juggling the football. The tendons in his forearms twitch. And then he's close enough that I see callouses on the hands I used to hold, off sailboats and up hills; off Jeeps and down boardwalks. My fingers itch to grab hold of the boy who used to be my anchor.

I dig my nails into my palm instead.

Mason huffs. "Maybe. But I think she misses us, deep down."

The crappy thing about reunions with people who really knew you is that they still know you, even though things have changed. Mason's right, but I'm not going to admit that to these two. "You know what?" I throw my hands in the air, clearly agitated. "I—"

I lose my train of thought.

The air temperature drops dramatically. The world in front of me fades away. It's such a drastic change I heave in great gulps of air, disoriented and breathless. And when the world comes into view like a tidy puzzle with all its pieces, I breathe again and taste woodsmoke. It's dark. Another blink.

I wrap my arms around my waist and stare at the bonfire, voices murmuring on the other side. I scoot around the edge to get a better look, skidding to a halt when I spot four figures. Two couples: one is my mother and Nathan. The other is the Sutton twins' parents, red-headed Rosie and dark-haired Gill.

"Rosie," my mom says, drawing the word out. "What are you going to do with twins?"

Mom's legs are crossed. Nathan's lying down beside her, his head resting squarely in her lap. She combs her fingers through his hair but she's not watching Nathan. Instead, she's staring wide-eyed at a pregnant Rosie leaning comfortably against Gill.

Gill pulls Rosie into his lap, his smile growing bigger as his hands cradle his wife's bump. "We'll have too much fun," he says. "Save the kids from twice the trouble."

Nathan's thumb lifts in wordless support.

Mom slaps it down. She looks at Rosie. "I'm excited for you, really, I am. But…" I wince at the hesitation in her voice, the hint that maybe she's not being honest. "Having a baby's a big deal. Two babies is even bigger. What did your parents say?"

Rosie laughs. "Mama 'bout died. Daddy brought her a whiskey. She doesn't drink, so you know it was a shock. Gill's parents didn't say much, but then what do you expect from a Sutton?" She grins at him. "Though I did overhear his mama on the phone with Blanche Dorsey, talking about mono-grammed baptismal gowns."

The conversation stalls, the roar of the fire filling the silence. Gill whispers something in Rosie's ear. My mother's hand drops to her side and Nathan pops one eye open. He pokes her in the leg, gently, and she rakes her fingers through his hair again.

"I guess I should have asked how *you're* doing. How do you feel about all this?" I recognize mom's tone. She's concerned, I think, but trying to be supportive. I can't tell if she's worried about the pregnancy in general, or the fact that there are two babies, not one.

"Wasn't what we planned on," Gil says. "Not this early."

"Figured we'd have a year or two before kids." Rosie agrees.

"But we got married young. Might as well be all in with it." Rosie's eyes grow misty in the firelight. Gill kisses the top of her head.

The scene shifts: a fire down to its embers. I'm alone with Nathan and Dewitt. They're wrapped in each other's arms, facing away from the shore and out toward the river. I have to move closer to hear them. "Dewitt, you know Gil's a good guy."

"No, I know. He's an amazing husband. He'll be good a father, too. It's just…" Mom shifts, turning in his arms to face him. "Rosie had plans. She was going to college. She might be fine with community college, but her first choice was UNC."

Nathan's head dips to the side. "And she can transfer if she wants to. I heard your Dad say they have some new internet courses, too. I don't know how any of that works, but this is Rosie we're talking about."

Mom smiles. "She's a force of nature."

Nathan hums in agreement. "Second only to you."

Mom laughs, standing on her tiptoes to kiss him. When they pull back, Nathan looks into her eyes. "You know…"

"Don't say it."

"You don't even know what I was thinking."

"I know you, Cartwright, and your one-track mind."

"So what was I going to say? Tell me." He's laughing.

She pokes him in the chest with a finger and smiles. "We are not getting married. I still have to graduate."

"June's a great month for weddings."

"I have art school. I'm out of here after graduation, assuming I can convince my father." She leans her head on Nathan's chest. He pulls her in tighter. "Assuming I don't continue to lose my mind."

Nathan's quiet, his gaze focused on the river. He looks conflicted from the set of his jaw. I hear him sigh, then he steps back and drops his hands to my mother's elbows. "Dewitt, I would follow you literally anywhere. You know I love you, right?"

"And I love you, but pretty words won't fix this."

"What is there to fix?"

"Me, for one. My family. That I'm leaving and you have your own plans."

"We don't have to get married now. But you're it for me, and you always have been. I don't trust people easily. Or ever. But I trust you."

"You trust me," she balks. "The town crazy."

"With every little piece of my heart."

I'm sucked out of the scene like I've been vacuumed, the pop of re-entry ringing in my ears. My butt hits the warm sand but my teeth continue chattering. Head spinning, I pull my knees up to my chest.

"Miss Lil, can I have that blanket?"

Strong arms and soft fabric swallow me whole. It's Ezra,

and in the worst of bad ideas, I lean my head against his shoulder and breathe deeply. The scent of ocean water fills my nose.

"Suppose I showed up late to the party," Lil says. "Looks like I missed a lot."

"She had a seizure, Miss Lil." It's Van. "At least I think that's what happened. She's never acted like this before, though…"

Ha — that's right. They think I have seizures. I never told them the truth. The fog in my head clears, the world growing sharper with each tiny increment. A gull cries overhead. I blink at the sun and look around, finally able to get my bearings. We left the point. They took me up past the ferry.

Ezra's carrying me to Lil's house.

"Put…put me down. Stop it."

He immediately complies. My stupid body misses his warmth, but his hand's still on my arm like he's making sure I can stand before giving me autonomy.

"I'm fine," I bite out. "Really. I just — Lil, could you call Nathan? I'd like to go home. Now."

I toss the blanket off, officially suffocating. That weird lump in my throat is back. I knew Nathan and my mom were close, but they were talking about a future.

What if Nathan is my dad?

"We'll take her home, Miss Lil," Ezra says with authority.

"I'm standing right in front of you, Sutton. Don't talk about me like I'm not here."

"*Hence the offer to take you home.*" His words come out slow, his tone a mix of care and condescension.

I hate this. I hate what I've done to all of us.

"I don't want your help," I say. "Call Nathan. He can pick me up. Or I'll walk home."

Ezra's lips form a flat line and his eyes narrow. "Past three barbed wire fences on private property."

"I've done it before."

Emboldened and annoyed, I step away, then stumble. Okay. So maybe I was wrong about the walking part.

Ezra huffs. "See, y'all? She's perfect. She can walk home just fine." He looks mad. It's in the set of his jaw, the way he's clenching the heck out of his fingers. But I know this stance. It's the same one he'd adopt if someone teased me about my mother. He's not angry at me, not really. He looks angry on my behalf.

Forget this. "I'm walking." I turn on my heel to retrieve my clothes. Halfway to the shore, the scent of honeysuckle envelopes me. "Do you run sprints in your spare time, Miss Lil? Or are you just outside the boundaries of space and time?"

"Well. I'm not as spry as I used to be, but I do walk quite a bit. Keeps these old bones healthy. How was movie night, shug?"

I'd hoped she'd forgotten about the camcorder. "Don't know. Haven't turned the thing on." She hums in response, a low murmur that for some reason infuriates me. "Look. Could you please just leave me alone?"

I'm breathing hard when I face her, my fingers curved into tight, angry fists. "If that's what you want," she says, "I'll respect it."

"Thank you."

"But I have something for you at the house."

Shrimp on a biscuit. "I'm not interested."

"It won't take five minutes." She puts a hand on my arm.

"There's this thing called consent, Lil. Ever heard of it?" I jerk away, remorse at her obvious surprise flooding through me.

My emotions are all over the place.

"I found the rest of the box," Lil calls, her voice strong over the wind off the river. I stop, every cell in my body alert. The sound of her footsteps grows close, and once again, she's standing beside me. "I have the box of memories. Thought there might be something in there you want back."

"I don't want it back. I left it here on purpose."

"Oh, I remember. And at the time, that was what you needed to do. Circumstances are different now." She presses a hand to my cheek, the gesture achingly maternal. "You need your friends. You say you don't, but I know you miss them."

I miss them like I miss everything else. Like my sense of control. My mom. My plans for the senior year fellowship.

Can you miss a life you've never had?

I rub at the ache behind my breastbone; watch the twins and Mason watch me from the yard. "I'll take a look," I say. "But I'm not making you any promises."

One side of Lil's mouth curves and the blue of her irises flash a hint of sparkle. "I didn't expect you would."

THIRTEEN

"Hello, ladies. Welcome to The Steamer. Can I start you off with something to—"

Our blonde server's eyes spark, then narrow in recognition. "Dewitt Griffin. I heard around town you were back."

Mom's smile is strained. "Rochelle. How's your mom doing?"

"Doing real well, *thanks*. Got a house in Merritt out highway 55. My husband's good, too. Married Tate Sherman. Fifteen years ago next month."

Are we competing? "That's wonderful," Mom says. "Tate was always a nice guy."

Rochelle skewers me next. "This your daughter?"

I smile and wave. "Nice to meet you." Rochelle's lip curls up like she smells raw sewage. Thirsty and hot and not a fan of her passive-aggression, I change the subject. "Could I get some water please?"

Mom orders sweet tea. Rochelle slinks away to place the

order. Mom snickers and leans in. "When she brings back our drinks, take a good sniff before you sip from it."

My lips twitch. "Checking for almonds?"

She jabs a finger at the table surface and hisses, "Exactly. That odor? Best tip-off for cyanide poisoning."

I snort. "What's her deal, anyway? Did you know her from before?"

"We ran in the same circles, I guess. She never liked me much. Your grandmother said it was jealousy…" she trails off, and my eyes flit to Rochelle as she fills our drink order.

"Guess she had a thing for Nathan." I lift my eyebrows as I turn back to my mom.

She stills. "What do you mean?" Her voice is wary. I wonder how far I should push. My gut instinct for this dinner date was a big fat no, considering she ambushed me on the upstairs porch as I wrote my way out of a meltdown. The trip to the point and the blink wore me out, physically and emotionally. The last thing I wanted was to go into town.

But the more I wrote about what I've seen since I got here, the more I realized I had a burning, pertinent question for my mom. Getting an answer, I decided, would be worth the conversation and the drive.

"Mae?" Mom's voice is still wary. "Why did you ask about Nate?"

"I saw you."

She lurches back.

"In a photo," I add quickly. "You were…cozy looking." I shove the panic from my voice and aim for mild interest. "Thought it might explain a few things."

Mom drops a straw into her tea glass and moves it off to the side. Fiddling with the straw paper in her hand, she leans her elbows against the table. "I dated Nathan. Rochelle was salty about it. But it's not like I owned him. We were over before I left."

My insides swoop as I lean forward, biting the inside of my lip. I'd wanted to focus on Nathan, but her response brings up additional questions."Did you leave because you and Nathan broke up?"

"No," she sighs, tearing the straw paper into tiny pieces. "Dad and I fought. A lot."

"About what?" I take a sip of my water, thinking I already know but hoping that she'll tell me.

"Everything," she says. "Especially art school. Dad didn't want me to go. He took my disorder personally, like I was pretending to be manic. He thought it was a ploy to ruin the family name."

I blink once. "I'm sorry?"

She gives a mirthless chuckle. "Yep."

A server comes — not Rochelle, The Unfriendly — and drops a hush-puppy basket between our drinks. Mom slathers butter on a hunk of fried dough and takes a bite, eyes closing in satisfaction. "These are so good. Couldn't get decent hush-puppies in Richmond." She tips the basket my way and shakes it. I shove one in my mouth and chew.

The break gives me time to put my thoughts together, specifically what she's said about her dad. "Your disorder embarrassed Pa."

She nods. "Nathan was angry about Pa's reaction. Thought we should go see Lil for help."

"With what?"

"Treatment, I guess. Support for art school. Dad, of course, found out. He's always disliked Lil, but as my symptoms grew he decided to blame Lil for them."

"You're kidding."

Mom shakes her head and grabs another ball of fried dough, dunking it into the butter. "That was kind of the last straw."

"You came back, though," I say. "Eventually. And I lived here for a while."

"While I got my life on track. I'd dragged you around enough, and by the time I went on that retreat, I was already slipping. I needed to heal so I could be better. And I wanted normalcy for you."

The openness between us spurs my next statement. "You could have reached out to my Dad." The words are just a whisper, one I'm not expecting a response to, really. But she sighs and runs a hand through her hair, to heck with buttery fingers. "Mae, your father…"

"Was a fling. I know. But are you being honest?"

"What does that mean?" Mom gapes.

"Exactly what it sounds like." My voice shakes, and I shove my hands under my thighs like that will somehow stop it. And then I ask her; toss it right out there in the open. "Is Nathan Cartwright my dad?"

Mom fumbles her tea and we scramble for napkins, blotting the mess as best we can with tiny two-ply squares.

"Nathan is not your dad," Mom breathes once we've managed the flood situation.

I study her. "I don't know if you're telling me the truth."

She drops a pile of wet napkins on the table, cringing when they audibly squish. "Nathan is not your dad." Her words are slow, the pace punctuating each syllable.

"That's not what I asked you, Mom."

"I'm pretty sure it is."

"No. I mean—" I take a deep breath and loosen my tongue, letting my jaw relax before I continue. "I did ask if he was my dad, but now I'm asking if you're lying to me." She looks down at the floor, studying the black and white tiles as though they hold the answers to life, the universe, and everything. Tension crackles in the air as I hold my breath, desperate to know what she's thinking.

"I'm not lying to you, Mae," she insists.

When she raises her eyes from the floor, I have no choice but to believe her. Her face bears no distress or deceit. Deflating like an overfilled balloon, I sit back and nod at my mother in acknowledgment.

"Okay," I say, and drop it.

Like usual, okay is all I've got.

———

MOM'S high school art teacher lives close to the restaurant, so of course she wants to swing by. I ask to take a walk — I'm in no mood for socializing.

"Sure, Bean. Meet back here in ten minutes?"

I set a timer for her on her phone.

We're in Oriental, a quirky sailing village about twenty minutes north of Minnesott. With a busy harbor and three marinas as their claim to fame, the locals like to say Oriental's got more boats than people. It's also super pet-friendly; it probably has more animals than boats.

Across the main street from the harbor is a half-acre fishing pond. Surrounded by cattails and high grass, it's mostly hidden unless you're on a deck or something. But on late afternoons when Nathan would take us into town, the twins, Mason, and I would tunnel through the grass and drag kayaks into the flat water. We'd talk and laugh and pretend to be older, waiting for the fireflies to come out.

Stepping through the tall grass and cattails is like entering another world. Sound is muted here, eclipsed by the scent of loam and life and earthiness. I kick my flip-flops aside and follow a dragonfly to the pond's edge, marveling at the soft mud beneath my feet. I'm alone and ensconced in my own little fairy world. I tip my face to the evening sun and breathe.

"One, two, buckle my shoe."

I stumble. What the heck?

A boy stands at the edge of the pond, his brown shorts and collared shirt a little too big for his frame. His feet are bare like mine. He's clearly playing in the mud, but even still there's an air of seriousness about him. Like he's a pint-sized professor looking for specimens he might dig up.

The boy continues his nursery rhyme, tossing rocks into the pond with each verse. He looks familiar to me. Maybe I've seen him around town? There aren't a lot of kids in Minnesott, and even fewer in Oriental. Especially kids dressed in vintage chic by what I assume are his unironic hipster parents.

Wait a second.

Awareness pricks the back of my neck.

"Hello," I say, calling to him. The kid doesn't look up. He reaches for a handful of sticks and lines them up along the edge of the water.

"Five, six, pick up sticks;

Seven, eight, lay them—"

A flurry of motion bursts from the cattails. The boy tips headfirst into the pond.

"Louie! I said play *by the pond*, not in it."

"You knocked me in," he sputters at the girl who crashed through the weeds. It's Effa. She's standing at the edge of the grass.

Effa laughs and slips her shoes off, rolling up the hem of her pants. She steps into the pond and reaches for him. "You're right. I wasn't paying attention. Here, Lulu. Let me help."

He stands up with a start and snaps at her. "Don't call me that. I'm not a baby. I like Luther or Louie, please."

"Alright, little brother." She sighs and lifts a shoulder. "Couldn't kill you to lighten up."

Air rushes out of me in an instant. *Luther.* This little boy is my Pa. In every record I've seen, in every story he's told, my grandfather has never had a sibling. He's supposed to be an only child.

Luther scowls. "I don't want to lighten up. I'd be like you, and you don't take anything seriously."

Effa pulls him from the mud and holds him close. "I don't want you to be like me. I want you to be yourself. My serious little man who is content with his books. Happy."

Louie swipes a muddy hand across his forehead. "I'd be happier if you were home."

Something about the tone of his voice gets to me, my heart aching for this little boy. Effa crouches down to meet his height, speaking softly. "You are my brother, my baby Louie. I'm here now, to be with you, and before you know it you'll be old enough to come along."

"To Asheville?"

"To anywhere. I'll take you anywhere you want."

Joy flashes across Louie's face for a split second before his brow furrows. "What about Father?" he asks.

A flicker of unease passes Effa's face. "Eh, he might get mad, but he'll get over it. And when Mama's better, *they* can come out."

When Mama's better. I roll the phrase around in my head. Effa hums a little tune as she slips back into her shoes, then reaches out to help Luther. The little boy looks lost in thought, his expression shielded. "I heard you in the kitchen. You told Father she wouldn't get better. You don't have to lie."

Effa stops for the briefest of seconds — a pause so microscopic I would have missed it if I weren't glued to the scene. She pats Louie on the foot and looks up, a bright, fake smile plastered across her features.

"I was just joshing. I promise. Everything will be fine."

The grass behind them waves eerily until finally, Patrick steps out. "Find Louie yet?"

Effa steps aside so Patrick can see him. "I had to fish him out of the drink."

"I'm feeling a little left out," Patrick pouts. "Y'all went mud wrestling without me."

"You're shameless." Effa kisses him on the cheek and paints a heart around the spot with a muddy finger. Louie grumbles and rolls his eyes.

"Gross," he says, disappearing into the grass and leaving Patrick and Effa to follow. I can hear his voice as it fades into the distance. "Y'all are yucky. I'm walking home."

FOURTEEN

Lil: Morning, shug. Check the mailbox

Me: It's literally 8:17 AM

Lil: It's early, I know. Left something for you when I was out walking. I suggest you get it now.

Okay, Lil. Like that's not creepy. I don't answer her last text. I barely slept last night, my brain desperate to reconcile what I *thought* I knew about my family with what I've learned over the last few days.

Bleary-eyed and nursing the start of a headache, I slip from the covers and slide my hoodie on. The foyer's quiet this morning, the outside air already damp and sticky when I step through the front door. Dew clings to my feet as I cross the front yard, and sure enough, there's a single envelope waiting for me in the mailbox.

Another text comes through from Lil.

Lil: You found it

Me: Stop. You're creeping me out.

I snap a pic of my find and send it through to her.

Good, she responds. *Open it up*

I text her back. *What is it?*

Lil goes silent and my stomach growls. Annoyed, I shove my phone and the envelope in my pocket and head back up to the house.

Pa's at the door when I climb the front steps, looking overly eager for this early in the morning. "Lila Mae. I was hoping I'd find you." The set of his shoulders makes me nervous.

"Morning, Pa," I clear my throat of its cobwebs. "You found me. What's up?"

Pa holds the front door open. "I just made a run for pecan rolls. Left the box on the kitchen counter for you. Go grab one. Bring it to my office and we'll chat."

Unsettled, I creep into the kitchen and discover there is indeed a Daughtry's box. Vanilla and sugar fill my nose, almost enough comfort for me to drop my plans for interrogation. *Hey, Pa. How are you doing? I was going to ask about your nonexistent sister, but this pecan roll is sublime.*

I grab a plate and a paper towel and carry my spoils through the office french doors. Pa's at his desk rearranging a few stacks of paper. "Excellent. Have a seat, granddaughter."

"I'm a little underdressed for an interview."

He laughs. "I just miss my girl. You've been busy, it seems. Out with the Suttons?"

I shrug and take a bite of my pecan roll, chewing thoroughly. "We've been forced together. It's not by choice."

"Well." His jaw tightens. "Let's avoid them in the future if we can."

I nod, because I don't disagree with him. I have a million reasons not to hang out with that crew. Not the least of which is my own past with them, the bitterness that clings to our interactions. Despite yesterday's sparse moments of relative companionship, we don't seem to like each other that much.

"The truth is," Pa says, and I snap back to attention. "While I do want to visit with you, I have a specific topic in mind." I shift in my seat, my brain jumping between his past and the envelope in my pocket. Does he know about it? He asks me, "What are your academic plans for next year?"

Of all the conversations I could have imagined, this was definitely not one. My mouth opens and shuts. I don't know what to tell him. I was supposed to leave for my Fellowship in August. That's definitely not happening now.

Pa tugs a red folder from his stack of papers, the front emblazoned with a golden crest. He slides the folder across the desk and taps it with his fingers. "Briarwood Academy. Take a look."

I flip the folder open with shaky fingers. There's a welcome packet on the left. *We're excited to hear of your interest in Briarwood, North Carolina's premier boarding program for girls…"*

"Boarding school?" The words come out slowly. "In…" I flip to the back of the folder, "Raleigh? The Research Triangle?"

Pa nods. "Top tier academics. And they have an excellent program for young women with special needs."

"Special needs? I don't...I don't have any." Unless you count blinking, which obviously, I'm keeping to myself.

"Life with your mom has dealt you a hand of trauma. I want to make sure you have a stellar education along with the support you need. If something happens—"

My stomach drops. "What do you mean *if something happens*?"

He shrugs. "There's a history."

A history of bipolar disorder. What about the history he's wiped clean?

"Pa, who's Effa?"

"I'm sorry?" His complexion goes white.

"You had a sister. You *have* a sister. Effa. I found a record of her."

Pa doesn't speak. He leans back into his chair, lips pressed in a line like he's waiting for something. I motion to his office shelves, filled to the brim with books on local history and genealogy. "The record I found didn't have a birth date. And she's not mentioned anywhere else."

A flush creeps up my neck and makes my hairline itchy. I may have made a mistake. But then he shifts, his voice tight as he says, "You're right. I had a sister. She died before I was born."

Before he was born? It didn't look that way yesterday, but I can't say that without revealing the truth. "Why isn't she in the books? The family Bible, or something?"

Pa sighs, the look on his face turning wistful. "My father didn't handle it well. He chose to grieve by removing every potential mention of her from our family records, as well as any public records he could access."

"That's…" Illegal. And really stupid.

"Sad. But our knowledge of her lives on."

"Except it doesn't," I say, and lean forward. "It doesn't live on if no one knows about her."

Pa holds out his hands like *I don't know what to tell you.* "I know about her. Your grandmother knows about her. And now, granddaughter, so do you."

The silence in the room is suffocating, Lil's envelope burns a hole through my shorts. I'm so tempted to pull it out. The paper's old. Could she have sent me a clue about my family? I shift and start to reach for my back pocket when my grandfather clears his throat.

"Mae, this isn't why I called you in here. I'm sorry Effa's story is a surprise. It didn't occur to me you would want to know, though in retrospect, I understand why it bothers you." Pa hands me the Briarwood folder. "But I'd like to get back to the matter of Briarwood now, if we could please. I think you should attend for your senior year."

First, he holds fast to the lie about our family. Now he's pushing this boarding school on me? "I'm not leaving my mother," I say.

He frowns a little. "Lila Mae, you're practically an adult—"

"And I'm capable of making my own decisions. I don't appreciate coercion, Pa."

"I'm not coercing you." His tone's conciliatory. "I'm asking you to consider applying."

Some of the fight leaves my chest, the anger deflated now that he's phrased it like ultimately, it's my choice. I'm still frustrated with him about Effa, but I'll put that on hold until I know more about her. I take the folder in my hands and run my fingers across the smooth surface.

"I'll think about it, Pa. Yeah."

———

BRIARWOOD ACADEMY LOOKS...NOT awful. But it's still three hours away from Mom. I'm not leaving her, not even for the robust writing program I got into. Couple the distance with what Briarwood calls the Magnolia program - their special needs department - and my interest is even less.

I toss the folder on my bed and flop down beside it, my eye catching on the camcorder across the room. My brain needs a break - there's so much that I'm overwhelmed and don't know what do with it. Mom. The blinking. The continued strain with the trio. And now I'm supposed to look at boarding school.

My phone lights up.

Lil: Open the envelope?

No, is all I text back

Lil: Suit yourself. But I do think you'll be interested in what it holds. That, and the footage on the camcorder

I shove the phone under my bed.

Restless, I grab my journal and head out onto the porch. Five minutes later I have one sentence. Ten minutes and I've revised it three times. Fifteen minutes in, I've got one phrase and a boatload of flowers scribbled in the margin. I'm sweating in the heat and direct sunlight.

I give up and go inside.

Lil's envelope is still in my pocket. I tug it out, then slide my thumb beneath the ancient flap. It gives easily, my fingers brushing against a vintage black and white photo. A family stands within the frame, and my eye's drawn first to a tall, light-haired man who resembles my grandfather. His arm curls around a dark-haired woman who's not quite smiling, her eyes focused to the left of the frame.

In front of them stands a girl - Effa. She's younger here than when I've seen her, a little fuller in the face. She's laughing, her eyes alive and her smile infectious. She has her hand on a little boy's head.

I turn the photo over. Something's scribbled on the back. I have to tilt it toward the light and squint to read the faded writing, but I make it out clearly.

The Griffin Family: Josiah, Annie, Effa, Luther.

That settles it.

My grandfather's lied to me twice.

FIFTEEN

It's a beautiful afternoon by Minnesott standards when Nathan pulls his work truck in the yard. I could care less, though, about the low humidity or the heady scent of plumeria. I fling a twenty-five-pound bag of fertilizer out of the truck bed and imagine it's my grandfather's head.

Nathan freezes. "You okay there?"

"Peachy." I grab a two-by-four.

"Mae, I, uh, appreciate the help," he ducks; the lumber's bigger than I realized. "But this is a hostile work environment."

"I am not hostile," I spit, cursing as my hand catches a splinter. I toss the wood into the pile Nathan started by the back porch. "I'm not heartbroken or on my period or any other male assumption you might throw at me." I stomp back to the truck and start unloading the brick pavers. "I'm just really." *Grunt.* "Freaking." *Argh.* "Mad."

Nathan's lips twist to the side, head bobbing. "Okay. It's always good to get it out."

Heaving, I go to climb up in the bed and grab another set of pavers.

"Woah, woah — wait a minute, Lima Bean."

"Get off me, Cartwright," I pull away from him, the motion dropping me back on the ground. "I can't...I don't...I just..." Stupid tears prick my eyes, and I growl in frustration. "Just please, Nathan. Let me do this. Let me work it out on my own."

Nathan stares at me, wide-eyed. I take a deep, hiccuping breath. My legs give out, and the next thing I know, I'm sitting on the ground by the wood pile. Nathan opens the cooler and hands me a drink.

"You done, kid?"

I scowl at him. He holds his hands up in a gesture of defense.

"Hey — I'm not judging. I've had moments." He takes his cap off and sits next to me, his long legs stretched out in the grass.

We stay like that in relative silence, listening to the muffled crash of waves on the shore. I close my eyes, willing away the tears as I sort through my emotions. I feel angry. Sad. Alone.

"I'm fine," I finally whisper.

Nathan answers, "I don't think that's true."

Not sure what to say, I put my arms around my knees and hug them tighter. "Pa wants me to go to boarding school in the fall."

Nathan shifts beside me, turning so we're face to face. "And?' he asks, like he knows there's more to the story. He's right, but there's no way I can tell him about my former friends or the memory box or the blinking or Effa. I stick to the school issue because it's safe.

"I'm not sure it's the right choice. Remember when you asked if I got into that writing program?"

"The day I came to get you? Yeah."

"Well, I did. I was supposed to do my senior year of high school at Keith College as a Lowell-Howard scholar. But I withdrew my acceptance after Mom's incident. I can't leave her like this."

Nathan hums. "You're worried about her."

"She quit her meds and overdosed."

"She's seemed pretty stable to me, especially lately."

"Seriously?"

He laughs. "What? I'm just calling it like I see it."

"And agreeing with everyone else."

Nathan turns his heel in the grass and tears at it, watching the way it spins under his shoe. "Maybe it's what everyone says because there's truth in it."

Okay, I'll give him that point.

"The thing with my Mom, though?" I say. "It's like, cycles. She'll be fine for a while, functioning, and then suddenly she's peeling plaster off the walls. There's always a slide back into her mania and then the depression. If that happens while I'm gone…"

"She's an adult," he says. "She can handle it."

I give him a look: *Yeah, right.*

"Obviously, you know her differently," he continues. "And I'm not even sure I know her at all. But I did know her once, and the Dewitt Griffin I knew wouldn't want you to put your life on hold because of a bunch of maybes. She'd want more for you than that."

I think back to my mom's repeated reminders that I don't have to hold her hand. I get it — I do. She thinks she can function. I want her to function.

Too bad we don't get what we want.

"Whatever," I say, and push to standing. "We should get back to work."

"No."

"No?"

Nathan stands, too, his arms crossed in front of him. "You need to go out and do something fun."

"This is fun."

"This is landscaping and manual labor."

"I like manual labor."

"Not today, you don't."

Nathan takes my work gloves and tosses them in the truck bed. "Saw the twins and Mason this morning at the Piggly Wiggly. Said they were hanging at the trestle today."

The trestle's not far. We hung out there all the time in the summer, a welcome reprieve from the jellyfish and the heat. But that spot was the beginning of the end for us, specifically for me and Ezra. We fell for each other, literally and figuratively. And then I broke his heart.

"No thanks," I say.

Nathan locks the tailgate. "Van says you won't respond to her texts."

"I blocked her." Along with Ezra and Mason.

"Figured as much," Nathan says, then he leans against the truck and scratches his chin a little, his gaze trailing off to the right. "I had a dog. Did I tell you?"

Where is he going with this? "Not that I remember, no."

"I named her Matilda."

"After the Roald Dahl character?"

"I've read that book, actually, but no. She just looked like a Matilda to me. This smart mutt who showed up at my front door half-starved and looking like she'd been through it. I couldn't get near her at first. She hung around, though. She wanted a human. And suddenly, I wanted a dog."

Nathan shifts on his feet, his smile wistful. "I put food out every day. She warmed up. Decided I was worth trusting. Best damn dog I ever had."

Nathan pushes off the tailgate and walks to the driver's side door, pulling it open. "Matilda taught me some things. She taught me what it means to trust. She taught me how to love unconditionally. And by the end of her life, she'd shown me there's a helluva lot more to it than holding your heart hostage." He studies me for a second, then taps his hand against the doorframe. "You might want to think about that."

———

THE CAMCORDER'S waiting where I left it, perched on the

corner of my desk. Fingers trembling, I turn it on, barely pressing the button to start playback. It's sensitive, I guess, because playback begins automatically. I'm staring at thirteen-year-old me.

There's no sound — I haven't turned it up yet. Just me with a huge smile, lying face up on the grass. The camera's focused on my eyes, my strawberry blonde hair spread around me in a halo. I'm laughing. The camera pans up and over, catching a smiling Van.

The scene cuts out and is replaced by a new one. This time we're on the shore. Mason, Ezra, and I are poking around the jetty, looking for something. I wish I could remember what.

Frame after frame, I watch us: four goofy, gangly kids. There are Jeep rides with Nathan. Bike tricks on the road. Rainy days we spent playing card games in the sunroom. The first time Ezra took us sailing on a Flying Scot.

Limbs heavy with so many memories, I let the camera fall to my bed. I must bump one of the controls, though, because it skips forward to more recent footage.

It's the Sutton twins shopping at Goodwill.

I'll admit, for a while, we filmed everything, even everyday stuff like taking out the trash. But the twins look older here: Fifteen? Sixteen, maybe? I'm a year younger than they are, and by the time I was fourteen, we'd turned our focus to adventures. By fifteen, I'd moved away.

Curious, I turn up the volume.

"Are you kidding me? She hates that band."

Ezra balks. "*I* don't hate this band. And this is supposed to be her reminder."

"Of crappy music?"

"No, dipwad. Of us."

"Makes sense to me," Mason says, his voice behind the camera.

"Don't encourage him." Van scowls.

"Why not?"

"Because the two of you are beyond frustrating! The point of this trip is to find items relevant to our *friendship*."

Ezra holds out the record. "Hence the album from Turning Jane."

Van was right — I hated that band, only listening because it was Ezra's favorite. Van throws her hands in the air.

"Fine. Whatever. Get the album. Anything else we get should be *for her*."

"But this is for her," I hear Ezra mutter.

"It's alright, dude," Mason says, so quietly I have to back up and replay to hear it. "I get what you're doing. So will Mae."

The expedition goes on for another ten minutes, cataloging items they pull for the box. When they're done, they approach the checkout counter and turn the camera on the guy at the register. I recognize him — Finegan? Felix? Franz?

"'Sup guys," he says, setting his phone down on the counter. "What's with all this crap?"

"It's not crap, Flanigan," Ezra mutters. *Flanigan.*

Van puts a hand on Ezra's elbow and his shoulders soften immediately. She flashes Flanigan a terrifying smile. "These are gifts for Mae," she says, and even I can hear the unspoken warning behind them. *You don't want to mess with us.*

Flanigan checks them out with a handheld scanner and

rattles off the tab. "I know y'all are friends with that girl, but I gotta be honest. Glad to see her and her freak show of a mom leaving town."

The camera stills, then slowly changes position until it rests at counter height. "What did you just say?" The voice is Ezra's.

"Good riddance. Dewitt's crazy. Her daughter's not much better, honestly."

A black shoe appears on the counter before the viewfinder screen goes dark. They gave me the memory box the night before I left, and the details of that moment make more sense now. Mason had a bruise on his cheek and there were cuts on Ezra's knuckles.

"What happened to y'all? Were you fighting?"

"Van was a little reckless with the golf cart."

For the second time today, heat pricks the back of my eyelids. I blink and wipe the liquid away. Mom's down the hall in her room — she was working in front of her laptop when I walked by earlier.

Me: Hey, Mom. How are you?

She responds almost immediately. *I'm fine, Bean. You okay?*

Me: Yeah. Just checking in. You know me. Always focused on your welfare

Mom: I can assure you I am both well and fair

Me: Good. Afternoon plans?

Mom: Yep.

Me: .....

Me: You gonna tell me?

Mom: You gonna hang out with Mason and the twins?

I roll my eyes.

Me: Maybe

Mom: HALLELUJAH

Mom: I'm getting coffee with Rosie. See you at dinner?

Me: Yeah

I back out of mom's conversation and pull up my contact list. My finger shakes as I scroll to the list of blocked contacts.

One's a telemarketer.

Two are Evan and Jane.

The other three are Van, Ezra, and Mason.

I hover over the last three and tap unblock.

SIXTEEN

Ezra's Jeep pulls into the driveway. It's Van behind the wheel. I'm so relieved it's not him that when I climb in, I blurt the most ridiculous thing I could possibly think of.

"Ezra lets you drive his Jeep?"

My cheeks heat in embarrassment but Van doesn't seem bothered. "He better," she drawls. "I rebuilt half of it."

Evangeline Sutton, mechanic? "Since when do you rebuild cars?"

Van pops the clutch and backs out of the driveway. "Since my Dad almost died."

"Lil said you might lose the shop," I sputter. "She didn't say anything about your dad."

Van just shrugs. "It was an accident. He lived through it. But the shop needed warm bodies so Ezra and I took over. I had to learn a bunch of stuff right quick."

I'm still reeling from the shock of Van's announcement when we turn onto a dirt road off Highway 306. We used to bike all the way, a decision that now seems monumentally stupid. I'm in an open-air Jeep and my thighs are sticking to the leather. How did we not die of the heat?

Van parks on the hill above the creek slope, the abandoned wooden trestle just ahead. I follow Van down the embankment on wobbly, adrenaline-spiked legs. I'm so slow, my feet so unsure on the jagged slope down that Van reaches the creek before I do. The boys stand in the shallows, arms crossed. Mason splashes out and walks up the embankment to greet us, his lips a grim slash of displeasure. "Didn't think you'd show up."

Then why did he tell Nathan? "Didn't think it would be a big deal."

Van stands like a wall between us. I don't know if I should be worried or glad. Begrudgingly, I settle for both, watching Ezra make his way up toward us, tanned skin almost glowing. My stomach does a flip and I pinch the inside of my arm, irritated at my reaction to him. I've affected him, too, it seems, but not in the same manner. His eyes harden when he looks at me. An ache burns in my throat, regret stinging the corners of my eyes. I watch the flex in his jaw as he mutters something to Mason, then walks past me up the hill.

Mason skips a stone into the creek before his eyes land on me. "You were in his head a long time, Griffin."

"Isn't that his problem?" I ask, immediately wishing I'd kept my mouth shut.

Mason's nostrils flare. "I was down to give you a second chance or whatever, but not after what you just said."

Hands shaking, I hoist my bag to my shoulder. I deserved

that. I know I did. But what I deserve and what I'm capable of handling are very, very different. "This was a mistake."

"Copley!" Van scolds. "Stop being a dipwad!" Van's footfalls track me up the hill.

I move faster, sweat sliding down the back of my neck. I hear a splash, and Van calls out something I can't quite decipher. I turn around just in time to see Ezra surface from the creek below me, water glistening like diamonds on his skin.

A hand closes around my wrist. Van's out of breath and panting. "Don't be stupid, Mae. And don't you ever make me run this hill again. I mean if you're dying, yes. I will haul my booty up here to assist you. But man," she leans over and puts her hands on her kneecaps. "These legs of mine are stunners, but they are not meant for chasing anxious dweebs."

"It was a mistake for me to come here," I reiterate. Van stands and grabs my arms.

"Decca Records rejecting The Beatles was a mistake. Those two and their crappy attitudes?" She gestures behind her at Ezra and Mason. "That is fixable." Her shoulders slump, and the fire in her gaze dims out a little. "I called you an anxious dweeb, but I want my best friend back. I've missed you. I want you in my life again even if getting there hurts."

My throat closes up and I wobble, the world shifting beneath my feet. "Just give the boys a chance," Van says, reaching forward to steady me. "Mason's thinks he has to protect me. I've told him I can handle myself. And Ezra—" I follow Van's gaze, our eyes lighting on her brother in the water. "You know Ezra can hold a grudge. But he's not upset

with *you*, really. It's more the circumstances. And with everything going on with Dad…"

She's right. I do know Ezra. I know Van and Mason, too.
Or at least I did, once upon a time when we were young and
the choices we made didn't feel so vital. I swallow the lump
in my throat, wondering if maybe the pain is worth it.

"I'll stay," I whisper, a chill running through me. I don't
know if it's a bad sign or not. But as I follow Van back down
the hill, back to the markers of our childhood, I'm going to try
to believe it's good.

————

"YOU MIGHT HAVE something with that Southern-Chinese-
fusion-whatever," Ezra muses, "but pork rinds weren't
invented in the South."

Egos have settled down, and the four of us are gathered on
an old beach blanket. Mason whips toward Ezra, a stray piece
of fried pig skin falling from his mouth. "No. No way. You're
lying. Don't do me like that, bro."

"Like what?" Ezra says, and the laugh in his voice is like
sunshine. "I'm just keeping you honest."

"Honest?" Mason squeaks, shoving Ezra on the shoulder.
"No, man. You're keeping me one hundred percent broke."

I turn to Van. "What's going on here?"

"They're discussing Mason's future plans."

"How'm I supposed to run a successful fusion-based,
gastronomical pop-up when my world-famous dessert might

not be authentic? Vanilla-pork rind ice cream is a culinary experience in the vein of Southern-Chinese fusion."

Van rolls her eyes. "Here we go with the vocabulary."

"I'm using my SAT words, Evangeline."

"No one calls a food truck a gastronomical pop-up," Van says to him.

"Well, I do." He tosses a pork rind at Ezra, who catches it. "It's trend-setting. Forward-thinking, if you will." Ezra smirks and tosses the pork rind back at Mason. It pegs him squarely in the nose.

Van hauled a bunch of stuff down from the Jeep earlier, including the infamous memory box. Lil insisted I take it home, but I conveniently *forgot it* in the boat's storage compartment. Van found it, I guess, and decided we should go through it. It's on the blanket next to her.

"Shall we see what we've got here?" she asks, and a cold dread creeps up my skull. Van starts pulling stuff out. A stack of festival tickets. A package of water balloons. Van throws me a look with each item. R*emember? How could you leave this? Leave us?* Two bites into one of the sandwiches they brought and my stomach's already churning. I get up and toss it in the trash.

"You owe me five dollars and sixty-seven cents, Griffin." Ezra's chin lifts in the direction of the trash.

"I don't have my wallet," I say, doing my best to keep my voice steady. "I can pay you when you drop me off."

He holds my gaze, the intensity of his stare making me nauseous. But I'm not going to back down. "Never mind," he says, looking away first, cheeks flaming. "I don't take Griffin money. I forgot."

Van rolls her eyes so emphatically they nearly get lost in the back of her head. "Oh, for the love of…hey!" Her reprimand on hold, she holds up an unopened box of sparklers. "Are these the ones we used the night of the Mailbox of the Unknown Trailer?"

I look at Ezra. "What's wrong with Griffin money?" He turns his body away from me.

Mason leans in, studying the box of sparklers. "Dude — I think they are. Crazy night. Almost got arrested for the bottle rocket."

"You also nearly blew off your hand, or have you forgotten?"

Mason's expression turns dreamy. "That night was so much fun."

"So much drama, you mean. It was not fun," Van continues, "because the Mailbox of the Unknown Trailer actually belonged to that scary old dude on the edge of the woods." She looks at the boys, snatching the box of sparklers back and shaking it. "The number of times we ran through that forest and y'all never even noticed. Least observant idiots I know."

"At least we were good-looking idiots." Mason winks and tugs off his shirt. Ezra peers into the box and roots around, shoving the contents to the side like he's looking for something. "That old camcorder was in here." He turns to me, the look on his face unreadable. "*It was in here*. Why isn't it in here now?"

Because it's back in my room on the bed where I left it

after watching half the videos. Van saves me from myself, waving a hand of dismissal. "Whatever. None of those videos matter. I had braces. And really bad hair."

"You were a goddess," Mason says. Her cheeks redden. "You always have been, always will."

Ezra groans. "Stop hitting on my sister." He stands and grabs his shirt at the back of his neck, tugging it over his head and shoulders.

I train my eyes on an interesting patch of moss.

"Copley," Ezra says. "You jumping?"

"Hell yeah, man. I'm in." Mason holds his hand out to Van and she grabs it, bounding up from the ground with a whoop. "Mae?" He's leaning forward, an outstretched hand in front of my nose.

"I'll stay here," I say. My voice is robotic. Van gives the boys a gentle shove.

"Just go," she says. "I'll be up in a second." Mason and Ezra climb the hill.

"You sure you don't want to go?" Van asks me.

"I'm positive."

"It'll be like old times," she sings. Van studies me, head tilted to the side. Understanding flits across her face: I know he's thinking of our last trip up here, when Ezra and I shared our first kiss. "You can jump for you, you know, if you want to. It doesn't have to mean anything."

"I know." I shift, touched by her kindness. Can I live this life again?

"Van, what you said earlier. About how you miss being friends?"

"Yeah?"

I take a deep breath and silence the fear. "I think...I think maybe I do, too. Miss our friendship."

Van nearly knocks me to the ground, arms in a death grip around my shoulders. "Van, geez. I can't breathe."

She lets go and pats my arm. "Sorry. You're good," she says. "Still breathing." There's a skip in her step as she heads off toward the trestle. "That's all I needed to hear."

SEVENTEEN

I was twelve the first time I jumped from the trestle. It was this weird, in-between stage where I wasn't *really* a kid, but I didn't feel like a grown-up, either. Scaling a decaying piece of infrastructure and leaping from it was a decidedly grown-up rush.

Now, though? The thought is terrifying. There's not even a hint of control. I can't predict where I'll land or what happens when I hit the water. It's like the whole of my life with my mom condensed into one terrifying moment.

I don't need to jump from the trestle. My whole life is a leap of faith.

I'm not complaining, though, as Mason and the twins take turns sailing into the water. I haven't been tracking but I think they're on jump number five. I push my toes into the mossy ground and lie back, closing my eyes as the sun's warmth washes over me.

"Griffin."

A fat drop of water plops directly on my forehead, star-tling me upright.

I must have dozed off. The sun's lower in the sky, the air suspiciously quiet. I shake out my arms, still heavy from my apparent nap. Checking for drool, I rub a hand across my mouth as Ezra shifts above me, his hand rubbing the nape of his neck.

I scramble to my feet, my legs a little wobbly. "Why are you talking to me?"

"Check your phone," he says, and I don't miss the flash of brotherly annoyance.

I have a text message from Van.

Van: Talk to my brother

Me: Your brother hates me. No

Van: He doesn't hate you. And I'm busy. Kissing Mason

"She can't be serious," I mutter.

"Oh, I assure you. She can."

The eye roll in Ezra's voice mirrors my irritation. My knuckles whiten as I clutch my phone.

Me: VAN. This is ridiculous

Van: It's fortuitous. Give me and Mason some space. You and Ezra smooth things over. Get back to where you left off

She sends a photo through, an old one from that last summer. It's of Ezra and me, hands touching, sitting alone at the end of the pier. My stomach flips, the sort of drawn-out swoop I used to get jumping from the trestle. Didn't I swear I wasn't doing that today?

Van: Go on. Chat a little. Make up while Mason and I make out

"Eww," I say, looking up at Ezra. He holds his hands up in a gesture of defeat. "I didn't ask to be in the same womb. She was there when I got there." And he's been dealing with her ever since.

"Those two are the worst," I grouse, settling back on the blanket, studying the sunlight's pattern through the trees.

"They won't admit it if you ask, but they've been into each other forever." I feel Ezra's eyes on me and I stiffen. We were into each other once, too.

"You thirsty?" Ezra asks me, raw emotion in his voice. He's being nice. I don't want him to be nice—it makes the back-and-forth more confusing. But my throat's super dry and my stomach's still flipping. I nod.

He digs through the ice and pulls two bottles from the cooler, tossing the second one to me. "I don't need a babysitter," I say, instead of a thank you. "I was fine here by myself."

Ezra stares me down, the green of his irises mixing with the steel in his gaze. It's an intense, darker shade, and every cell in my body regrets what I just said to him.

I hurt him once. I keep hurting him. What is wrong with me?

Ezra scowls. "I don't care what you do, Griffin."

If I were a better person, this is where I would apologize. But my anxiety's at the helm, now that I'm face to face with Ezra. "You...jerk face. I *wanted* to lay here in peace."

"Jerk face." Amusement plays across his features as he settles on the stump across from me. "Are we in second grade, Mae? Do I have cooties?"

I ball my hands into two fists, then unclench them when I

realize I am, in fact, behaving like a grade schooler. "Whatever. It was nicer than what I wanted to say."

"Which was?" He's taunting me. I turn my body away.

"Why do you want to know?" I ask.

"No reason. Curiosity, maybe."

Why is he curious?

Why am I still sitting here?

The blanket shifts as Ezra sits on it. Everything grows hot. My neck, my cheeks, the center of my belly. I scoot forward on the blanket, as far away from him as I can get.

"I wasn't supposed to be here this summer," he murmurs.

"Funny. Neither was I." It's biting and mean and absolutely a defense mechanism. He doesn't deserve it. "I'm sorry."

"It's fine." The blanket shifts again. "I got into Broward for nautical engineering. Summer term started this month."

"Congratulations," I say, and realize I mean it. Getting into Broward is huge. He's loved boats and anything to do with them since he was small, and Broward's one of the top programs in the country.

"Thanks," he tells me. "I'm not going."

I gasp and turn around. "Why aren't you? Broward's been your dream for years."

Ezra huffs a dry laugh. "You remember that."

"Of course I do."

"Dreams aren't exactly cheap." Ezra pulls his knees to his chest, trapping them in with his forearms. "There's a niche market for vintage-style sailboats. I built a few wooden prams. I saved enough money to pay for at least the first year's tuition."

"But?"

"The money's gone. Half of it went to support Sutton Seafood. The other went to Dad's medical bills."

My hand goes to my mouth. "Are you kidding?"

"Not even a little bit. Dad was contracting out because the shop's had some trouble and two kids in college ain't cheap. Found a temp job on a yacht build over in Morehead." Ezra pulls a blade of grass from the ground and rubs it between his fingers. "He fell twenty-five feet from a yacht scaffolding. Freaking lucky he even survived."

My throat goes tight. That poor family. My voice shakes a little when I speak. "I saw Lil. She mentioned something about the shop. Said y'all were having trouble and I was sorry to hear it."

There's a tightness to his eyes when he laughs. It's humor-less. "You should be. Considering it's your grandfather's fault."

I rear back. "I'm sorry?"

He sneers at me. "You heard what I said."

I mean yeah, I did, but that doesn't mean I understand it. "Are you accusing Pa of pushing him from the scaffolding?"

"What? No. Your grandfather's a jerk, but he's not violent. He started a whole bunch of rumors about the shop."

I shake my head. "He wouldn't do that."

"Oh, he would. And he did."

"But that doesn't make sense. Sutton Seafood's a

Minnesott institution." If anybody wanted to protect it, it would be my history-loving Pa.

Ezra stares at me long and hard before pulling his phone from his pocket. He swipes the screen a few times and hands it to me. "See for yourself," he says, and my eyes go wide as I take in the webpage Ezra's showing me.

A Letter to the Editor in the county paper, titled, *Sutton Seafood: Institution or Menace?*

"He accused your father of subpar sanitation practices," I marvel.

"Keep reading. There's more."

"Shoddy business practices? *A rat infestation*? Holy cow, Ezra. He implied your parents are dealing drugs!"

Ezra takes the phone back. "That was just the first one. The paper's published three so far. He writes one about every six months, I reckon. And because your grandfather's such a pillar of the community, people believe the lies."

"Ezra, I..." don't understand. Why would Pa do this? I don't know my own grandfather anymore. Lil's insistence that I help takes on a new, pressing urgency. The Sutton's struggles are my family's fault.

"I can...I can talk to him."

Ezra goes completely still. He watches me like he's trying to figure out some great mystery of the universe. "Why would you want to help us out?"

Hurt blooms in my chest. I deserve that. "You really do think that poorly of me." Ezra stirs at my side, getting up on his knees and reaching for the memory box. He retrieves the green ceramic frog. I inhale as he sits back on his heels, kneeling, sort of, in front of me. I exhale as he takes my hand.

"You left without saying goodbye, Mae." He presses the figure into my palm. I squeeze my hand around it, the points of the feet digging into my flesh a little.

"I missed my mom. I thought she was better." It comes out like a whisper. "I thought…I *wanted* a fresh start."

What I don't say, and what I don't know if I can ever tell him, is that the blinking was getting worse. I was slipping through the cracks with alarming frequency, convinced I was losing it. I'm still not sure I was wrong.

Ezra shifts to sit down next to me, his long legs spread out in the waning sun. "We all wanted that for you, too. And we were happy for you, really. But you cut us off, and I—" he clears his throat. "*We* lost the one person we trusted with all of our secrets. We told each other everything." I study his face, and in its sharp, masculine lines I see traces of the boy I hurt. Loved. There's a softness in him now, a vulnerability when he continues. "I got back from sailing practice that morning. Found this box on my front step."

"I didn't—" I gulp. "I didn't mean to hurt you."

He studies me and I don't breathe. "It was a long time ago," he says.

"But it still matters." I huff a watery laugh and drag my finger beneath my eyelids. "I don't blame you for hating me, Ezra."

He exhales a short sigh. "Is that what you think? That I hate you?"

I lift my eyebrows. "Um, yeah?"

"I don't hate you, Mae." He smiles a little. "I know. It doesn't makes sense. I tried to burn that whole box in a trash fire once I realized you weren't going to answer my messages." He rubs at his bottom lip and I fight the urge to reach out and adjust the lock of hair that's fallen over his forehead. "That's how the box ended up at Lil's."

His little laugh is soft, like warm honey. I should say something to push him away. I sift through the words in my head, trying to choose a response that's detached yet conciliatory. But then he speaks, and all hope of that is ruined.

"When I saw you at Daughtry's, everything I thought I felt changed. I couldn't think. I couldn't speak. It was honestly like you'd never left here. And I realized hatred wasn't what I felt. It was emptiness. I missed you. You left a giant, freaking hole."

I missed him, too, I think. More than I realized. More than I wanted to admit. But now I'm here, surrounded by the ghosts of who we were and all the pain that's followed behind us. "Do you...do you want to start over?" His eyes widen and I rush to clarify. "I mean, as friends?"

He rubs the back of his neck like he did earlier. "I don't know if I can trust you, Mae."

Oh, Ezra. "I don't know if you should."

Long shadows fall over us both, and Mason's voice sounds from above us. "They're sitting close enough to kiss."

"I'm withholding judgment," Van says, her shadow flanking Mason's. "Just until I know they have all their limbs."

The moment between us snapped, Ezra lobs a pinecone at

Mason. He catches it and tucks it in his bag. "You're gonna find this, E. When you least expect it."

Ezra smirks and makes a rude gesture as he stands.

Ezra reaches out to help me up, his eyes telegraphing a secret. Like even though he said he's not sure he can trust me, he has enough faith for us both.

"Y'all ready to go?" Van asks. "Or are we interrupting something?" Her gaze pings back and forth between Ezra and me, assessing. But Ezra only nods. He tears his eyes away from mine with what seems like a hint of reluctance. He's been brave so many times, not just for himself, but for me, too, when I needed him.

"Wait." I say, and three heads swivel my way, their faces expectant. "I think...I think I want to jump."

Mason's grin is wide. Van is beaming. And Ezra? There's confusion and something else - joy?

I tug my coverup over my head to reveal a modest two-piece and Van whistles. I toss the dress at her head. My steps are slow but sure as they lead me one, two, three steps closer to Ezra. I don't miss the way his eyes do a quick sweep of my body. I reach out to him with a settled hand. He looks down at my arm. I'm not breathing. And then he takes my hand in his.

EIGHTEEN

"You realize there are child labor laws, drafted for situations such as these."

Nathan tugs his cap down over his eyes and hands me a pair of heavy-duty work gloves. "I'd say a decent sunrise's worth a run-in with Sheriff Kelly."

"This is criminal," I mumble, shoving the worn leather over my hands. "My friends have actual, paid jobs and they don't have to get up this early."

"Quit your whining and pull up the dang pot."

Sunrise is the best time to pull the crab pots, apparently, which is what we're doing right now. They're chicken wire traps, roughly three feet by three feet, cube-shaped, and with an entrance-only doorway. Two days ago, Nathan baited the inside with raw chicken before tossing them in the water and securing them to the pier with eight feet of line.

It's super early but it's hot out here already. The pots are heavy and they stink. I feel so bad for the buggers trapped inside, waving their claws around like drunken sailors with switchblades. I have half a mind to spring the traps and dump them out.

"Release those critters and you're getting 'em back by hand, lady."

"That's creepy, Nathan. Don't read my mind."

"Not that hard to tell what you're thinking." I stick my tongue out at him. "That was classy," he grumbles. "Nice of you to keep me in line."

Twenty minutes later we've emptied the crab pots and put the spoils in a cooler under ice. We lug it down the pier and secure it to the golf cart. "You're lucky," I say, "as far as keeping things classy. You could have Van as your lackey, you know."

"Yes, I know. And no thank you. She'd have tossed me off the pier by now. Twice."

Nathan and I wince at the high-pitched whine from the golf cart's ignition. It ends when he turns the key. He presses down on the pedal and the cart lurches forward, bumping us up the hill and across the grounds toward Pinecliff. Nathan spares a glance in my direction. "Speaking of, you got plans with those kids today?"

Actually, that's a really good question. I don't know if I do. Yesterday's events were *charged*. And I don't just mean how things went with Van or the come-to-Jesus meeting I had with Ezra. The jump from the trestle was electric, too. Every step up that ladder shot tiny sparks of life through a part of me I thought was dormant. And then at the top, the breeze lifting my hair; the loud rush of sound as I leaped into the water.

The exhilarating rush of entry.

The adrenaline from holding Ezra's hand.

It was good — so good — but exhausting. I don't know if I can live through that again. I open my mouth to give Nathan a lame, noncommittal answer but snap it shut almost immediately. Heavy guitars and female vocals blast from the sunroom. The hair rises on the back of my neck.

"What time is it, Nathan?" I ask him, my voice steady. He slows the cart and glances at his watch. "Five of eight," he says, the words slow and deliberate like molasses. He peers at me and puts a hand on my shoulder. "You okay there, kid?"

That blast of music is my mom's preferred band for painting, but only when she's in a manic episode. "I was just curious," I say. "Don't have my phone on me. Mind if I take a bathroom break?"

Nathan nods. "Ten minutes?" He gestures to the cooler. "I'll meet you 'round back after I get these critters squared away."

Apprehension steals my breath as I climb the porch steps and make my way to the sunroom. The music's stopped. Mom's sitting in the corner of the room facing the water. The beginning brush strokes on her canvas are already a work of art.

"Mom?"

She looks up, not startled in the slightest. Like she expected me to be there when she turned. "Sorry about that blast of sound," she says. "Did you hear it? Scared the crap out of me. It's the first time I've used the speakers in here. Moses. They are way more powerful than I thought."

Sweet relief washes over me. "Maybe your parents are party animals."

Mom smiles at me and winks conspiratorially. "More likely, they're just going deaf."

I laugh and hug her awkwardly so I don't share too much of my stench. I head back outside where Nathan and I work until lunchtime, when, sweat dripping, we take a break in the boathouse shade.

We're a little worn out for conversation, so I replay a thought I had while I was arm-deep in Deebie's heirloom rose. What if my mom wasn't honest with me? I could go right to the source.

"Cartwright, were you born here?"

Surprise passes over Nathan's features. "I was."

"What about your parents?" I ask.

"Early Crystal Meth users. They grew up in Grantsboro, up the road."

A rueful smile tugs at his lips as he pops a chip in his mouth, munching on it. "I wasn't exactly planned. I was eight when they left. Got home from school to an empty trailer. They didn't even leave a note."

I gasp. "Oh, Nathan."

He waves a hand. "It's not as bad as you think. Lil used to keep an eye on me since our trailer was right across the creek from her farmhouse. She came by around dinner time and found me crying in the kitchen." He trails off, unfocused eyes staring up into the tree line. "Went to a foster home for a bit while Lil got things sorted, but after that, I went and lived with her."

I open my mouth a few times, dumbfounded, then shut it when I can't think of anything useful to say. I knew Lil was his guardian, but I didn't know the story behind it. Nathan drops a fatherly hand on my shoulder. "It's alright, Bean. I found family, anyway."

"You mean Lil?"

"Yeah, Lil. And Gil and Rosie. And there was this other girl. You might know her, too." His smile's wistful with a hint of teasing.

"My mom," I say. He cuts his eyes to me, and I'm surprised to see there's barely a hint of longing. "Yep. But she left, so…" He shrugs.

"And yet you kept working for my grandparents."

"It was a solid, well-paying job. And I figured, if your mama ever came back, the best place to be was here. Not that I was waiting around for her, or anything." I quirk an eyebrow. "Okay, okay. I waited a little." He winks at me, then looks away.

I drop my head against the wall and squeeze my eyes shut. It's hard not to be angry at my Mom. She did what she had to do, I guess, but she left behind a wake of collateral damage.

Just like she always does.

"Kiddo. Hey." I feel a nudge at my sneaker. Nathan's face is etched with concern. "She left, and it killed me, but I've moved on. And when she finally came back, she brought you. You're not my blood, but you're the closest thing I've ever had to a daughter. I'd go through it again if it put you in my life."

Thick, heavy emotion washes over me, lodging at the back

of my throat. He's just confirmed I'm not his, and yet he loves me like a daughter anyway. I pull my knees to my chest and drop my head down, feeling so very small and unsure. I had hoped. I would have been mad at my mom for lying, yeah, but I would have let go of the anger. Now I'm back at the start, back to an endless cycle of wondering.

What a gift Nathan is to me, though.

"Thank you," I whisper.

"Absolutely."

Nathan helps me up. I throw my arms around his neck and squeeze, trying to telegraph my feelings into the stiff posture of his shoulders. But I think he gets it, because while he pats my back a little awkwardly, he clears his throat and blinks hard when I pull away.

"Now, come on," he says. "We got work to finish. I'm not interested in causing more trouble for Miss Dora Bell."

"Me? Cause trouble?"

"Definitely." Nathan points to the roses I trimmed, now substantially thinner. My face heats and Nathan claps me on the shoulder. "How 'bout you pay attention next time?"

———

I'M FILTHY. I need a shower. I'm covered in fertilizer and I smell like a swamp. "You skip your deodorant, Mae?" Nathan is smirking.

"I'm offended."

"Well, kiddo, so's my nose."

Nathan gives an exaggerated grunt when I elbow him in

the stomach. "Man. You and your mama throw a mean elbow to the gut."

"I'll pass that info along with your compliments. Can I go take a shower?"

"Might as well. But do me a favor? Take this out to the boathouse." He hands me the bucket and shovel we used to dig the weeds from the back flowerbed. "I'll put the tractor in the shed."

Face scrunched in mock displeasure, I mutter a grumpy, "Fine." I hear him laughing as I head across the lawn, trying to fight the smile threatening my own features. What in the world was wrong with my mother? Nathan is such a good man.

There's not much of a breeze in the backyard, typically, and the air out here is humid and thick. It grows heavier with each step, same as the bucket and shovel in my hand as I walk to the boathouse.

"Mama!"

I set the bucket down.

Foreboding turns in my stomach. I breathe in, then out, through my nose. Then I close my eyes and count to ten, hoping that when I open my eyes, I'll be back in my own reality.

I don't know if I can hope enough.

I open my eyes and find the boathouse in front of me. It's unpainted, just the bare wood with which it was built. The trees are smaller, too, like this younger version of my grandfather. Red-faced and covered in sand, he's practically vibrating with excitement. He can't be older than seven, I'd guess.

"Louie!" A voice calls from behind me. "Louie!" He doesn't turn around. Louie's jumping up and down, desperate for his mother's attention. His mother — Annie, I know, from the photo — is kneeling at the edge of the boathouse, digging. She hasn't acknowledged her son.

"Mama, look. I have something to show you. I found a fossil. A real one. At the shore."

Annie's lips move but she doesn't speak, her focus on the dirt below her. "Mama," Luther says, leaning on her. "Mama! Look what I found!"

Despite my frustration at Pa and his lies about his sister, my heart hurts for him as I watch. "Mom?" The word is weaker now, his energy less obvious. "Fine," he huffs, turning back toward the house behind me. "I'll show you later. Never mind."

"Lulu. What are you doing?" Effa's voice is frantic as she moves toward him across the lawn. Louie doesn't flinch. He just grins super wide and takes off at a run toward his sister. "I wanted to show Mama my fossil. I found it all by myself."

Effa's eyes flit toward the boathouse. "I'm proud of you, Lulu."

"Mama, do you want to see it?" I cringe as he tries one last time, running back to find Annie still focused on the ground, still oblivious to her surroundings.

"She'll want to see it later, Lou. I promise." She turns him toward the house.

With a backward glance toward Annie, I follow Effa and Louie across the yard. "Let's get you inside," Effa says. "Get your hands clean before Patrick gets here." Effa tugs the screen door and we walk into the kitchen. A younger version of a petite, mocha-skinned woman I recognize stands cooking over the stove.

"Miss Mary, I need your help for a minute." Effa sets Lou at the sink. Miss Mary puts her spatula down and leans in as Effa whispers. Mary's eyes widen. "Absolutely," she says, removing her apron. "Don't you worry. I'll go right now."

Mary sets off at a trot through the back door and I watch her through the window as she runs.

"Are your hands all clean?" Effa asks, and when Lou nods, she hands him a towel.

"Mama's in a mood again, isn't she, Effie?"

Effa's shoulders tighten. "She's gardening. Miss Mary's gone to help her finish up."

I glance out the door and see Mary holding Annie, a wide smile on Mary's face. Mary's rocking Annie back and forth, singing to her. Maybe talking. I can't hear them. I can only watch from inside the house.

The scratch of a chair brings my attention to the kitchen. Luther's plopped down, his head on the table surface. "Oh come on, little Lu. Don't you want to ride into New Bern with Patrick?"

"Why should I? Father says the Suttons ruin everything they touch."

I'm pretty sure Effa and I have the same reaction: the color drains from our faces. Hers I can see; mine I can feel in the slight sway of my body and the cold, clammy sensation I'm currently experiencing.

Patrick's last name is Sutton.

My great-aunt loved a Sutton boy.

Effa takes a deep breath and begins swapping out Luther's clothing. "What Father said isn't true, and you know it."

"What about Mama and her gardening?"

"What about it?"

"Father says she wouldn't garden all the time if you and Patrick weren't friends."

"Now you listen to me. Mama's gardening has nothing to do with the Suttons. And has Patrick ever harmed a hair on your head?"

"No."

"Father says things he doesn't mean when he's frustrated. Or when he's angry. Which is all the time."

Luther looks down at his shoes, wheels turning. "But why would he say something like that?"

"I don't know," Effa says, but I can tell she's lying. "Quite frankly, it's not our mystery to solve."

"Who's Frankly?"

Effa smiles, some of the tension leaving her. "He's no one, darling. Just a figure of speech."

A knock reverberates through the foyer. "That'll be Patrick," Effa says. "Let's get out of here quick, before Father can raise a stink at us."

I watch them exit through the kitchen, their silhouettes fading into nothing. I step back with a jolt. Back in the heat, back in my time, back to the boathouse and its blue-and-white siding.

Back to having no clue what's going on.

NINETEEN

"My sunscreen, Mae. It's *melting*." With her accent, the words sound like what Van means. "If you've seen one old man in a shrimp costume driving a motorized wheelie cooler, you've seen all of them. I'm not getting heatstroke because you're obsessed with an ill-advised, questionably traditional parade."

I crane my neck to see what's coming. "Shrimp Fest Weekend *is* the Fourth of July." I'm not missing out, not after a week of doing Nathan's chores, watching my mom, and avoiding Pa while I figure out what in the world to say to him. Not to mention waiting for another blink.

Nine days have passed since my last glimpse of history. I'm not brave enough to ask the twins about Patrick. Lil's the only one who knows about my blinks, and if I ask the twins, I'll either have to lie or tell them. I don't want to do either, actually.

"This parade *is* dumb," Van says, mocking my use of emphasis. Van shoves her weather app under my nose.

"Eighty-nine degrees at Nine a.m. And the humidity's what? Ninety percent? Soup city. If I don't get shelter, shade, and water immediately, my underwear will grow legs."

"Van. Be a lady," I warn. "There are children present."

She scowls at me.

"Get me air conditioning. Then we can talk about manners, Lima Bean." A drumbeat sounds to our right. The crowd shifts like a herd of lemmings. I hold up my souvenir flag.

"Goober," Van whispers.

"You're unpatriotic."

"I love my country," Van teases. "I'm just not a dweeb."

Van gets a good-natured shove in the shoulder before I turn back to watch all the floats. They're mostly pick-up trucks, their beds hung with streamers and glitter and big, bright decorations. Each one has a theme: Noah's Ark for the county animal shelter; little merpeople for the swimming school. I elbow Van in the side when I see the float for Sutton's Seafood. Rosie's behind the wheel.

"Your dad's the king of the castle! You decorated his wheelchair like a throne?"

"Yeah…" She squints at the truck, then huffs a little.

"It looks great. What's the matter?"

"My stupid brother. He's supposed to be helping out."

I squint into the sun. "I don't see him."

"Funny. Neither do I. There's a dragon suit. You know, to go along with the castle? I told Ezra if he wore it, I'd do the dishes for a month."

Van's mad, and I don't blame her. Ezra's been quiet on the

group text. And while he and I aren't at the stage where I expect him to tell me everything, we have been talking. That he's missing is admittedly odd.

Loud pop music streams from the float behind Sutton Seafood where four of Deebie's friends are decked out. Van looks past them and stills, grabbing my arm as she curses.

"What?" I say, and stand up on my tiptoes. Van doesn't answer me, but...*oh.*

A fleet of cars, mostly classic convertibles, makes its way up the street. It's the pageant contestants, riding in place order after last night's competition. The newly-crowned Shrimp Fest Queen pulls up in the last car, a red Mustang. It's Molly Evers, hair swept away from her face and not a hint of sweat on her. She's stunning in a flowing floral dress.

I've talked to Molly twice since I got back here. That night she was in the truck with Bex Bennett, then a few days later at the dry goods store in town. She recognized me first and complimented the necklace I was wearing. She was thoughtful. Warm. Nice.

Since then, I've learned Molly is a talented pianist and in the running for valedictorian of her class. She volunteers at the county food bank and spent spring break working with Habitat for Humanity. If anyone deserves to win the Shrimp Fest Queen title and scholarship, it's Molly.

"Did you know Ezra was her parade escort?" Van asks.

I shake my head instead of speaking because suddenly, my mouth doesn't work. I shouldn't care that he's playing a role typically reserved for dads, brothers, or boyfriends. I shouldn't care because yes, we've smoothed things over, but our relationship's still tenuous, at best. I shouldn't care because dating him is out, for the sake of our hearts and my ability to take care of my mother. Van scoots closer to me, and I'm not sure if it's a gesture of solidarity or if she's just trying to see better.

Something wet and cold hits the back of my neck.

"Holy Moses what the — Mason."

He's standing behind me, holding an offensively cold, wet monster in his hand. "One double chai shake for a Miss..." he checks the name scribbled across it... "Lilly Mar Guffin?" He squints and tilts his head sideways. "I don't know her. Is that you?"

He'd be annoying if he weren't so adorable, all dimpled cheeks and rumpled blonde hair. He's dressed for his band, The Treetorns, set in a faded white tee, his skinny black jeans tapered at the ankle. He's chosen a pair of vintage Tretorn shoes for his feet.

I take the drink and point to his footwear. "How meta."

He winks at me. "I'm the front man. Gotta rep my band."

"Where's my drink?" Van asks, still glaring in Ezra's direction. Mason slides an arm around her waist and presents it with a flourish. "One mocha chocolate shake with a shot of espresso 'cause it's early, topped with sprinkles and extra whip."

Van takes a sip while he holds it, eyes not straying from her brother's face. She holds up two fingers and points to Ezra, then to her eyes and back again. *I'm watching you,* the motion says.

"I'm missing something here. What am I missing?" Mason drains a quarter of Van's shake.

"Death vibes for Ezra." My stomach's in knots, and while I'd like to lay blame on the drink I just inhaled like it was oxygen, I'm pretty sure it has nothing to do with that.

"Eh, he deserves some Van voodoo." He takes another long sip from the straw. "Guess he followed through with Molly, yeah?"

Van whips around. "You knew about this?"

"You didn't?"

"Wrong answer," I say.

"Mason Matthew Copley," Van says, her face growing redder, "how could you let this travesty take place?"

"Because he can make up his own mind?" He stands back, shoulders lifted. "And it's not like I knew he'd said yes. Last we talked about it, he just mentioned that she'd asked him."

"Oh, for the love…" Van mutters, shifting her gaze toward me. I have to shut this down. Fast.

"Hey, you know what? I could really use a fried Twinkie. Something awful I can eat off a stick."

Van's nose scrunches up. "You're deflecting."

"I am not." I am, totally. "I just want a Twinkie now, before the food trucks get swamped and I have to wait in line for an hour to mainline my calories."

I grab Van's hand and tug, walking away from the parade as fast as I can in the direction of the food trucks. I turn around to make sure Mason's still with us, just in time to see Molly take Ezra's hand.

———————

THE DAY PASSES in a whirl of sound and color and fried junk food until I'm standing on Main Street in a borrowed mid-length dress. It's bright blue, a seldom-worn selection from Van's more fashionable closet. She also insisted on doing my hair.

Live music blares from the stage by the waterfront. The last traces of sunset cling to the sky. I'm an observer here, the twinkling lights, crashing guitars, and crush of people swirling around me. It's suffocating — the loneliness, the fear, the uncertainty that had waned but is back with a vengeance.

I feel like the tiny plastic figurine in the middle of a souvenir snow globe, at the mercy of whoever picks me up.

"Mae! Come dance with us!" Van's face is a brilliant blur. Mason spins her around, then dips her. They two-step back to me.

Van's dress is deep red, cap-sleeved with a sweetheart neckline. The full skirt fans out on a final twirl. My heart twinges when they come to a stop, the sweetness of their shifting bond overwhelming. "Impressive."

Mason grins and cuddles her close.

Van and Mason insisted I join them at the street dance despite me making it clear I didn't want to go. We left Shrimp Fest around two. I'd checked in with my mom, gotten a shower, and was writing in the loft when Nathan barged in and tossed a Nerf ball at me. "Van says y'all are leaving in an hour, and if you don't come on and get dressed she'll drag you in whatever you've got on."

I could have stayed in the loft and worn the barn cats like a weighted blanket, basking in their softness and warmth. But being alone with my thoughts and a dozen cats felt a little too crazy-lady-in-the-attic.

I refused to be the protagonist in a southern gothic novel, so I gave in and climbed my way down.

Ezra was absent when I got to the Sutton's house. Despite my best efforts to quash it, a weird mix of rejection and disappointment coiled in my chest. I must have looked tense because Mason reached out to squeeze my shoulders. "You look beautiful," he told me, then leaned in to whisper, "Don't worry. Ezra's going to meet us there."

But he's not here, not yet, and the band shifts into a ballad. Mason pumps his fist in the air. "Excellent. Miss Griffin, would you excuse us?" He steps back and pulls Van in, waltzing her across the dance floor.

"Get out here," Van calls. "Come dance."

I look right and left and hold my arms out, empty. "No partner." And no interest in a solo waltz.

"I mean, there's always me."

I spin around. Ezra's standing there in a white button-down shirt, the sleeves rolled up to his forearms. Faded jeans hang just right on his hips.

My cheeks flush. I drop my eyes to the ground. Which is a mistake, because even his feet are handsome. They're tanned and calloused and shoved into a pair of dark brown leather Havanas. Why (oh why, oh why) does he have to be the epitome of all my brooding surfer boy daydreams?

"I've gotta go, actually. I'll see you later?" Never mind I

have no idea where I'm going, or how I'm going to get there at all.

"I thought you got a ride here with those two." He makes a face, and I swivel around to see Mason whispering something to Evangeline.

"Nathan," I say.

"What about him?"

"Nathan is...um...coming to get me." As soon as I text him. Assuming he has his phone.

Ezra looks at me like I'm a puzzle, one he's not quite sure how to solve. I should welcome him to the club, I guess, considering I have no idea what's going on with me, either. "I'm just tired, and it was a long day in the sun, and I'm here because Van is persistent."

Ezra shoves his hands in his pockets and quirks a brow at me. "She's tenacious. You can be honest among friends."

Friends. I don't know why, but that word from his mouth takes me down a couple notches so I'm not standing on the edge of Awkward Cliff. I am, however, still working my way down Fight or Flight Avenue, leaning toward a hard left down Flight.

Ezra steps back like he can tell I'm about to run for it. "We can take a walk if you want."

"A walk."

"Yeah. You move your feet, typically one in front of the other? It kind of propels you forward, and—"

I step forward and shove him on the shoulder. "Shut up."

"There she is," he says, and I look behind me expecting Molly. But there's no one there.

"There who is?"

"Your smile. Haven't seen it much lately."

I'm so catty. "You've been otherwise engaged."

Ezra sighs. "Yeah, I know. Molly—"

"Needed an escort. I heard." Derision drips from my mouth, hardening Ezra's expression.

"Wait a minute. You're angry at *me*?"

I'm not angry at him. I'm jealous. And really, really angry at myself.

"I'm sorry," I say, and mean it. "Van says I'm emotionally constipated."

His jaw ticks again. Whatever he says next, I know I deserve it.

"My Peepaw takes prune juice for that."

I shake my head. "What?"

"Oh, and light exercise. You know. For regularity."

"*Emotionally* constipated, Ezra."

A slight smile cracks Ezra's scowl. "I can check the bar for some prune juice?" He rocks back on his heels and shoves his hands in his pockets. "Or we can go for that walk."

In the end, it's the dimple that wins me over. Despite my better judgment, despite the warning bells in my head. That little divot in his cheek reels me in, and softens what resolve I have to keep him at a distance. We step away from the crowd without a single thing between us, save the fireflies in the evening air.

TWENTY

I cross my arms as we leave the street dance. Ezra's so close I feel the heat from his skin. He bumps me with his shoulder. "You in there?"

I jump, my flushed cheeks grateful he can't see them. "Yeah. Just lost in my thoughts for a minute."

Thoughts about us. Him and Molly. Thoughts about why I even care. Ezra Sutton stirs up big feelings I don't want to analyze. He always has, even when we were kids and the way he looked at me meant I mattered. That I wasn't just the abandoned kid with the mom in a mental hospital. I was Mae Griffin, one of Ezra Sutton's best friends.

Now, a handful of years later, I don't know what he sees when he looks at me. Am I Mae Griffin, a girl worth the effort? Or am I Mae Griffin, the girl who left?

The farther we get from the street dance, the more the sounds of the river eclipse the night. It was dead calm this morning, but by afternoon, the winds were roaring. Shrimp

Fest officials canceled the Salty Regatta, the festival's just-for-fun sailing race.

"Were you racing today?" I ask Ezra.

He exhales through his nose and looks toward the water, disappointed. "Yeah, actually. I was."

"That's a bummer," I say.

"It was a good call. The winds were too high."

"Will they reschedule, you think?"

Ezra shrugs. "Maybe? I won't compete in it if they do."

I'm tempted to ask why but I don't want to push it. He'll tell me if he wants me to know. Our pace slows down—we've reached the waterfront. We walked all the way to Point Park.

A broad, waterfront space on the edge of town, Point Park marks the spot where the Neuse River widens before flowing into the Pamlico Sound. The current here is swift, the potential for large waves more likely than up by my grandparents. As if the river can hear my thoughts, water slams against the Point Park dock and its wide concrete wall jutting out into the water. I can just make out the end of the dock's long platform thanks to the streetlights on the access road.

I sit down at one of the picnic tables with my back to the river, scraping at the surface with my fingernail. Ezra slides next to me on the bench, positioning his body so he faces the river. He props his elbows on the table behind him, his arm resting next to mine.

"Wanna hear something funny?" I startle. We've been quiet for a few steady beats. I look up at him, and heaven help me with that dark hair, that sharp, angular profile. And the almost-smile on the corner of his mouth.

"I thought you were a mermaid the first time I saw you."

"A mermaid?" I bark the word like an elephant seal.

"A mermaid," he confirms. "I was fishing on the jetty. I saw you sitting on the shore by yourself. The sun hit your profile just right and —" he breaks off, shaking his head — at the memory? "I mean, I was twelve and an idiot. You looked so beautiful and at peace. Exactly like a mermaid."

"Says who? Hans Christian Anderson?"

"No. That story's messed up. Mom took Van and me to the Maritime Museum. They had that mermaid exhibit going on. I got kind of obsessed. Started looking for real ones. And then one day, there you were."

My heart stutters in my chest. This should be a sweet moment. But instead of swooning, my skin starts to crawl. I remember that day, my first at Pinecliff. I missed my mother so terribly. I knew where she was, that an inpatient stay would help her. But I couldn't chase the feeling I was being sold to the highest bidder. I ran down to the shore to get away from the feeling, dropping my stiff-legged body in the sand.

"Glad I could indulge your fantasy for a minute."

"Mae, that's that's not what I meant."

I know it's not what he meant. But it's the stark difference in our points of view that unfolds a much-needed reminder: my life isn't normal like his.

I'm out of my seat and across the grass in an instant, my feet carrying me toward the dock. I hear Ezra call out, then the sound of his footsteps. I run, thankful I refused when Van tried to put me in her platform wedges. Flats are much more effective when escaping the ghosts of your past.

The soles of my shoes slap against the dock surface. Breathless, I slow to a brisk walk. I reach the end of the dock and sink down, my body turned into the wind and my legs dangling over the water. I'm facing downstream, the red and green lights of a dozen channel markers visible in the distance. I don't see Ezra on the shore. The glow from the street lamps is far away. It's a new moon, so there isn't much moonlight. It's just me on this dock in the middle of the river, my company the darkness, the water, and the wind.

Something's moving on the shore, too tall to be a dog, not willowy enough to be a random tree branch. I squint, tracking the shape as it moves closer to the water's edge. It's a woman, I think, and I raise my fist in solidarity to our mutually crappy evenings. Guess I'm not the only one with major street dance regrets.

A loud boom sounds in the air behind me, the water glittering in a shower of red light. It's the fireworks display they do every year, the one I forgot about because I was out here, wallowing. Each blast lights up the night, intermittent bursts that mean I can see the woman more clearly.

Dark hair in a braid.

Skirt flowing.

Shrimp on a biscuit. That's my Mom.

I scramble to my feet. What's she doing here? Did she text me and I missed it somehow? My phone's lit up with notifications but they're all from the group chat, texts of the "Where the heck are you?" variety. I jog down the dock and onto the sand, yelping as I step on an errant seashell. I power down my phone and nestle it in a tangle of tree roots away from the water just in case I have to go in.

When I asked my mom if she'd come tonight, she said no, that being out late would mess with her sleep. I guess it's possible she changed her mind, but I can't let go of what she said, especially if something like this will throw off her recovery. I need to get her home.

"Mom! Mom! What are you doing?" I move faster toward the water's edge. Another boom; another blast of light. I look up just in time to see my mother walk into the water.

What the hell is going on?

Cursing softly, I sprint forward. I make it three steps into the surf before I'm smacked by a wave. My startled gasp is sucked away by the unforgiving current. I force my body to relax, remembering a trick Ezra taught me about letting my buoyancy bring me to the surface. Both annoyed at him and thankful, I breach the surface and cough up what feels like the contents of the river.

Brackish water tastes freaking gross.

Maybe I should be panicked, but I'm angry. This is exactly why I don't trust my mom. She's not stable enough to be left alone regardless of the state of her therapies. I dive under a wave, grinding my teeth and cursing beneath the water until it occurs to me.

Is she trying to end her life?

I push to the surface, sputtering and gasping. She's not in front of me. I spin around. She's gotten behind me somehow, and in the sustained blast of light from the fireworks finale, I watch her lie back and sink beneath the surface.

"Mom!"

The scream is deep and guttural, the sound burning its way from my throat. I choke on a sob and dive again, only to realize my strokes aren't taking me forward. I'm moving sideways. The current's pushing me toward the dock.

It happens so fast I don't have time to get my bearings or pop to the surface for a breath. My lungs burn and I careen to the left, kicking as hard as I can to push my way to the surface. I drink in the night air, trying to stay in one place when my mother's form rises above the water. She turns toward me, the light just enough that I get a decent look at her soft teen features.

Sweet Mother Molasses.

I'm in a blink.

Caught off guard by the realization, I don't see the wave that strikes me from behind. I'm under the surface again, helpless as the current sends me straight into the concrete bulkhead.

Blinding pain reverberates through my left side, but it's not just from the force of the collision. The current pushes me again, dragging my skin across a colony of knife-sharp barnacles. Bloodied and bruised, I push up with my legs and break through the surface. Something organic — warm and fleshy — grabs hold of my arm and tugs.

"No! Stop! Stop it!" I kick out hard, my bare foot connecting with a solid mass. It's pulling me; water fills my nose as whatever this is drags me through it.

Oh, dear God in heaven. What if it's a shark?

"Mae. Mae! Quit — ow. Would you please stop kicking? I *would* like to have children someday."

"Sharks don't —" I was going to say "talk," but a wave smacks me in the face and takes the rest of my sentence with it. I cough hard, right into the face of my very human savior, river water spewing from my nose.

"Not a shark," he spits. "Just a Sutton. Would you please stop — ow — fighting me so I can get us both out of here?"

Maybe it's the sound of his voice that finally gets to me, a honeyed growl frustrated and fond. Or maybe it's not him at all, and the limp, jelly-like sensation in my limbs is just the adrenaline leaving. Whatever the case, my body goes slack. Ezra's strong arms wrap around me and I rest my head against his shoulder, too exhausted to care what he might think. Even soaking wet he smells like himself, a potent mix of ocean water, pine, and metal.

His touch is respectful. Achingly gentle.

I give in to the pull of sleep.

TWENTY-ONE

"Is this where I ask what the other guy looks like?"

Van's face sours. "The other guy was a concrete bulkhead, Miss Lil."

"A worthy opponent, then," Lil muses, "though typically not aggressive." Lil tapes a gauze pad over the gash on my thigh, then leans back to look at her handiwork. "Which one of you's going to tell me how you ended up at my house?"

I squirm in my seat, the bright light of Lil's kitchen reminiscent of an interrogation room. "I'd rather not talk about it. I'm just sorry we troubled you."

"It's no trouble, Mae. Really. I would prefer advance notice, though."

"Noted," Van huffs. "We can text you. 'Miss Lil, Mae's been in a bar fight with the broad side of a barn.'"

"So much sass. You picked that up from Rosie." Lil affixes one final bandage to my wounds and pats me gently on the knee. "You, Mae, are sufficiently bandaged." She turns to face the trio. "The three of you? Get out."

"What?" Van says.

"We're not leaving her." That's Mason. Ezra scoots closer to me in his chair. All I want to do is go home and hide in the boathouse, maybe bury my face in a barn cat's fur. But I also can't lie to myself: I do want answers.

"I'll be fine," I say to them. "It's okay."

Van stares me down, gaze terrifying in its assessment. Whatever she sees must satisfy her. "Five minutes," she points at Lil, "and we're coming back for her."

"Five minutes," Lil promises, holding one hand in the air like she's taking an oath of office.

"I can grab the Bible if we want to make this official." Mason ducks out through the doorway before Lil can smack him on the head.

Extra bodies ushered out, Lil turns to me with her hands on her hips. "You've built quite the pack here. Y'all remind me of the crowd your mama used to run with. Thick as molasses for years."

She nods toward the wall and I turn, taking in the collection of famed photographs behind me. Images of my mom as a teen posing with Nathan, Rosie, and Gill. Afternoons on the shore, evenings on the front porch swing. Mom and Rosie leaning on a car. Carving pumpkins in the fall: Nathan and Gill crouching down in front of two jack-o-lanterns carved with band names. Halloween costumes, Christmas presents. Mom radiates joy in each shot.

"I don't understand," I whisper, but Lil hears me.

"Why she left this behind?"

"I mean, that I kind of get. But tonight…" I pause, remembering I said I don't want to talk about it.

Wondering if maybe I'm lying to myself.

"I fell into a blink," I say. "During the street dance."

"You saw her." Lil taps the glass on a photo of my Mom.

"Yeah," I nod. "I was on the dock."

"But you didn't stay on the dock."

"No, I didn't."

"It's okay if you don't want to tell me."

"I think my mother tried to drown herself."

The words are loud, much louder than I intended. I wince like there's an echo of it in my ear. Lil doesn't say a word. She just stands there, waiting for me.

Waiting for me to do what, I'm not sure.

My mouth decides to fill the silence, spewing all the sordid details of the night. About Ezra at the parade. About our walk to Point Park and the idiotic way I ran from him. About watching my mother walk into the water and going after her, not realizing the whole thing wasn't real.

"I was so stupid, Lil. I couldn't even tell the difference between reality and the *thing* I'd fallen into. And not only did I almost drown, I forced Ezra into the water." Heat rushes through my veins, and the emotions I've been holding back burst forth like a dam breaking. "I'm mad, Lil. Mad at myself. Mad at my mom. Mad at Pa and this place and what it does to my brain when I'm down here. My family is not normal. *I* am not normal. And those idiots outside are going to get hurt." I slump to the cold tile floor, drop my head between my knees, and fold my arms on top like a miniature fortress. I'm morti-fied I let Lil see me like this.

Beyond the roaring in my ears, I hear shuffling. I feel movement, make out a muttered curse. "These old bones," Lil says. "I swear. I don't get down on the floor much, shug, but for you, right now, I will make an exception." Huffing like she's out of breath, she pulls me in, her fluffy arms much stronger than I was expecting. I lean my head against her shoulder and sob.

Lil doesn't speak. She just holds me in her arms and rocks me, humming a sad, quiet tune. Snot leaks from my nose. I try to apologize for the way it's spreading all over her housedress. "Hush," she whispers, then goes back to humming the song.

I don't know how long we sit there but she doesn't move until I do. My sinuses are full and I've got a headache three times the size of Texas. Lil hands me a tissue. I blow my nose.

"You have every right to be angry," Lil says. "You haven't had a typical childhood. And now you're here, where time and space are as fickle as the weather. I'd be beside myself."

"Lil," I yelp. "Do you *see* me?" I throw my hands out to display my general mess. "I am beside myself. I don't even know what's real. I'm pretty sure I'm going crazy."

Lil grabs my hands and holds them steady "You know better than to use that word, Lila Mae. It's a careless excuse used by ignorant people." She pauses, inhaling deeply. "You aren't mentally ill. There are imprints, Mae. After-images. They're woven into the river and the land. Some of *us*," she emphasizes the word, and I know she, herself, is included, "are…sensitive to them. The moments you see? They're real. And whatever magic this is, it's very personal. Your blinks —" she looks at me. "I think that's what you call them? They are pieces of your story to solve."

I drop my head against the wall. "I hate puzzles."

She laughs and pats my knee. "I know you do. You want everything to be normal. Clear." Lil takes my face in her hands, the twinkle in her eye like the first pinpricks of starlight in the bluest evening. "There's no such thing as normal. Only the wonder you're meant to become."

———

"YOU KNOW, we — ouch! — Probably could have gone in through the front door here, people," I mumble.

"And risk waking up the whole house?"

I roll my eyes at Mason, because in what universe is using a ladder and the trellis any quieter?

"Alright. I'm ready," Ezra says, his green eyes bright in the darkness. "Put your hands up and I'll pull you over."

"This is ridiculous," I mutter.

Mason's voice sounds from somewhere above me. "I don't know. I'm having fun."

"Mason Matthew Copley, " Van snaps, "I have my hands on Mae's butt. And while it is a lovely specimen—"

I cringe. "Thank you?"

She pats me with a barely perceptible movement of her fingers. "Anytime, lady. Anytime. But, Mason, this is stressful and, in hindsight, ridiculously stupid. Now be quiet and get her over the rail before my hands slip and we have an international incident."

With a tug on my arms and a few grunts of exertion, I land on the porch outside my bedroom with a groan.

On top of Ezra. Neither one of us breathes. Our eyes are wide, matching orbs in the darkness. Mason taps me on the shoulder. "You good?"

I roll off to the side, lightheaded. Ezra lets out a strangled cough. We're both embarrassed, I think, but he squeezes my hand as Mason leans over the rail to pull Van over. She waves him away and vaults it like a track star. "Tell me you left the french doors unlocked."

"She did."

We all freeze at the voice in the doorway. It's Pa's voice, and he's *mad*. "Would someone like to explain why my grand-daughter is soaking wet and covered in a number of bandages?"

"Mr. Luther! Hey!" Mason's voice is remarkably neutral. "We were just…making sure Mae got home safely."

"That was a rhetorical question." Pa holds up his phone to reveal a dozen or so notifications. "I've been made abreast of the situation, thanks."

My stomach sinks. "Y'all," I say, kind of strangled, and falter when I try to stand. All three of them help me up, refusing to let go even when I'm standing under my own power. "I, uh, think maybe it's time for you to go," I say. No one speaks at first, until the dam breaks loose and releases a million words and excuses.

"It was our fault, Mr. Luther." Ezra.

"Don't be hard on Mae." Van. "We had too much fun —
sober fun — and things got a little whacky."

"We can explain everything, Mr. Luther." Mason. "It all
started when —"

"Mr. Copley," Pa roars. "Shut your mouth and get off my
property. Preferably through the front door."

"But—"

"Leave now. I need to speak with my granddaughter."

Pa opens the door and we shuffle through, defeated. Van
hugs me in the hall. "You got this, Mae," she whispers. "Text
me when this is over, please."

I nod, my heart swelling in gratitude. Mason chucks me
under the chin. "Blame it on me," he says. "I can take it." I
roll my eyes and shove him out the door.

I hold my breath as Ezra brushes past me. He stops and
opens his mouth like he's about to speak. But then he closes it
again, reaching out to brush a wild strand of hair behind my
ear, fingers lingering. I smile in spite of myself.

Pa closes the door behind them. He turns to face me.
"Sit."

"Yes, sir." I have half a mind to rush the door and grab my
mother, but I think better of it. Lil would tell me not to poke a
sleeping bear.

"Talk," Pa says. "What happened this evening?"

"I thought you already knew."

I watch the vein in Pa's forehead flex, regret coursing
through me. "Sorry, I just…" dove headfirst from the bulkhead because I thought my mother was drowning. "I tripped

on the dock during the street dance. And then I sort of…fell in."

Moses, do I hate lying. But what am I supposed to say? If I tell him the truth, he'll have me hauled off to Briarwood tomorrow and I know for sure that's not what I want. Never mind where I'm spending my senior year — I need more time if I'm going to help the Suttons. I need more pieces of the puzzle, as much as I'm dreading figuring them out.

Pa's face is impassive. He places his phone face-up on my bed. There's a string of texts on the home screen, each one more damning than the last.

From Miss Mary (she has a cellphone?): *Luther, have you heard from your granddaughter?*

From Nathan (the traitor): *Mr. Luther, something's happened with Lila Mae.*

From Sheriff Kelly: *Mae went in the water. Sutton boy pulled her out. She insists she's fine; refused medical attention. I told the kids to take her home.*

I roll my lips between my teeth and set the phone down. "I don't know what you want me to say. I fell in. It was rough. I got hurt, but nothing Miss Lil couldn't fix with a first aid kit. It was an accident, Pa. That's all."

Pa stands, shoving the chair behind him. He paces back and forth. "I just got your mother straightened out. And here you go, causing a scene in front of God and everybody. You've put our reputation on the line."

That he's worried about our influence shouldn't surprise me, but hearing him say it is a punch to the gut. "I could have drowned," I whisper, so softly I don't know if he hears. I'm going to hope that's the case, because otherwise, his response is too brutal, too caustic.

"Your behavior was an embarrassment. After all the damage control I did for your Mom—"

"Damage control?" My hands shake; my heart wants to pound from my chest. "You were proud of Mom once, before her disorder. Before you decided she was a liability." My stomach sinks. I just realized something. "That's why you want me at Briarwood, isn't it? So I won't be a problem for you, too."

Pa's nostrils flare. He presses his lips together. "Neither one of you is a problem. I am *fiercely* proud of you both."

"If that were true," I respond, "your *damage control* wouldn't matter."

Pa's mouth twists to the side. His stare goes cold, and he gives a quick, disgusted snort before moving to stand above me. "This behavior is a disgrace, not just to the way you were raised, but to the entire Griffin family. What in the world has happened to you?"

I laugh a small, strangled sound, bereft of any lightness. He wants to know what's happened to me? Only a million shattered hopes. A million broken promises and lies. Reminders that I'm on the other side, that I will never be close to normal. Stiff-legged, I moved to the door. The knob turns with a click in my hand. "I don't know, Pa," I breathe. "But I think we're done here. Maybe you should ask yourself what happened to *you*."

TWENTY-TWO

"What" *thwump* "is the actual point" *thwump* "of a beach umbrella if it" *thwump* "refuses to stay in the ground." Van makes a final stab with the stake and collapses underneath it, panting.

"Entertainment," I say. "Watching you struggle? Ten out of ten would recommend."

Van shoots me a rude gesture and I reach for her finger, using her hand to pull her to her feet. "Thank you for protecting our skin from UV rays," I say, apologizing. Van grumbles as she rummages through the cooler, scrunching her nose at me before opening a Coke.

I had planned to write this morning, hoping the process would clear my head. It's been a week since my incident at Shrimp Fest and I'm still managing the emotional fallout. But the Suttons pulled up at nine, surfboards mounted on the back of the Jeep and beach gear nestled in the wheel wells. Mason charmed my mother and grandmother, who in turn put the reins on my grandfather. One ferry trip and a forty-minute drive later, Van and I are sunning ourselves on the shores of the Atlantic while the boys tumble around in the surf.

A salty breeze tosses my hair and I reach for it, tying it up into a tidy knot. I grab water from the cooler and settle down on my towel next to Evangeline.

I haven't said much about life since the Shrimp Fest. She doesn't know I've been texting Ezra every day. It's not groundbreaking stuff — just bits of our day, funny memes, random thoughts and observations. We've also flirted a bit, enough to make my heart race and my mind wander.

Van's been doing her best to figure out what's going on between me and her brother, God bless her, but she's not as subtle as she thinks. "So what's up with you and my brother?" Van asks me, and I startle. I guess today we're going with direct.

"What's up with you and Mason?" I take the drink from her hand.

"Eh," she muses, spreading out her towel. "I guess that's fair. You're just so transparent. I can tell you're crushing on my brother again."

I flatten my lips together. "This topic is off limits."

Van ignores me like I knew she would. "You can't tell me there isn't a vibe between you two. Ezra's all googly-eyed, and as far as you're concerned, well…"

"Well, what?"

"Let's just say you should never play poker."

"There's nothing happening." My voice is an octave higher than normal.

Van quirks an eyebrow at me. "Uh-huh."

Frustrated, I dig my heels into the sand below the towel. A lot of things have *happened*, but nothing is *happening*. Not when it can't, not when Lil's kitchen wisdom isn't cutting through my mental static.

Not when real life is indistinguishable from a blink.

"Doesn't Molly Evers have a thing for him?" Distraction.

"No. He's been restoring a boat for her dad. Mr. John has MS. It's gotten worse, makes it harder for him to do things. Molly's dating a kid from New Bern. Has been since," she counts on her fingers like it's been ages. "I don't know. July?"

"It's July right now." I deadpan.

"Which is why Molly asked Ezra to be her escort. It was still early days with Brandt...Beau...Buford — whatever the dude's name is. She thinks Ezra's safe and easy to talk to because they have stuff in common. You know, because of our dads."

I nod, embarrassed. Could I have been any more self-absorbed?

"You gonna make a move, then?" she asks. "Make it official?"

Ha. Not likely. "You're certainly one to talk."

I poke Van in the arm, fully intending to distract her with a conversation about that blonde-haired, blue-eyed boy in the surf. But she's the master of strategic burns, so she just looks at me, lips curving. "As of Wednesday, Mason and I are *officially* a couple."

My mouth drops open. "What?"

"You heard me." She smirks.

"It's Saturday. Wednesday was four days ago. Four days, Van. And you're just now telling me?"

Van slips her sunglasses down her nose and leans back like a swimsuit model. "'I've learned that we're all entitled to have our secrets,'" she quotes, batting her eyelashes. "Audrey Hepburn said that."

"Van. That's from *The Notebook*."

"Audrey Hepburn's notebook, yes."

I roll my eyes. "Nicholas Sparks, you weirdo."

"Audrey, Nicholas….same thing."

I stifle a laugh and follow her line of sight toward the water. Ezra rises out of the waves. The sunlight catches his skin as the water sluices downward. "Why are you so pale and vampiric when your brother's so darn tan?"

Van's eyes burn a hole right through me. Her lips form a thin straight line. "Sure. No attraction at all. Ridiculous." Her eyes scream *I told you so.*

"Fine. Yes. I'm attracted to your brother. When he looks at me, I feel like I can't breathe. And it's not just the fact that he's built or has a jawline and cheekbones that would shred parmesan—"

Van lifts an eyebrow.

"He's honest and generous to a fault."

She nods abruptly. "Agreed. But?"

"But…everything. I'm not a typical teenager. I don't have a normal life."

"Your mom's doing amazing."

I nod, wishing I could tell her the truth. That it's not just about my mother. It's about the way I slip between realities. It's about my family tree.

I hug my knees to my chest and bury my nose in the space between my kneecaps, steeling myself to talk about Mom. "She's doing amazing now, but how long will it be before she has a relapse? Or before I'm the crazy one?"

Van sits up and I know I'm in trouble. She's got that *hold my earrings* vibe. "The Minnesott Beach mayor has a mummified chicken wing collection, and not the kind you get from Popeyes, alright? Our postmaster, Miss Rudy, is terrified of envelopes. She can't handle them without wearing latex gloves. And we have a whole group of old men who put engines on wheeled coolers *just to play Jimmy Buffett and pop wheelies during parades.* Our whole freaking town is nuts, and you're worried about your sanity?"

I toss my hands in the air, huffing in frustration. "Our town is *eccentric,* Van. Eccentric is amusing. That's not my family's brand."

Van makes a face and goes back to leaning on her elbows. "No offense, but the Griffin *brand* is snobbery and old money."

"Which your brother absolutely hates." I laugh. "I'm surprised you don't, too. Ezra told me what Pa did — about the articles. I'm sorry." I shove my hands into the cooler and fish out a second bottle of water. Collect myself while I take a sip.

Van scrunches up her nose. "First of all, you're about as

connected to that whole debacle as a possum is its first set of teeth."

"What?"

"You have nothing to do with your grandfather's axes, whatever they are to grind. And as far as my brother is concerned, you do realize you're not a *Griffin* to my brother? He keeps *you* and *your family* completely separate."

"He shouldn't," I say.

"Oh, my word."

Van shakes her head and takes a long pull from her soda, punctuating it with a heady burp. "Everybody knows Griffin women are different. And what people know," she uses air quotes around the word, "and what the truth is are two very different things. Your family's not unique because of mental health issues. There's nothing to be ashamed of there."

"But —"

"But I'm not finished," she says, wagging her index finger at me. "We got the best gift in the world when you came to town. You are brave, you are smart, and aside from that two-year span where you ditched us, you are loyal. Bottom line? We love you," she glances at her brother, "some of us a little more than the rest. That didn't change when you left. That didn't change when you spent those years ignoring us. We know who you are deep down, and we love you for it. There's no way that's going to change now."

My vision blurs and my nose tickles. I bite the inside of my cheek. Van clears her throat just as two long shadows fall over us, dripping water on our towels.

"Y'all are worse than a bunch of dogs in the river," Van fusses. "Quit dripping on us. Yeesh."

"You love it." A saucy grin slides over Mason's features. "And I'm here to give you a kiss."

I watch as Van tips her head back and smiles at him with impish affection. "I'd prefer some ice cream, please."

TWENTY-THREE

We trounce the boys in mini golf. Mason is not pleased.

"We were robbed, E. I'm telling you."

Van pats Mason on the head. "You weren't robbed. You were *beaten*. By two strong, strategic, beautiful women who relied on physics and determination. You should be reviewing match footage and taking notes."

"I am not denying we may have been outgunned in the practical approaches department. But I still maintain there was tomfoolery—"

"Tomfoolery?" Ezra smirks. He joins the line of cars waiting for the ferry and shifts the jeep into park.

"Tomfoolery, yes," Mason answers. "I saw a YouTube video about it."

I turn in my seat. "A YouTube video."

"Don't ask," Van hisses. "He'll show it to you."

"*That* is an excellent idea."

Mason pulls out his phone and swipes through it. Van

buries her face in her hands. "I saw it last week...no, not this one. Was it this channel? No...no...okay. Found it. They trick out the balls by weighting them improperly. That must have been what happened to ours."

"Bless your heart," Van sighs, and I stifle a huff of laughter. The jeep lurches forward as Ezra eases it down the ramp. A deckhand guides us to the starboard side where we park under an awning. My muscles strain with a pleasant sort of ache.

I exit as soon as we're allowed to, folding the seat forward to let Van and Mason out. Van clambers past me with a whispered, *"Talk to my brother."* She grabs Mason's hand and heads for the bow of the boat, Ezra trailing along behind them. Like Lil says when somebody looks a little lost and clueless, I just stand there with my teeth in my mouth.

Lunch and mini golf gave me ample time for emotional progress, but Van's nudge sucked the air from that balloon. It's not purposeful, I don't think. She's not trying to make me nervous. But my chest tightens up again, the lump in my throat growing thick and chalky. I don't know how to be this person, the one not toeing the ledge before it falls.

A flash of black crosses my peripheral vision and my skin stings like I've been bit. I yelp and look down at my hand, expecting a welt from a horsefly. I spot a black hair tie on the passenger seat.

"Did you just slingshot me with a hair tie?" I ask Ezra. He's approaching the side of the jeep.

"What are you gonna do if I say yes?"

I close my fingers around the band, Nathan's voice in my

head from water balloon lessons. *If the distance is short, put your line of sight just below your target.*

I lift the band and point it at Ezra's chin.

Ezra's eyes go wide. His lips part and I cackle. I shoot, my aim too true for him to avoid. The band snaps him in the nose with a fleshy ping and he flails to the side, yelping in pain when his hand smacks the driver's side mirror. I'm doubled over the side of the jeep, laughing, when my feet up and leave the ground.

"Ezra, you big dummy. Unhand me!"

He tosses me into a fireman's hold. "You bully!" I shout into his back, pummeling his kidneys for good measure. "First you shoot me, then you abduct me. Put me down right now!"

Ezra's back vibrates with laughter. I'm giggling so hard I can't breathe. I'm still flailing around when he sets me down and my fist connects with his cheekbone. "Dang, Mae," he says, breathless with laughter. "You've got a mean right hook."

I raise my guard and bounce a little. "Nathan taught me everything I know."

Ezra gives me *that grin*, the sort-of crooked one that makes my stomach flutter. His green eyes sparkle and the air leaves my chest.

"I said *talk* to him, Mae. No physical violence." Van's voice floats down from the observation deck.

"He shot first," I say, pointing at Ezra.

"Whatever, Han Solo." Van glares at me. She's communicating with her eyes, silently. *Go on, girl. Get on with things.*

"'*Being a twin is amazing,*' they said," Ezra grumbles.

"*'You'll have each other. It's great...*'" Ezra's arm twines with mine as he guides me port side. I can't decide if I should pull away.

"My sister is obnoxious," he says.

"She's persistent."

"Persistently frustrating."

"She has flair."

"Whose side are you on?"

"Do you really want an answer?" I'm teasing him. Ezra stops laughing and the air around us shifts.

"Yeah," he breathes, "I want an answer." When he inhales, he takes all the oxygen. The way he's looking at me makes me dizzy, with his lips parted and his green eyes wide. "I have something to say," Ezra says, "and I need you to listen."

Anxiety zips up my spine.

I start looking for a way out, somewhere to run if this gets awkward.

"We're on a boat, Mae. There's nowhere to go."

I crinkle my nose. He's right, clearly. I stand up straight and fold my arms against my chest. I'm afraid of what he's going to say. I'm afraid of my feelings for him. I'm afraid of standing out on the ledge.

Ezra takes a deep breath and starts talking. "That night at the street dance, if you hadn't woken up after I pulled you out...." He trails off on a huff, running a hand through his hair and shuffling his feet a little. "As much as I'm still kinda mad, and as much I'm still learning how to trust you, I realized something. I care about you. More than I should."

Any other girl would respond appropriately, closing the

distance and kissing him squarely on the mouth. But I'm me, so I open my mouth and insert my foot in it:

"I had an idea about Broward. You know, if you still want to go. I got into this Fellowship thing, also in Charleston, but I backed out because of my mom. I could maybe get back in and we could go down there together, you to Broward, me for the Fellowship. I could convince Pa to submit a retraction to the paper. Maybe recommend you to the County Board for their scholarship."

Ezra's face goes stony. He steps back and clenches his fists. "I don't want his help. I don't want *your* help — not like that, anyway."

"Sorry. That was stupid." What in the world is wrong with me? The boy tells me he cares, and I start throwing out future plans and fix-it scenarios that, given my current relationship with my grandfather, aren't just unhelpful. They're incredibly farfetched.

"It wasn't stupid," Ezra says, softening. "It was..." he looks up at the sky like there's an answer in the clouds. "The transition was a little sharp. You ignored what I said. Brought up the thing I hate more than anything."

I shrink back. "My family?"

He reaches out to touch me and I flinch. I'm raw, every nerve ending on fire with emotional upheaval. If we could just start over, maybe reboot the conversation —

"Can we, like, back up?" he asks. "Start at the beginning? This isn't going how I thought it would."

I blink against the glare from his sunglasses. He looks as though he's spun from gold. The warm afternoon light threads strands of it against his skin, through his hair, and along his jawline. The tilt of his mouth bears the weight of regret.

"It's not going the way I thought it would, either." My voice is barely audible above the wind. Ezra steps closer, the broad span of his chest so close I could fall into his arms with the slightest of movements. He nudges my palm with the back of his hand.

My gaze dips to his mouth. He links our pinky fingers. There's silence save for the rush of blood in my ears. Sparks crackle in the small bit of space between us. I'm pretty sure this is how lightning is made.

"I don't hate your family," he says to me. "I hate this feeling of being trapped. It doesn't matter how much I want or how much I plan, everything crumbles. The first boat I sold? I made more than enough to pay for a year of room and board at Broward. And then the Lady Sue's engine went out."

The Lady Sue is the Sutton's shrimp boat. It's old, even by commercial vessel standards. "You paid for the repairs?" I guess.

"And then there were the hospital bills," he says, nodding, "so I told Mom and Dad they could use my college savings for that." Ezra lifts a hand to my cheek, the rough callous of his thumb a gentle friction against my cheekbone. "Everything goes to them now — anything new I earn from boat sales."

"I'm sorry," I say, my heart aching for him.

"Please don't be. It's not your fault. It's just effort all the time. Work until I'm weary."

"What if I knew a way to make it right?"

The words are out before I can stop myself. Ezra's hand falls from my face. Our pinkies unlatch, and he steps back from me, eyes flashing. "Please don't start this up again."

"We don't have to deal with Pa," I say, hands waving. "Getting a scholarship can be all you. You just fill out the application and send it off to the organization or whatever. There might be an interview, too, but you'd be brilliant."

"Brilliant? I prefer people when they're not talking to me. At all."

The anger fades from Ezra's eyes and I smile at him. "So what does that mean for me?"

Ezra closes the distance between us, wrapping his hands around my upper arms. "You're not people," he says, his breath in my ear and the scent of him filling my brain with memories. "I'll take whatever you'll give me, Mae."

There's no air in my lungs. I'm dizzy. I stumble from his grasp. I'm across the deck and at the ship's rail without remembering how I got there. I pretend to study the water when really, I'm trying to steady myself.

His footsteps sound behind me. He's inches from my back. "Mae, I —"

Nope. Not gonna talk about it. Too many hidden pieces. "Hey, look," I say, pointing at the water. "There's a jellyfish."

The creature's a deep red, tentacles streaming out behind it. I lose sight of it once or twice. Ezra leans against the rail next to me, eyes on me instead of the water. I scrape the black paint off the railing with my thumb.

"How long are we going to do this?" he asks me.

"We're at the halfway point in the crossing, so I'd guess ten, maybe twelve minutes, tops?"

"That's not what I'm talking about," he growls. We've crossed some sort of line, the kids we used to be lost to the ether. There's no going back to the place where shark tooth hunts and dock chats fixed everything. I'm not sure I'd even want to go back.

Ezra's eyes narrow as he steps forward. I lift my chin and hold my ground. His voice is firm but gentle when he leans forward and speaks, just above a whisper: "I'm not a fan of this game we're playing, the one where I tell you how I feel and you push me away."

"There's a lot you don't know, Ezra. My life is complicated."

"I like complicated. I build boats."

"But there's no blueprint for this. I don't even know what's happening, really. I mean I do, but there are rules, and the rules keep changing, and —"

"Tossing you in the river?"

"What are you talking about?"

"I've known you for years, Mae. I know about your mom. I know you tally her meds and text her to check in because you worry that she might not answer. And I know that sometimes," he cages me in, one long, lean arm on either side of me against the railing, "the world slips. And whatever happens, throws you somewhere."

I stare at him, dumbfounded. "I have seizures."

"No, I don't think you do. There would have been tests. Hospital trips. You would have had to tell your grandparents and your mom when they happened." He runs a fingertip around my wrist and my heart speeds up. I'm on fire. "You'd wear a medical ID bracelet on your wrist."

"The point is," he continues, "I don't care about any of that, except that it's part of you. And as much as you frustrate me with the way you run, as much as you hurt me when you left and cut us out, as much as you keep trying to throw your family at me to fix things, I have feelings for you." He stops, his eyes searching my face, and I can tell he's wrestling with something. "I've been in love with you for years."

He can't be serious. "You — you mean the way you love Evangeline."

Ezra's smile is sad, the laugh accompanying it a little hollow. "Nope," he says, looking at me. "Not like Evangeline at all."

It's not the rumble in his voice or the intensity of his stare that convinces me, nor is it the exhaustion that makes me give in. It's the truth on his face and the memories that exist between us. It's his sincerity, his honesty. The kindness he's always had.

"You should kiss me," I blurt.

Surprise flashes across his face, the growing tilt of his mouth setting my butterflies into a frenzy. His eyes flash with determination. "Oh?"

"Yes. I mean, we wouldn't want to miss this —" I wave my hand in the air — "romantic opportunity."

"The sunset is pretty nice, now that you mention it."

"I didn't mention it."

"Huh. What do you know? Too bad."

Tension hums like a string between us. "I'm going to kiss you now," he says. "Unless you've changed your mind, or something."

"Nope." Nope, nope, nope. Not ever. "Definitely no mind-changing here."

Ezra's touch is feather light when his fingers cradle my jawline. His lips are a soft brush against my skin. I run my hands up his arms and around his neck, fingers twirling the soft curls at the nape of it. He pulls away for a moment, barely breathing, and presses our foreheads together. Then he's kissing me again, gentle and soft but with infinitely more purpose — right as the ferry captain blows the horn.

TWENTY-FOUR

We're coated in salt and sand, and ravenous from the sun exposure when we pull up to my grandparents' house. I'm so addled by the day's events — my talk with Van, that kiss, Mason's *If those two kiss, blow the horn, please* pact with the ferry captain — that I don't notice we've got company.

"Miss Dewitt," Van says, her voice carrying from the porch steps. "Didn't realize you'd be painting tonight."

My mother's on the porch, and yeah, she's painting, but there's not a single canvas in sight. Instead, she's on her hands and knees, wide paintbrush in hand as she drags great swaths of paint across the porch floorboards. It's after sunset.

My mother's painting the actual porch.

"Mom?"

"Hey there, Bean." She sits back on her heels. "How was the outing?"

How was the outing? I cut a glance at my friends. "The outing was fine." Ezra takes my hand. Mason grabs my bag from the car while Van hooks my free arm with her elbow. "Why, uh…why are you painting the porch?"

"Well, it's a funny story…" I take inventory, starting with her speech. It's measured but not too slow — two positive signs in our favor. "I was out here this morning after you left, working on a project. Knocked my pallet over and then couldn't get the paint to come up. But then I remembered you and Nathan had painted the porch a couple weeks ago, so I checked the boathouse for leftovers. It was so peaceful once I got started, I guess I just kept going." She tosses her arms out, motioning to the floor and flinging splotches of dove gray around her. "Now I'm almost down to the stairs."

Mom's pleasant smile is natural, the happiness clear in her eyes. Her clothes are a little rumpled, but aside from painting woodwork in a pair of linen pants and a crop top, the explanation for all this seems *mostly* valid. She sets the paintbrush down and pushes to her feet, grabbing a rag and wiping her hands with it. "Tell me all about it," she says to us. "How cooperative were the waves?"

Mostly. There's that word again, creeping its way in from my Richmond past. This is *mostly* ordinary. She's engaging in conversation and responding appropriately. But something feels off, and as Mason rambles on about cutbacks and aerials, I realize I don't remember the date of her last psych appointment. I tap the calendar app on my phone — she's supposed to go weekly.

I don't have records for the last three weeks.

"Mom." I clear my throat. Am I overreacting? Should I

even ask about this at all? "Have you — did you get something to eat?"

I was *going* to ask about her appointments. She was laughing a moment ago. Her smile was wide, her peals of joy ringing out like church bells on a Sunday morning. Now her lips are frozen in a grimace while she drags a paint-streaked hand across her cheek.

"I had something, yeah. There's lunch meat in the fridge if you're hungry. I can..." she wipes her hand across her face again, startling at a smear of gray. "I must look a mess," she says, and her eyes start to crease at the corners. Van tightens her grip on my elbow. "Nothing a rag won't fix," Van says.

"We're fine, thank you, Miss Dewitt," Ezra says to her. "We've got the cooler here. We'll take it down to the beach. It has everything we need in it."

Mom gives a brittle laugh and jams her fingers together. "Oh, of course not. Y'all can hang out here."

"It's fine," I say, gaze locked on the front porch. "Don't want to mess with your progress."

"Progress?"

"Mom. The porch." Ezra squeezes my fingers tight while my mom looks bewildered, sweeping the space behind her with a blank expression until recognition dawns.

"Progress! Yes. Porch progress."

I climb the steps, careful not to spook her. I lean in and lower my voice. "Mom, are you okay? Have you been —"

"Taking my medication?" She scowls and twists the rag in her hand into small, knot-like pieces. "I am *fine*, Mae. I just got a little distracted. I don't need a babysitter, remember?"

I don't move. I study her face, looking for signs of insomnia. "I know what you're doing," she says to me, "and you need to stop."

"What am I supposed to think?" I hiss. "I come home and find you painting the front porch for no reason."

"*Not* for no reason. I was covering up the mess I made."

Mom looks over my shoulder, cupping her hands around her mouth. "Mason. Van. Ezra. Y'all, come up here and get my daughter. She's forgotten how to have fun."

"Will do, Miss Dewitt." Mason's at the top of the stairs in an instant, his arm snaking through mine. Mom swats me playfully with the rag. "I'm gonna finish up and head in, probably get a shower. I'll turn in early, Mae, unless you need me."

What I need is to come home and not find her being reckless.

What I need is to keep better track of things.

What I need is a normal life, one where I'm not the adult, where I don't have a so-called gift that means I'm solving other people's problems. "You don't have to," I say, grabbing the handrail and taking the steps backward. "I'll see you in the morning, Mom."

———

I DO, in fact, see her in the morning. First thing, to be exact. I'm on the newly-painted porch, taking in the sunrise when the screen door creaks. "Hey," Mom says, coffee mug in hand and voice tentative. "What time did you get home?"

I hide my clenched fists and lean over the railing, one hundred percent *not* in the mood. The sky just traded her blues for pink, her optimism for a new day washing over the river. I breathe in, hoping to bottle it.

I get early-morning river stench instead.

"Mae?" Mom's light touch lands on my elbow. I jerk away from her and sit on the steps. Out of everything I've given up, the loss of yesterday's joy feels unforgivable. She steps toward me and crouches down, the loose knit of her dress draping over her knees like dark water. "Mae, please. Just listen. I know what it must have looked like last night."

I flinch at her tone, so achingly maternal. I twist my fingers together as she talks. "I'm still taking my meds," she says. "I've been to every single therapy session. What happened last night was a mistake. I got carried away fixing it."

"Like you tried to fix things with the lithium?"

Her sharp intake of breath knocks me sideways. "I'm sorry, Mom. I —"

"No," she says. "You're right."

"What?"

She nods. "I've made mistakes. I regret them because they hurt you. You can be angry at me." Mom leans back against the post and we sit there, wrapped in a heavy fog of silence.

I *am* angry. So angry I can't see straight. "I'm not angry, Mom. I'm just tired."

She leans closer to me and takes my hand. The better part of me squeezes her palm. "Nothing has changed, Mae. I'm independent. Capable. Don't let my disorder destroy your dreams."

I give a dry laugh. "You should print that on a motivational poster."

Mom chuckles. "I probably should."

Tension settled for now, she shifts until she's sitting next to me on the porch steps. "I talked to Gemma," she says.

"Gemma Broaden?" My pulse threads erratically in my throat.

Mom nods, letting go of my hand and folding her legs on the step beneath her. "She told me about Lowell-Howard. That you withdrew your intent."

"*That* was confidential information."

"Not for your mother. Gemma wants you to apply again. She put in a good word with the admissions committee. She says your portfolio's outstanding, and while it's not a sure thing, they might reinstate the offer." Mom studies me for a breath, then her shoulders sag as she looks out over the water. "I'm just...hopeful, I guess. I know you want this. You shouldn't drop out because of me."

"It's not just because of you," I blurt, and I'm being honest. The last few blinks have been difficult to cope with. What if they follow me wherever I go?

"What else is going on?" Mom asks me. "Is it Ezra?"

"What? No! I mean, he got into Broward and that's a whole mess, but it has nothing to do with me and the Fellowship." I shift in my spot while she studies me. "There's something you're not telling me," she says.

I look away, too rattled to keep eye contact. I inject a hint of humor to my voice. "I'll be eighteen, soon, Mom. What seventeen-year-old girl doesn't have secrets?"

"Oh, please. You're a model daughter and you know it. That's not what I'm talking about." Mom has that look, the one Lil gave me at the beginning of the summer. Of insight. Of *knowing*. "I should have noticed it a long time ago."

My throat closes up. I can't clear it. I grab her coffee and take a long sip. "What — what are you talking about?" I ask, but I already know what she's going to say to me.

"Once upon a time, on the banks of a mighty river —"

"No, Mom," I beg. "Please stop."

My insides twist at the reminder of my bedtime stories, a routine I let go of when her disorder became more disruptive. They were stories about a dark-haired woman who loved the sea, a free spirit who had eyes the color of the ocean. "You used my bedtime stories as code."

"Not code, no. I wanted you to know the truth. I wasn't sure how to do it without scaring you, especially because of my illness. You needed to be prepared in case…"

"In case we came back here," I whisper.

"In case it happened to you."

I breathe a bitter laugh. "You've known about my blinks this whole time."

"That's a good word for it," she says, the small smile on her face apologetic. "I used to call them my *trips*. Deebie wrote it off as my *vivid imagination*. Dad ignored it until Effa came up. It made him so mad, I stopped talking about any of it. It was easier to bike up to the courthouse and do my own research there."

I take a long moment to process what she's told me. Our past interactions shift and change. It's like I'm staring at the inside of a foggy kaleidoscope, watching the images coalesce as I turn it all over. "You lied to me."

"Because I didn't flat-out tell you about it?"

"No, because of that whole *reputation* thing. You said you were talking about yourself when you meant Effa and Annie."

"You're right." Mom's gaze drops to her hands and the paint on her fingers. She rubs at a blue splotch with her thumb. "Griffin men are intensely private. They're super prideful, too. Anything different, *other*, has to be hidden, especially if you can't root it out. I don't know a whole lot, but I get the sense Annie embarrassed Josiah. And then Effa was out of control, a whirlwind of opinion and energy…"

Mom stops rubbing at her hand. She pulls her arms around her waist and stares out toward the water, a sigh streaming out from her lungs. "Josiah was Dad's only influence, and his attitudes aren't going to change. I'm sorry I lied. It was a pretty lame attempt at trying to protect you. I want you to get out of here, Mae; be the one to break the cycle. Dad's baggage doesn't have to be your future. That's why I want you to reapply."

I lean back against the rail, processing. I get what she's saying — I do. But there's more to this story than she knows, more lives wrapped up in my grandfather's burdens. "Pa's baggage isn't just holding *me* back."

Mom stares at me in wary silence. "What do you mean by that?"

I tell her about Pa's letters to the editor, about the boats

Ezra built, and the bills. "How much money did he have saved?" she asks, eyes narrowed.

"Enough to pay for his first year."

Mom curses under her breath, her knuckles whitening. "Has he talked to Nathan at all?"

"About this stuff? No. Why would that matter?"

A quiet flush creeps up Mom's cheeks. "Nathan was supposed to go to Broward. It was a long time ago. I don't know what happened with that, but I wonder..." Mom's eyes meet mine, their grey-green stormy. "Maybe Nathan can help."

TWENTY-FIVE

Ezra drops from the dock, barely disrupting the surface. The sun is warm, and while I brought my notebook, I haven't written a word. I've been too distracted by the boy, too busy telling him about Nathan.

"Nathan builds boats," he says, repeating what I just told him.

"Yeah. He used to, at least."

"Huh," Ezra says, his attention focused on a dock line curled around a cleat. My attention's on the way his tongue peeks from the corner of his mouth. I wrench my eyes away and open my notebook to the first page, which is glaringly empty. "You should ask him about it."

Ezra's hands still over the knot he's tying. "Any specific reason why?"

I shrug, trying to play it off like I'm not vibrating with excitement. "I just think you should ask him, is all."

"Why are you bouncing?" he asks.

"Bouncing? I'm not bouncing." I'm bouncing, dang it.

"Mae," he says. I can hear him grinning. "What exactly did you do?"

It's a challenge not to jump in the water and throw my arms around his neck. "I *might* have mentioned Broward to Nathan. And he *might* have connections there. And he *might* be looking for a paid apprentice in construction. Marine construction." I finally look up, biting my lip in anticipation. "You know. Like for building boats."

In a flash, Ezra's out of the water and sitting next to me, creek water spilling from his shorts. "You told Nathan," he says. "About Broward."

I flash a huge smile as Ezra shakes his head. "You are the absolute worst," he says, laughing.

"We can both go to Charleston," I sing.

His head tilts the side. "I thought you weren't going?"

"Mom and I talked about it. I decided to reapply."

Ezra grabs me — there's no other word for it. He just reaches out and holds me tight. And then we're standing, and he's lifting me off the dock and spinning me in a circle. He's beaming when he sets me down.

"I can't even be mad at you for meddling. I'm so proud of you. This is huge."

"It's not that huge," I mutter, desperate to look away so he won't see my cheeks heating.

"Haven't you wanted this program forever?"

I slide my arms around his waist and smile up at him. "We'll see if they take me back."

"They will," he says. "I'm sure of it." He leans in for a

kiss, then tosses his head toward the boat he's been prepping. "Let's get this girl out on the water." He's grinning. "Time to see what she can do."

EZRA TAUGHT me how to sail the summer I first moved here. The boat was a castoff from one of the camps. "I don't know — this looks a little sketchy," I said, standing on the shore in my bright orange life vest. "Are you sure it's going to float?"

"She's fine. Got a couple leaks in her, but I'll stay close enough that we can swim."

I stepped back, mouth open in horror, while Ezra let out a voice-cracking laugh. "I'm teasing, Griffin. Geez. It's totally seaworthy."

"It better be." I scowled.

Ezra pulled the boat into the shallows and stood there, the life vest too big for his frame. He had to keep tugging it down, and I think that was the first time I felt something…other… about him. It was awkward and cute and, I don't know — equalizing. Like suddenly, we were on the same page.

It was late spring so the water was still chilly, even though the sun was so warm. I inched my way toward the boat, goosebumps on my arms as Ezra kept the craft steady. I held my breath as he towed me out and let the boat go, briefly panicked that he might not reach me in time. But then he was up and over the side, splashing me with brackish water. He settled in and we were off.

Ezra taught me the basics, like which ropes to use for

what. He taught me starboard for right, port for left, and that the rudder goes in the opposite direction of where you're headed. He handed the tiller over to me so I could steer, my heart brimming with exhilaration. I was floating along just like always, but on that day I wasn't adrift.

That floating sensation is back now as we navigate out of the creek. The gangly boy I used to know is gone, and I can't help but admire the man he's become. I try to remember what I learned, but it's difficult.

I'm distracted by the muscles in his arms.

Thwack. I'm pulled out of my blatant ogling when an empty water bottle lands in my lap. "Look alive, Grif. Grab the painter?"

I jump and pull tight on the rope, grimacing. "Sorry."

He smirks at me. "You got some drool on your chin."

We pick up speed as we exit the channel, the calm water shifting to gentle swells. Our focus is on the angle of the wind as we move out into the open river. Once we're settled, I cross to the port side and sit next to him on the bench.

"Thank you," I say, squinting into the sunlight. It's a gorgeous day, clear and warm.

Ezra scoots in my direction until our knees are touching. "You're welcome. I've been itching to take you sailing for a while."

"I'm not talking about the sailing. It was a thank you for forgiving me."

Ezra blinks, his expression unreadable. Maybe thanking him was a bad idea?

I move to stand, desperate to put some space between us

even though there's not much room to move. "Wait — hold on." Calloused fingers circle my wrist and I freeze, too embarrassed to look at the boy they're attached to. "Hey. Bean. Can you look at me? I was just…processing what you said."

I turn around, bracing myself for emotional impact. I feel like I've messed everything up. But when I meet his gaze, there's no anger there, just confusion. He tugs on my hand, pulling me toward him. I don't sit as close as before.

"You don't have to thank me for forgiving you," he says, brow furrowed. "You make it sound like it was hard."

"It is hard," I say, thinking of my mother. Of all the anger and the blame I've heaped on us both. "It's hard for me, anyway, and I figured for you, too, since you're not historically well-known for absolving people."

"Ouch, Griffin. I'm not that bad."

Eyebrow raised, I tick examples off on my fingers. "Seventh grade. Brent Hadley cut in front of you in the lunch line. You didn't speak to him for an entire month. Summer after seventh grade. Coach Warner. You filled the glove box in his car with day-old fish. Eighth grade —"

He suppresses a laugh, holding his hands up in surrender. "Alright. You proved your point." But the tiny smile fades, and suddenly, an awkward silence stretches between us. He props his elbows on his knees and stares at the floor of the boat like it's fascinating. I consider jumping overboard.

"I'm sorry," I say, desperate to fill the quiet.

"Don't be," he says softly. "You were right. How much do you know about my dad's recovery?"

"Not much."

Ezra shifts in his seat, jaw muscles tightening. "The mighty Gill Sutton has a drinking problem."

I study his face, schooling my reaction. I'm gobsmacked, but I don't want to make it weird. "That sucks," I say, using the response I'd want if people knew about my mother.

I don't want pity.

I want people to understand.

Ezra chuckles a little. "It does suck. It started after the accident. Did you know he called me, drunk, that day we went surfing?"

I scan my memories of that day and come up with nothing. "I don't remember you being on the phone."

"We were stopped for gas. You and Van were getting slushies. Dad couldn't say two words without slurring. He had lots to say, specifically about my big plans for Broward. He doesn't know I decided not to go."

"Ezra..." I breathe.

"It's okay," he says. "The point is that when my dad fell, the anger I'd been holding was just lost years and wasted energy. Because if life can change that fast; if my dad can go from the strongest man I've ever known to a drunk-dialing jerk, why was I carrying all this misery? When you fall, everything you're clinging to crashes down with you." He sits back and scrubs at his neck, staring out toward the shore beyond us. "The extra weight makes it hard to get up."

Ezra just called me out and he doesn't even know it. I sniffle, then wipe my nose with the back of my hand. I've let fear and anger hold me down, let them dictate my life choices.

Just like my grandfather, Luther Griffin.

Maybe this is what Lil meant about blinks and secrets. Maybe the healing means *I* learn to let go. I don't have to fear my blinks. I don't have to hide them from the people who love me.

Maybe Ezra deserves the truth.

"I have to tell you something."

"Okay," he says. "What's going on?"

"You were right. I don't have seizures. I have…something else." Ezra listens while I tell him about the blinks, the way I slip through time without warning. I explain how it makes me feel. Sometimes, my body's turned inside out; other times, it's like mist in a meadow. "It started here, that first summer. It's a big part of the reason I left."

Ezra furrows his brow. "I thought you wanted to live with your mother."

"I mean, yes, that was part of it, too. But I was so afraid. I was afraid y'all wouldn't want me anymore if you knew I wasn't normal. It just seemed easier to disappear."

Ezra pulls me into his lap, presses a kiss to my temple. He squeezes me tight and whispers something. "Normal isn't real."

I cough a laugh, incredulous. "Then what are you? And Van? And Mason? And all the other kids in Minnesott? Y'all do normal things. With normal people."

I feel the vibration of his laugh. "Have you met my sister and Mason? They're freaking weirdos, Mae. And I'm glad they're weird. The blinking — whatever it is that happens to you — it doesn't make you wrong or broken. It's just one of the million-and-one beautiful parts that make up Lila Mae Griffin. Part of the girl I love."

I lay my head on Ezra's shoulder, breathing in his ocean scent while I sob. When I've run out of tears and can only cringe at the amount of junk I've smeared all over his t-shirt, Ezra hands me water and a box of tissues. I tell him about my latest blinks.

"Wait," he says, putting two and two together. "My great uncle and your grandfather's sister?"

"It sure looks that way, yeah."

"Woah," he says. "That's like, incest adjacent. We're going to have to break up."

I smack him playfully on the shoulder. "We haven't even defined what we are."

"Should we make it official, then?"

Once upon a time, I wouldn't let a boy distract me. I promised myself I wouldn't make friends. But here I am in a boat on the middle of the river, quietly loving this boy's presence in my life. He takes my hand and twines our fingers together. "Our goals are in the same place," he says. "In Charleston."

"Are you going to Broward, E?"

"Thirty minutes ago, I was not. But if you've reached out to your program, I want to live my dream alongside my girlfriend."

"Your girlfriend."

He raises a brow, a silent, *"Yeah?"* in the motion.

I nod once, then again, then a million times over.

I think I'm ready to start living again.

TWENTY-SIX

Things with Ezra are perfect. I can't explain it any other way. We spend most of our free time together, sometimes down at the dock, sometimes around town with Van and Mason. Ezra's apprenticeship with Nathan has padded his savings. He hopes to start at Broward in the fall.

I'm still waiting to hear back from Lowell-Howard, which Van has taken as a personal affront. I'm fine to wait, but I'm worried about the board's personal safety. Van's liable to take action the longer it takes for them to let me know.

Mom has been thriving lately, and I feel better after that night on the porch. She's settled into a routine, one that alternates therapy and psych appointments with social time and work for a gallery she signed with — plus the glaringly obvious Nathan avoidance.

There is one wrinkle in all of this: Lil's not doing well. She's been slowing down, and while she insists she's fine, the hollows in her cheeks border on skeletal. I'm trimming back her hydrangeas this morning as Nathan's unofficial spy.

"I could have done this myself," Lil says, her voice rough with irritation. Sweat beads at the top of her brow.

I set down the shears and survey my progress. It's decent and Lil needs to rest. "You totally could have," I say, climbing the front porch steps to retrieve her. "And you would have been done in the half the time. But I like to help, and Nathan didn't have anything for me to do this morning." I shrug and tuck her arm into my elbow. "Sometimes it's nice just to supervise."

Lil sighs a grumpy *humph*. We make it to the trailer door before she speaks to me, eyes narrowed. "You tell Nathan to stop sending you up here. I like having you around, but not this way."

"What way?" I say, feigning innocence.

Lil's lips flatten. "Like a half-rate, half-wit spy."

I text Nathan on my way back to Pinecliff.

Me: Gig's up. She's on to us

Nathan: Is she mad?

Me: I wouldn't say mad. Annoyed, maybe

Nathan: Eh, she'll get over it. You heading back now?

Me: ETA two minutes

NATHAN: Good. Mail's here

Me: ....

Do you want me to get it?

Nathan: Nope. Miss Rudy came up to the house

I stop walking for a moment, nervous. I haven't checked

my email today. Would Lowell-Howard have sent a letter? I don't think so. But Nathan's acting funny…

I decide to pick up the pace.

I'm practically running by the time I round the corner and see Nathan and Miss Rudy up ahead. Nathan's got a clipboard in his hand, the one Miss Rudy carries for signatures. She smiles at me as I approach, then holds out a large, manila envelope. "I believe this is yours, sugarplum."

Miss Rudy climbs in her car with the Post Office lights on it and backs down the driveway. Nerves buzzing, I tear the envelope.

Congratulations! The Admissions Committee for the Lowell-Howard Fellowship is pleased to inform you that —

They took me back. "They took me back!" I dance a jig and lunge at Nathan.

"There you go, Lima Bean," he murmurs into my shoulder. "Didn't I tell you they would?"

"You did," I squeal. "Thanks for believing in me."

He blinks and mutters something about stupid allergies. "Whoo, boy. I'm proud of you, kid."

I all but skip up the driveway like a first grader, texting the good news to my mom and the trio.

Me: Lowell-Howard took me back!!!!!

Mom: That's my girl. I'm so stinking proud of you, kiddo!

Ezra: Charleston, baby! Heck yeah

Mason: Paaarrrrrrtaaaaayyy tonight

Van: My bestie's a freaking rockstar

Van: Also, Mason? No

Ezra: No?

Me: No?

Mason: What do you mean no?

VAN: If there's a party, I'll plan it. I don't trust anything you cook up

I laugh, silencing my phone and shoving it in my pocket. My heart sinks when I realize I still need to tell Pa. We've danced around Briarwood enough. It's time I take ownership of my decision. He's in his office with the door open when I come into the house.

"Lila Mae," he says. "I'm a little busy. Is this something we need to talk about right now?"

"I just have good news," I say. "My acceptance letter."

He leans back in his chair and pulls off his reading glasses. "Yes, I got an email. Well done."

Wait. "You got an email?"

"From Briarwood Admissions, yes."

"No, Pa. I..." My hands shake as I fumble for the envelope. I hold it out for him to see. "The Lowell-Howard Fellowship took me back." My stupid voice is shaking. "I start September first."

Pa sighs and leans forward, rubbing his eyes with one hand. "We talked about this. The program's not appropriate."

The room spins. "We talked about it briefly. Weeks ago."

"Yes, where I made my preference clear. It hasn't changed."

"But I've changed, Pa. Mom's doing great, and Ezra's going to Broward..."

"A Sutton." His lips flatten.

"Yes, a Sutton. My boyfriend."

That was a tactical error.

The vein in Pa's forehead bulges. "Boyfriend," he says.

"Yes." I tip my chin up, aiming for polite defiance. Pa stands from his desk and walks around it, stopping in front of me.

"I received your admission to Briarwood three days ago. You start on the twentieth. Less than three weeks."

A nervous sweat breaks out under my armpits even as my blood runs cold. "But I — we — we hadn't talked about it. And I decided not to apply."

"Your mother may have given you the mistaken impression that this is a house in which what you say, goes. I am not a cruel man, Mae, as much as you may feel that way at the moment. Your attendance at Briarwood will provide the necessary therapeutic resources you have so far been denied."

My jaw drops. "You want me to let the Fellowship go — again — so I can go to therapy."

The fire in his eyes dims just a bit. "The Lowell-Howard Fellowship is prestigious. I *am* proud of you for earning a spot. But I'm not inclined to send my granddaughter to a school where she can fixate solely on her interests *before* she has received appropriate counseling services."

"I don't...I don't need therapy."

"Once you get started, you'll find it helpful."

"But I'm not Mom!"

He stares at me long and hard. Then he turns, grabs the keys to his truck from the hook by the door, and walks past me into the hallway. "No, but your mother's illness has had an impact on you," he says, stopping in the foyer. "This summer, you've disobeyed me at every turn."

I stumble into the foyer behind him, fires of rage at the side of my face. "And you've lied! Over and over again, about our family, about the Suttons. Ezra showed me the letters you wrote. Do you realize what you've done to their business?"

Pa throws his keys to the floor and roars at me. "Do you realize what they've done to us?"

I freeze, dumbfounded. He's never yelled at me like that. "I don't," I say, my voice small, the missing pieces of this puzzle swirling around me. We stand rooted here in the foyer, Pa's sharp echo ringing in the air. The truth is *right there,* murky and obscured like it's pressed inside a piece of amber. The answers I don't have.

"It doesn't have to be this way," I whisper. "You don't have to carry all that weight."

"What in the world is going on?" Deebie rushes in from the kitchen, clutching a damp dishrag in her hands. "Raised voices in this house aren't rare, but I've never seen a conflict between you two. Luther," she puts a hand on his arm, his shoulders instantly tightening. "What are you yelling about?"

Pa's face flushes red, any hint of vulnerability leaving. He jerks away from Deebie, jaw set. "Ask your granddaughter, DB," he spits out, then wrenches the front door open. The screen door slams as he crosses the yard.

I stand at the door as Pa climbs into his truck cab. He leaves a dust trail as he speeds down the drive. Deebie sets a hand on my arm. I shrug it off, murmur, "I'll be back later."

I don't come back until after dark.

———

THE PACKAGES START ARRIVING a week later. I don't think anything of them at first. A new deal with a new gallery means Mom has been busy. Her supplies must be getting low.

But worry coils in my gut by the fourth delivery, because how many new brushes does she need? I pick up the latest box marked *Brush And Bramble* and climb the stairs, a little nervous. I tap gently on the door to her room.

"Hey," I breathe, not wanting to startle her. The scent of turpentine stings my nose.

"Lima Bean, hey." She glances up from her work and flashes a quick smile. "Let me finish this detail and I'm yours."

My gaze travels the room. Aside from the piles of boxes, her belongings are organized and out of sight. Bed made, clothes put away, surfaces clear, and desk free of clutter.

Except for that stack of envelopes.

"Okay. Done." Mom claps her hands and walks toward me. "The UPS truck came again?"

"Yep. Brush and Bramble this time." I set the boxes on the desk, right next to the stack of envelopes. "Do you —" I pause, not sure if I should even ask this.

"Do I?"

"Do you want me to go through your mail?"

Before my mother was in treatment, it was my job to sort the mail. It served two purposes, cutting some of the clutter and allowing us to stay on top of bills and important notices. She hasn't needed my help in a while.

"My mail?"

I point to the envelopes.

"Oh! No, I know what they are. New credit cards. Only a couple have been activated."

My stomach clenches. "Credit cards?"

"Yep! Got an offer for the bottom one. A Visa. And then I figured, what the hell. Why not?"

I count four separate offers as I leaf through them. "That's cool," I say. This is bad. I set the envelopes down. I breathe in through my nose; plop down into her office chair and spin three turns exactly.

"Great stuff you've got here," I say, motioning to the boxes. "It must have cost a ton."

"The owner of that gallery I signed with offered a bonus for three additional works. I was low on supplies, and the bonus will more than cover the charges."

The balloon of stress in my chest cavity deflates a little. "So you'll be able to pay this off."

"What? Oh. Yeah. I'll have enough to cover it." Her attention's back on painting now.

"Is this one of the pieces you promised?"

Mom looks at me, her grin sheepish. "No, actually. This is just for me."

Mom shifts the easel. I see the beginnings of a landscape. It's the view of the shore at Pinecliff, two figures — a parent and child, maybe? — are bent over and combing the sand.

"Who are they?"

"Eh, just people. Needed something to add texture here."

I nod, and because I can't let it go I turn the conversation back to her finances. "Why do you need the cards if you got a bonus?" I ask her. I'm not ready to let the topic go.

"The bonus posts next week, unfortunately. I needed the paint and stuff sooner than that." She studies me, and I get the feeling I'm being evaluated. "Mae, we've had this conversation over, and over, and over. I promise you. I'm fine."

I take a breath and loosen my shoulders. "Old habits, I guess."

"Old habits you have to let go. You're heading out of here soon. Studying your passion. And it's a Friday. Shouldn't you be getting ready to wreak havoc with your friends?"

I grind my teeth. She doesn't know about Briarwood. Nobody knows, actually. I haven't figured out what to say. I can't even look at my grandfather. "We don't wreak havoc. And yeah, we're doing something tonight."

"Don't wreak havoc?" She raises an eyebrow at me. "Have you met Mason Copley? And Van?"

"I know them quite well," I manage a smirk. "But I still don't think we wreak any sort of havoc."

Mom reaches for my hand and squeezes it. "Well. We'll see about that."

TWENTY-SEVEN

Van's voice floats from my closet. "She's opened four new credit cards?"

"Yeah," I sigh, studying my nails.

"But she's buying art supplies, right? Not hats for chickens?"

"No, no hats for chickens. Just paint and brushes and stuff." I flop back on my bed and Van emerges from the closet. She's holding a wispy blue top.

She's coming for me, I know it. Sitting up, I grab a faded hoodie and shrug it on. "What are you doing?" Van barks, and she sounds remarkably like my tenth-grade biology teacher.

"I'm getting comfortable."

"You're not wearing that to Brent's party."

"I'm not going to the party. I'm staying in."

Van crosses the room in two quick strides, struggling to pull the hoodie off me. She succeeds, and my vision is once again obscured. She slides the wispy top over my head, smoothing it against my tank layer. "This is much better." She stands back, appraising her effort. "Miss Dora Bell sure knew how to dress."

I recognize the top — it's an old kimono-sleeve blouse of my grandmother's. It's definitely cute, and it highlights my curves without exposing them. But there's no point in wearing this if I'm staying home to keep tabs on my mother. "I'm serious, Van. I'm not going. Wild credit cards are on the loose."

Van pulls me up by the arms and walks me to the mirror. "The boys are expecting us in," she squints at her phone, "fifteen minutes. And Miss Dewitt said you should go out."

"So we're trusting a woman with a history of mental illness?"

She rolls her eyes at me. "No, we're trusting your *mom*."

"That was a low blow," I hum.

"Sorry. But I think you need to flip the script. Because you can ask *all* the what-ifs and expect them to be negative. But did you ever stop to think that maybe, the possibilities could be good ones?" Van turns so we're face to face. Her eyes blaze with conviction. "*What if* we go out and it's fine?"

———

BODIES PACK the wide-open space near the Hadley's guest cottage, figures aglow in a thousand twinkle lights. The group's a mix: vacation preps in khaki and Lily Pulitzer dresses; locals in cut-offs and faded tees. Van tugs on the straps of her 1950s romper. It's both adorable and perfect for the heat.

"Have you heard from my brother? Or Mason?" she asks me.

"I don't have a signal here."

Van wrinkles her nose. "I was kinda hoping your phone was magic."

"Sorry," I shrug, scanning the crowd for the boys' familiar faces. "Pa went with the basic plan."

Van shoves me playfully on the shoulder. "And here I thought the *Sutton family* ruined everything. Buy me a drink and I'll forgive you. Probably."

"Weirdo," I mutter, leading her toward the drinks.

The drinks are free, actually, in one of those get-what-you-pay-for ways. Brent's older brother sprang for a few cheap kegs and filled a half-dozen coolers with generic options. I snag a grapefruit seltzer (*SnapBubbly!*) while Van roots around a little more. "It's all light beer," she complains. "And it's fake stuff from the Dollar General." Van cups her hands around her mouth like a megaphone and shouts in Brent's direction. "I'm not a fan of knock-offs, Brent!"

A few heads turn in our direction and I beg the earth to swallow me whole. "Could we go out *once* without you causing a scene, Evangeline?"

Van blows on her nails and rubs the surface of them against her romper. "That was not a scene," she says. "It was a community protest."

"A community protest."

She shrugs at me, dead serious. "I'm a champion of human rights."

I shake my head and thread my arm through her elbow. "Let's go find the guys."

While my grandfather's mostly a hobby farmer, Brent's parents run a full-scale operation on their land. The house sits close to the road with the rest of the outbuildings behind it. All told, the Hadleys own and work about four hundred acres surrounded by piney woods.

Van and I walk out past the guest house toward the edge of the Hadley's fields. We can see the corn up ahead, tall stalks of Silver Queen swaying in the moonlight. It's thick and fully grown, a bumper crop the family will start harvesting in the next week or so, I imagine. The sounds of an acoustic guitar and Mason's rich baritone float across the field.

Ezra's face lights up when he sees me, and how I love that crooked smile on his lips. He looks so perfectly him in faded jeans and a worn concert t-shirt. It steals the breath from my lungs.

"Look. I know I was one of y'alls biggest supporters, but do we have to act like lovestruck idiots when we're within twenty yards?"

"Yes, we do. And I do believe you're the one who ditched me at the trestle for your famous musician, so I don't want to hear about it."

We reach the edge of the group listening to Mason and his guitarist, Caleb, a new-to-the-Treetorns kid. Mason's in the grass with his elbows on his knees, belting his way through the last lines of an old emo song about love and loss and the aftermath of infidelity. He looks lost in memories of his dad.

Ezra wraps me in his arms and we sway a little as Mason's

voice fades out. For a moment, there are only crickets and the hum of conversation from the guest house. Then the small crowd bursts into applause.

Caleb's younger than we are — a sophomore. He stands, all swagger and smirk. Setting his guitar to the side, he pushes his straight black hair out of his eyes and pulls a joint from his pocket. He's two hits in when the sweet, earthy scent reaches Mason.

"Dude. You're still in diapers," he blurts.

"It's just a joint, man. I've got extra." A cloud of smoke dances upward from his lips.

"Oh, you sweet, summer child," Van sighs with derision. Mason shakes out his limbs and cracks his neck. He turns his back to the crowd, muttering something about idiot kids with drug habits. He's got opinions, courtesy of Eric, his dad.

Mason spins around and points at Caleb. "You play decent guitar. But my band is clean. If you get caught with that thing, Sheriff Kelly's attention is gonna be on you, and then us, and I don't need that. I don't want that. So if you have even the slightest interest in continuing to play for the Treetorns, I'm going to recommend you put the damn thing out."

Caleb deliberates for a second, looking at Mason through hooded eyes. Ezra steps forward and holds his hand out for the joint, but Caleb doesn't give it to him.

He tosses it, still smoldering, into the corn.

Nobody moves for a second — we just stare at Caleb, open-mouthed. Ezra recovers first, a strangled, "That was still lit!" disrupting the moment. "You're gonna start a fire. What the hell?"

Ezra and Mason dive into the corn, crashing wildly. I giggle, nervous and caught up in the absurdity. "I'm not finding the humor here," Mason shouts from the stalks, and I fuss at myself for laughing even harder. Van knocks me in the shoulder, then dissolves into giggles herself.

It's dark, the rows of cornstalks crowded. I grab Van's hand and dodge an ear of Silver Queen. "Anybody see anything?" I shout.

"Nothing yet." Ezra's voice is close, but not close enough that I can reach out and touch him. Mason yells from farther away, the sound of his voice more distant. "Follow the smoke with your nose!"

Van drops my hand and I lose her, the only sign of her direction a curse about bumper crops. The smoke thickens and I push forward, right into a dense patch of it. Not thinking, I breathe in a lungful of smoke.

Acrid fumes sting my insides and I cough desperately, tears streaming from the corners of my eyes. Desperate to get out, get away, get into wide, open spaces, I drop to the ground and crawl.

My hands and knees are raw from the exertion by the time the smoke thins enough to breathe. Not sure where I am, I stop and pull my hair from my face, listening. The rumble of tires against pavement pulls my attention. If there's a car, I must be close to Highway 55.

I push to my feet, tripping right and left as I stumble toward what I hope is the open road. It's not the fastest way back to the house, but I can follow the road until the cornfield ends and cut straight across Brent's property. Arms flailing at the stubborn stalks, I push toward the edge and then tumble forward onto the wide shoulder.

Straight into the lights of an oncoming car.

I try to scream. Jump up and down or something — warn the driver of the deer standing in the road. They're everywhere down here, especially along 55 with its farms and thick pine forests. Most people know to take it slower at night.

This driver, though, is either careless or clueless, driving at a high rate of speed. Tires squeal as the driver slams on the brakes, then swerves in my direction. I end up sideways in the ditch, my hands flying to my ears at the unholy screech of metal. Helpless, I watch in horror as the vehicle flips and comes to rest on its roof.

Silent. The world is silent. I stand on shaky legs. Taking in great gulps of air, I scramble from the ditch and pull my phone from my back pocket. It takes me three tries to call 911.

Nine one one, state the nature of your emergency... The operator sounds far away.

"I just witnessed an accident on Highway 55. Hadley Farm area."

State the nature of your emergency...are you there?

I say it again, spacing my words like I'm talking to a three-year-old. "I...just...witnessed...an...accident."

Static blasts my ear as the call drops. I growl in frustration and try to bang out a text. But none of my contacts will come up, not Van, not Ezra — no one. And then I can't see the screen because yet another car's lights are streaming up behind me. I shield my eyes, the sudden movement sending me backward. I'm back in the ditch on my butt.

The stench of burnt rubber fills my nostrils, pungent against the freshly turned earth. My heart pounds and my hands tremble as I push to stand, willing my legs to support me. The second vehicle is old — definitely vintage — but whoever owns it has kept it looking brand new. The driver's side door opens with a sharp creak, the figure of a man emerging.

"Effa!" he yells. "Effa Griffin!"

Lord, have mercy.

Oh, no.

Waves of nausea roll through me. I sink down into a crouch. My long, deep breaths do a decent job settling the contents of my stomach — until ten-year-old Luther Griffin tumbles from the second car.

"Father, wait! I'm coming!"

I turn and vomit into the grass.

"Get back in the car, Luther…" Josiah rasps, and I wipe my hand across my mouth, stomach heaving. My legs don't want to work, but I push up and try to stumble forward, the irrational part of my brain eager to help. But it's no use, and not even because I'm blinking. Patrick's halfway out of the car. His white shirt twinkles in the night, bits of windshield glass in their own twisted constellation.

I choke back a sob at the angle of Patrick's neck.

"Luther!" Josiah roars. "Get back in the car like I told you!" But Luther doesn't move an inch. He just watches, stoic and still as his father tugs on the passenger door handle. The car rocks on its roof with the effort. Patrick's body shifts. The wheels spin.

There's a pop of glass and a scream of metal. Josiah's wrenched open the door. "It's alright, Effa," he rasps. "It's alright, love. I've got you."

Effa opens her eyes.

"There you go," Josiah huffs, voice taut and breathing ragged. "We're going to get you help."

Josiah groans as he moves to his feet, cradling his daughter so gently. "In the car, Luther," he commands once more, and the boy startles to life, scrambling for the vehicle. Josiah's nearly there, panting, when he lurches and comes to a halt.

He drops to his knees. "Effa? No. No, no, no, no, no." He lays Effa on the ground in frantic, jerky movements. She's gone completely limp.

Fresh tears spring to my eyes as Josiah spins around toward Patrick. The tortured man heaves a fractured cry. "Ef —" he huffs, leaping to his feet, hands in his hair as he looks back at his daughter. Everything goes quiet.

So quiet.

Until the ground shakes with an unholy roar.

Josiah storms the short distance to the wreckage. The first blow lands squarely against Patrick's chest. "Stop!" I yell, even though it's no use. He can't hear me.

I wish I couldn't hear him.

Patrick's already gone, but that doesn't matter to Josiah. His violent screams ring through the night. There's the crack of bone. The fleshy squelch of soft tissue.

My great-grandfather's beating a dead man.

A whimper sounds to the right of me. I wipe the snot from

my nose with my arm. I turn back to Josiah's car and see Luther on the ground, holding his sister in his arms as her blood soaks through his shirt sleeves. "I told you," he cries. "I told you they ruin everything. I told you. I told you…I told…"

I sink back onto the ground, exhausted. Every bone in my body hurts. I squeeze my eyes shut, blocking the horror I've just seen. But I'm here all alone with the wreckage of my family, feeling the cries of a lonely little boy. A little boy I know; a little boy irreparably broken. Begging the only person he ever thought loved him

to please,

please,

wake up.

TWENTY-EIGHT

I wake to the stench of burnt popcorn. Fortunately, the fire never got very big. The boys managed to put it out fairly quickly, but the pungent odor still permeates everything.

Fires in a cornfield are the worst.

Also the worst? Lying to Ezra, Van, and Mason about what happened when I got separated from the group. The tears were from the heavy smoke, I said, and I was quiet because I was tired. I couldn't talk about the accident.

I scrub my hair three times in the shower, then rub my skin raw in the hottest water I can take. I need to feel something other than the ache in my chest, the pain of watching four lives destroyed in an instant. Josiah and Pa didn't die in that accident, but something inside them did.

My fingers are wrinkled when I step out of the shower and tie my wet hair in a messy knot. I toss on a blue knit dress, the most professional-looking thing I can find in my closet. Pa left me a note: he wants to meet about Briarwood. Even if my heart's a thousand percent not in it, I might as well look the part.

A quick glance at my phone says I better get moving. I better plan, too, what I want to say. Because as much as he wants to *chat* about school, I've got headlights and deer on the agenda. Patrick and Effa's accident was just that — an accident — and I don't think Pa knows the truth.

I walk out into the hall on autopilot, running conversation scenarios through my head. Do I tell him about the blink? What will he say if I do, and how do I keep him from losing his mind over it? So far, I'm coming up empty. What the heck am I going to do?

I'm nearly past my mother's bedroom when I feel a shift in the air. Mom's door is ajar, spilling early morning light into the hallway. It's too weak and too watery for the sun that streams in after nine.

Nathan's voice floats through the door and I steel myself against the memory of the night my mother overdosed. His voice has the same youthful lilt and I peek through the door, knowing what I might see but not quite prepared for it. Nathan's there, alright. He's shirtless and grinning. And definitely all of nineteen.

His legs are clad in faded denim. He tugs a worn navy t-shirt over his chest. Mom's standing there, too, wrapped in a soft, white sheet, her bare shoulders peeking out above the cover. She leans forward and kisses him. I mean, *really* kisses him. I smack my hands over my eyes. This is weird.

It's probably less than thirty seconds, but it feels like an eternity before I hear them part. "I've gotta go," Nathan says, the reluctance in his voice obvious. Mom nods, clutching the sheet with one hand and rubbing the other across her forehead. Something's wrong — she's worried. I can tell by the way she's chewing her lip.

"Hey. You okay, Dewie?" *Dewie?* Nathan takes her free hand in his.

Mom nods, her breathy laugh failing to convince me. And from the looks of it, Nathan, too.

"No, something's bothering you. Are you worried about practice tonight?"

Mom's shoulders relax and her head bobs forcefully. "Graduation." She forces a chuckle. "It's kind of a big deal."

"It's easy," Nathan says. "You can do it. All you do is walk across the stage. And I'll be there. Front row. Wouldn't miss it."

Mom sighs and presses her lips together. "Easy. Yeah. Okay."

My mother is lying to Nathan, but if he notices, he doesn't press. He pulls her into his arms and kisses her temple, then walks backward across the room. The window squeaks a little as he tugs it upward with one sharp pull. Then he's halfway out, his legs on the roof above the back porch and his torso leaning into the bedroom. Two circles of pink bloom across her cheekbones as he winks at her. "I'll meet you at Lil's after graduation practice. 7:30, alright?"

Mom nods as Nathan exits the window and climbs down to the ground below. She sinks into the chair at her desk, her eyes closed as she regulates her breathing. I grip the edge of the door with taut hands, completely and utterly helpless.

My mother is freaking scared.

"Stop it, Dewitt," she says into the silence, snagging a t-shirt from her desk. She pulls it over her head and stands; the sheet falls to the floor in a pile. Mom pads across the hardwood floor and tugs at the top of her dresser. I cringe at the loud squeak of wood. She rifles through the drawer, teeth tugging at her lip as she excavates its contents. Finally, she stops.

Removes her hand from the dresser.

And stares down at a used pregnancy test.

————

"LILA MAE. Let's go to my office." Pa's voice barely registers through my rage.

"I'll be late," I bite out and leave him in the hallway. "Deebie!" I yell. "Where is my mother?"

Deebie jumps, a little coffee from her mug sloshing out onto the kitchen table. "First of all, Mae, a lady never yells for attention. As for your mother, I believe she's painting. In the boathouse loft."

I bust through the back door and make a beeline for the boathouse, blood roaring in my ears.

"Wow. Last night must have been a rager," Mom says, barely glancing from her canvas. I just stand there, my shoulders tight. The gentle scrape of brush and paint stops, and she looks at me, alarm on her features. "Mae, honey. What's wrong?"

I hate the way she asks me, like it's a simple question we

can discuss. Like there aren't layers upon layers of heartache and deceit, tearing at my heart and pushing distance between us. "Everything, Mom. You lied."

She rears back, eyes wide open. "I don't...What are you talking about?"

"My dad wasn't a one-night stand. You were pregnant with me when you left here." My ache and rage bubble out like lava. "Nathan," I spit, "is my dad."

Color drains from Mom's face, her lips trapped in a frozen o-shape. When she recovers, there's a quiver in her voice. "Let's talk about this."

"We already did! I asked you, point blank. You lied to me, Mother. You made it clear the answer was no."

"It's — it's just — "

"Complicated."

Relief plays across her features. "Yes."

I dig my nails into my palms so I don't punch something. "You got pregnant and you left without telling Nathan. Seems pretty simple to me."

Mom sets down her brush and tugs her hair with paint-stained fingers. Her eyes are red when she looks at me. "You think I wanted to leave? I agonized for weeks. But in the end—"

"In the end, you left because you were a coward."

She rears back like I've slapped her. "You have no idea what bravery means."

"It means sticking around, Mother. Sticking around and showing up. It means choosing to face the consequences of your actions — something you've never done."

"Don't you *dare* assume you know anything about this. I chose to put you first. I chose to get out of here because I knew what would happen otherwise." She leans forward. "Mae, I chose to live."

My heart pounds in my throat. The Street Dance. "You were going to end us both."

"I was. I was scared out of my mind. But all the fear in the world couldn't dampen my love for you. I changed my mind and then I left."

"Nathan would have gone with you."

"It would have ruined his life."

"How? Your parents absolutely adore him. Lil thinks he hung the moon. You decided what everybody got because you thought it was the best decision. *That* sounds like selfishness, Mother. It doesn't sound like bravery to me."

Mom stands from her stool and walks toward me, reaching out to grab my hand. I pull away, embarrassed by the way my voice shakes. "No one knew I existed, Mom."

"That's not entirely true," Mom says. Her lip wobbles.

"What do you mean *that's not entirely true?*"

Mom sniffs, rubbing a knuckle beneath her lash line. "Lil Rooney, Lima Bean. She knew."

————

LIL'S CAR IS MISSING. I don't bother to engage the kick-stand on the bike. I let the thing fall into the sand at the edge of the drive and run straight for the trailer.

"Lil! Open the door, Lil. I mean it!"

Silence. No response.

"Damn it." I kick the doorframe, then dance up and down in pain and rage. Every adult in my life has lied to me, except for Nathan.

Why do people treat me like a child?

It's in the corner of my eye at first, the movement. I turn, the familiar vacuum pulling me in. I see my Mom and Lil on the front porch of the farmhouse, both so much younger. Lil's worrying her braid, desperately pleading with my mother. Mom's shoulders are back, her chin up resolutely. She stands there, shaking her head.

The blink ends just as quickly as it started, but in its wake, I spot something tacked to the farmhouse door. I jog across the lawn and leap up the steps, snatching an envelope emblazoned with block letters.

It's addressed to me.

From Lil.

DEAR MAE,

I'm going away for a while. I bet you're probably ready to smack me upside the head. But it's necessary. I have things to figure out that can't be helped in Minnesott. I hope you'll forgive me for this.

I know, Mae, that you're not going to like this next part, that I'm going to be asking forgiveness of you again. But what is it they say? Better to ask forgiveness than to seek out permission? Well. Here it goes, anyway.

Your grandfather has never liked me, but he came to see

me last week. He told me about Briarwood, about your desire to attend the fellowship in Charleston. It was a tense conversation, and believe me that I very nearly told him to stuff it. But I listened and held my tongue.

Mae, he made some excellent points.

You, my dear, are an amazing young woman. You have taken on so many tasks above your pay grade that I admit, I am concerned. I wasn't strong enough to help your mom in the way she needed me. I'm not going to make the same mistake with you.

Go to Briarwood. Do a year there. It's a good school and it will serve you well. Your writing can wait. A certain young man can wait if he really loves you. Your focus should be on yourself right now, first and foremost.

I love you, Lima Bean.

Be good for me.

Lil

I KICK the door so hard I feel the force of it, up through my bones and into my teeth. I crumple the letter into a ball, scraping up my hand as I shove it back through the mail slot.

I sit down on the porch steps and cry.

TWENTY-NINE

The rest of the day passes in a haze.

I don't eat. I don't answer texts. I avoid Nathan and my grandparents. I have no idea where my mother is, nor, frankly, do I care.

I'm stretched out on the shore like a bleached and bloated jellyfish, totally over it.

My family and its secrets can take a flying flip.

A shadow crosses my face.

"I don't think she's dead," Van mutters. Something nudges my leg. I smack the offending thing, pleased when I hear it curse as I roll over.

"Ow, Mae," Mason sputters. "That hurt."

"Go away. I'm busy."

Van snorts a little. "Getting up close and personal with the sand?"

"I'm hoping if I lay here long enough the sand fleas will end my misery."

"That's hideous."

"Yeah, well. Welcome to my glamorous life."

My tormentors eventually stop speaking, long enough that I think they've given up. But then two strong sets of hands lift me up and drag me to the river, dunking me. I emerge from the water with a gasp.

"What the heck did you do that for?"

Van and Mason stand in front of me, lacking the decency to look chagrined. They actually look mad, which makes no sense considering they're the ones who tossed me in the river. Van leans in, her index finger stabbing the air like she wants to poke me. "Why are you acting like a recalcitrant crab?"

"Excellent use of an SAT word." Mason pats her on the shoulder.

"Why thank you, Mr. Copley. I try."

Wiping salt from my eyes, I fumble up the shoreline and shove both of them as hard as I can. "I asked you to leave me alone." I'm breathing hard, my temper flaring. "I told you to go away. I'm not answering your texts for a reason. Just…" Traitorous tears threaten my eyelids. "Just please," my voice wobbles, dang it. "Really. Please just go."

I flop back down on the sand, my hands shaking, the river's soundtrack the only noise. Until I hear Van speak, her quiet urgency not directed at me but to her phone. To Ezra. "We found her," she says. "On the river. Pretty stupid not to check here first."

Mason shakes open a beach towel and wraps it gently around my shoulders. Kneeling in front of me, he tucks it in tight. "There. My mama used to do this after I'd fall in the creek by the trailers."

His touch is so gentle I sob.

"Hey, now." Mason sits down beside me. "Everything's alright."

It's not alright. Nothing's alright, and it never will be. My whole life is a lie.

"What's your ETA?" Van asks into her phone, and I assume she's still talking to Ezra. "Okay. See you in five." Van ends the call, then sits on the other side of me. "Ezra went up to the trestle to find you. He says he'll be here soon."

Nobody speaks for the next several minutes. We sit in silence, staring out at the river and her waves. Van rubs small circles on my back and it's oddly comforting. Mason fidgets, digging holes with his feet in the sand.

I'm trying to decide what I'm going to tell them, if anything, when I'm enveloped in Ezra's arms. He smells so darn good — like days at the beach and good memories and the salt air that blows through my bedroom window. "Hey. You had us a little worried."

"Sorry," I mumble, my voice strained and thick with snot.

"Anybody get ahold of Lil?" Ezra asks, probably to Van and Mason.

"You can't," I say. "She's gone."

"What do you mean, *gone*?" I don't have to see Van's face to know it's pinched.

"I mean I went by the house and she's gone somewhere. Left town, apparently."

"She probably went into New Bern or Oriental," Mason says.

I shake my head. "Nope."

Van shifts in the sand and pokes me with a finger. "Mae, if you have something to say, just go ahead and tell us. We left twenty questions in elementary school."

I pull away from Ezra's embrace and fumble upward, gripping the towel at my throat. "Okay, fine. My grandfather hates your family because he blames Patrick for his sister's death. And all these years I thought my dad was a loser one-night stand? He's freaking *Nathan*. My mother lied to me about it. *Twice*. And our fabulous Lil has left town on personal business. Left me a note on her door. She's friends with my grandfather now and agrees with him that I should ditch Lowell-Howard for a boarding school in Raleigh."

"Raleigh?"

"Raleigh. So I can get therapy. Mental help."

I'm ridiculously warm under this towel. So hot, my skin feels like it might slough off. I rip it away, flinging it down on the sand and stomping my foot like a three-year-old. "I am so tired of my life being decided for me. Of everything I believed being a pack of lies! Of having to hide who I am and lie to you, because by the way, I don't have seizures. I'm a freaking time traveler."

"Mae —"

"Ezra, no." I step back, then turn and scream into the wind. "All I want is a normal life," I yell, throat burning. "No time traveling. No crazy mom. No out-of-their-minds ancestors or grudges or any of the rest of it. I never asked for any of this."

Spent and drained of just about everything, I fall on my knees into the sand. A hand touches my shoulder and I flinch, then melt as three sets of arms pull me upward.

"We've got you, love. We've got you," Van whispers.

Mason sings my favorite song.

Ezra kisses my hair. Holds my hand. Whispers that he loves me.

I let the people I love more than anything hold me while I cry.

MOM'S ROOM is empty when I stumble through her doorway. Worry ignites at the base of my skull. It's a distinct kind of distress, sharp pinpricks of fear I haven't felt since that night in Richmond.

The night I pushed my mom to overdose.

Bile rises in my throat. We fought this morning. I was angry and horrible. Trying not to assume the worst, I take the stairs two at a time to check the main floor and the sunroom. No Dewitt. No anybody, actually. I head down the hall and into the kitchen, hoping she'll be there when I turn the corner.

My stomach turns.

She's not.

"Hey there, shug. How has your day been?" Deebie glances up at me, her hands sudsy from the dishes in the sink.

"It was…" incredibly awful. "It was fine," I say. "Have you seen my mom?"

"Not since earlier. She came downstairs around four fifteen. Said she was heading to the loft. Might still be out there."

The boathouse. I should have checked there first.

I curse under my breath when the boathouse is empty. The knot in my throat tightens as I jog to the shore. It's empty, too, but Deebie's on the porch when I come back from the water. "Find her?" I don't lie. I just sort of…sidestep her question.

"Oh, you know my mother. She's been busy today. All over the place."

Not that I have a single clue where.

Deebie hums. "Well, there's a plate for her in the refrigerator. There's one in there for you, too."

"Thanks," I say, the word garbled by my panic. I'm having a hard time keeping it together, here.

I open the door and sprint up the stairwell, reminding myself to think. I head back to Mom's room, my eyes lighting on the pile of art supplies in the corner; on the stack of envelopes with new credit cards. A yellow card sits on the desk addressed to Lila Mae Griffin. My fingers shake as I pick it up. She's written something on the back —

You are golden, Mae, like sunlight on the river. None of this was ever your fault.

I curse. Is this what I think it is? Dread takes residence in my bones. I tap a stiff text to my mom.

Are you hungry? Where are you?

There's no response.

I stare at the screen, waiting. I stare at it a while more. Nothing comes through, and the underlying fear of the last thirty minutes explodes into abject terror. I start to send a message to Nathan.

I pull up the group text instead.

Me: I need help

The response is immediate.

Van: Coming. Let me find my metal bat

Ezra: I hid that thing for this exact reason. Mae, are you alright?

I'm not alright - not even close to it.

Me: I can't find my mom

The thread is silent for a beat until it flares to life with rapid-fire responses:

Ezra: On my way to you

Mason: Late to the party. What's going on?

Van: Mae's mom is missing. I'm coming to you, Mae. Call 911

Mason: Check the loft. Is she painting?

Me: No. I've looked everywhere

I shove the note in my pocket and scurry to the backyard. I take off for the woods once I hit the boathouse, springing until Ezra steps out from the trees. He grabs my hand, and the two of us run to his trailer together. Van and Mason meet us at the Sutton's front door.

"Mae, we should call the sheriff." Van's face radiates concern.

"Not yet," I gasp. I'm out of breath, both from the run and the fist of panic my lungs are fighting.

"What do you mean *not yet?*"

I purse my lips at Van and pull the card out of my pocket.

Ezra takes it from me and swallows hard. "Is this a —"

"I don't know."

I can't move. We *should* call the sheriff. We *should* tell Nathan or Deebie and Pa. But I'm frozen to the spot, memories of Mom's lifeless form passed out on the floor of her bathroom. "I can't do this," I gasp. "Not again."

Ezra's keys shake on the chain as he pulls them from his pocket. He herds us to the Jeep. "Van, Mason, one of y'all call Sherriff Kelly?"

Van nods. Mason says, "On it." Ezra starts the Jeep and pops the clutch.

I try to buckle my belt but my arms are heavy. I can't get the darn things to work. Foot heavy on the brake, Ezra leans across my lap to pull the seatbelt over me. His lips brush against my head. "We got this," he whispers, and I believe him. "We're gonna start by tracking her phone."

THIRTY

My earliest memory is of lights.

We were in the car, Mom and I. It was nighttime, and I was three or four. We were in Atlanta, I think, because I started preschool in Georgia. I don't remember where we were going.

I don't remember much about that moment at all.

But I do remember the lights out the window, the way they'd get close to us and then arc on by. Bright, buzzy stars, coming just close enough that if I reached out, I thought I could touch them. They were there and they were happy and they were beautiful for a moment.

And then in a split second, they were gone.

That, I have learned, is living with my mother. Brief glimmers of hope that flash and disappear. It's the story of every Griffin girl, whether her life ends in a rush of twisted metal and headlights, or the rotating flash of an ambulance, the kind that bathes everything in red and white, throwing the road and the trees and the night into a kaleidoscope of crimson before it fades away in the distance.

Like my mother, as they try to revive her.

Like every good thing in my life.

THIRTY-ONE

"Took me a while to find you," Pa says, his voice weary.

I shrug. "I'm not trying to hide."

"Didn't say you were." Pa's hands are in his pockets as he settles down in the chair across from me. We're in Craven County Hospital's observation lounge.

It's late, close to midnight. The lights in the room are dim. I wonder if it's intentional, so the poor souls who find their way to this room can see the lights across the river. Watch the quiet hush on the waterfront.

"You and your friends saved your mother," Pa says.

I sink deeper into my chair. Mom went down to Baird's Creek. Cut up her wrists pretty bad before wading out into the water.

Ezra spotted her first.

"Your Sutton boy ought to consider a career as a paramedic."

"He's going to Broward, Pa." I look toward the door,

wondering why the boy in question hasn't come back yet. He went to get coffee a while ago.

I'm pulling out my phone to text him when my grandfather clears his throat. "I'm grateful for y'all, really. You got to her right quick."

I don't respond, because what is there to say? This was Mom's second attempt in three months. The second time I pushed her over the edge, forcing her to make a life-altering decision. I don't want to talk about it, think about it, or analyze it. I want to crawl into a hole and sleep.

"I've been thinking about what you said, about those letters in the paper," Pa says. The muscles in my jaw clench hard. "I have good reasons for what I did, though I may have been short-sighted." Pa pulls his hands from his pockets and leans forward, his voice quiet. "I will do what I can to make amends."

I laugh a little, internally. "They don't want your help."

"That may be true," Pa shrugs. "It would be a shame, though, if word were to get out regarding Gill Sutton's *habit*. People don't take kindly to drunken mechanical work."

My skin crawls. "You wouldn't," I grit out.

"I won't," Pa says, hands up in surrender. "*If* you agree to certain terms."

Holy Moses. "You're blackmailing me."

"This is....*motivation*, I'd say. You know by now your best option is Briarwood."

I don't want to admit it, but he's right. Briarwood will be closer to Mom. Not that I plan to go within five hundred feet of her since my presence in her life is so complicating. But I want to keep an eye on things; be close enough to make the trip if necessary. Briarwood's campus is only half an hour from Mom's new facility. The drive from Charleston will take five.

Pa seems unbothered by my silence. "You leave tomorrow morning at eight. Once you are securely in the dorms, I will draft and submit a letter to the editor praising Ezra Sutton's heroism. No one will hear about Gill's *issue*, not from me, anyway. Their business will pick up. Briarwood will give you a well-rounded education and provide you with services. And with the return of their customer base, the Suttons will be able to assist Evangeline and Ezra with college tuition. This is a scenario in which everybody wins."

I don't win. Not really. My second chance for the Fellowship is gone. All my plans. All the hopes and dreams I shared with Ezra. "What if I say no?"

Pa's face hardens. "I wouldn't recommend that, Mae."

"What if I tell them the truth? I'll tell Ezra everything."

Pa lifts his hands in a *so what?* gesture. "I have no problem with revenge."

And there's the truth of it, really. My grandfather doesn't care. Either way, he wins, because no matter how desperately I want to go, the fellowship's out of the picture. I'm *going* to end up at Briarwood. He's not standing on the ledge — the Suttons are, my decision their assassin or their savior.

I don't want to hurt them anymore.

Ezra was right — my family is poison. *We* are the destructive force. I stand, and as I do, I hear the ping of a notification from the group text. I block each number one by one.

I walk to the door and step out into the hallway. I'm not shaking; not angry. I'm numb. I turn back toward my Pa, still sitting in the lounge chair. "It was an accident, you know."

Pa startles. "What are you talking about?"

"When Effa died. There was a deer in the road. Patrick swerved to avoid hitting it." Pa's eyes grow wide, then narrow with anger. And then I tell him the truth. I give the one indisputable fact that could have prevented everything. "Patrick didn't kill your sister. You've spent your whole life clinging to a lie."

THIRTY-TWO

Ten months later

"So. Tell me. How are your exams going?" Dr. Towers, my therapist, crosses her legs and sets her legal pad in her lap. I lift a shoulder to shrug off the weight of my anxiety. "Eh, you know. Standard. They're basically killing me."

Dr. Towers's laugh reminds me of wind chimes, of summer nights on a front porch. "Exams here are tough," she says. "Birdsall's is a monster."

I cringe at the memory of my Intro to Philosophy final. "I took it yesterday."

She shudders in sympathy. "At least you got through it alive. You have how many left?"

"English and Government."

"Those should be a breeze for you."

Despite aiming for calm and genuine, my responding smile is tight. They'll be a breeze for me, yeah. Lots of writing. Lots of dry, factual analysis that requires no creativity. Nothing like what I used to write.

"Have you heard from your grandmother?" Graduation is next week. Each senior gets four tickets to the ceremony. I left three of mine on my roommate's bed.

"Deebie's coming up on Friday. Said she'd be here about mid-afternoon."

"And your grandfather?"

I shake my head. Dr. Towers's face falls, the motion tugging at my conscience. She's worked so hard to help me. Too bad some things can't be helped.

"No one else is coming for graduation? What about Nathan?" she asks.

"I'm not ready for that."

"That's fair," she says, nodding. She taps her pen against her legal pad. "You're spending the summer in Minnesott. How do you feel about that?"

I squirm in my seat, not sure how she's going to take this. "I've decided not to go back."

Dr. Towers makes a note, pen scratching. "I thought you'd want to go home for a while."

Head shake. "I don't. I'll be at State for the summer."

She makes a high pitched noise, a little *hmm* sound. "Interesting. What can you tell me about that?"

I sink my nails into my palms as I consider what to tell her. I've been dreading this all day.

Dr. Towers knows more about me than most people, but there are still a few things I haven't said. Like she has no idea about the blinks. They've stopped, so why tell her? I don't see the point in opening that mess. She knows the bare minimum about Minnesott, so whatever I tell her will probably lack *oomph.* Not that she'd care — it's more me who needs convincing. I need to know that what I'm doing is still right.

I left the hospital that night with my grandmother. Didn't speak to a soul. Packed my bags and loaded Pa's truck at five thirty the next morning. Left the camcorder on the Suttons' doorstep, and then I was gone.

Pa did keep his promise, not that Mason or the twins have any idea. The county paper printed his letter on the front page, above the fold, accompanied by a photo of Pa and Ezra. They stood next to each other at the Town Hall, Pa's wide smile glinting. Ezra looked stone-faced. Sad.

My friends have moved on with their lives, thankfully. Mom fills her weekly emails with updates from Deebie and Van's mom. She sent me a link just last week: Ezra won the award for outstanding first-year student.

I already knew about it. I stalk Broward's Instagram.

I can't go back. They hate me. They'll hate me even if I tell them the truth. That I walked away *for* them, that I didn't see any way out other than through the path ahead of me. That my cancer of a presence would be a shadow over everything for as long as I remained in their lives.

When I'm lying in bed and staring at the ceiling, too wound up to sleep, I wonder if I messed up. If I should have just talked to them about Pa's threats. But what has talking ever done? Two of those, and my mother tried to kill herself. And Ezra didn't want Griffin help, no matter how much he needed it.

I made sure he got it anyway.

"I'm ready to move on, Dr. Towers. Ready to live the next part of my life."

There's a quick twitch of her mouth and I wonder if she sees through me. "Do you remember our first appointment?" she asks.

Color heats my cheeks. Of course, I remember. I sat on this couch in absolute silence for forty-nine minutes and fifty-seven seconds.

Dr. Towers's smile is conciliatory. "You were hidden behind a brick wall. One that you'd built, one I wasn't sure you had any interest in disassembling. But you've opened up, and I have to say I'm very proud of you and your progress. You've exhibited a great deal of growth."

"Thanks," I say quietly, my eyes cast down at the floor. Dr. Towers leans down and into my line of sight, her brown eyes bright with inquiry. I look up, and mutter a quick *sorry* for my first session behavior.

"Oh, Mae. Of course, it's alright."

Dr. Towers tosses the legal pad behind her. It lands solidly on her mahogany desk. "Let's take a different approach. What's a boundary?"

"I didn't realize I had an exam for therapy."

"Humor me, Mae." She winks.

I internally roll my eyes, then straighten my back and answer. "Boundaries are relationship tools."

"And what do they do?"

"They set limits. They're like, rules for interaction, I guess."

"Would you say you've mastered that skill?"

I stop and think for a moment. "Yes, I think I have. I'd had practice setting boundaries before, so it was easier for me than some of the other techniques we've covered."

Dr. Towers leans forward. "You said you had practice. Are you referring to *before* you came to Briarwood?"

I nod, suddenly nervous. "I set some boundaries with Pa."

"What about —" she checks her notes, "Van, Ezra, and Mason? The friends you've mentioned here and there. You've made it sound like you don't keep in touch, and yet, they were very important to you."

Oh boy. Here we go. "I don't talk to them anymore."

Dr. Towers tilts her head. "Is that a boundary?"

"Yes."

Dr. Towers hums a little. "Because it sounds like an avoidance technique."

My phone buzzes. I flinch, but otherwise ignore it. It's probably my mom. Dr. Towers is right. I didn't have to cut them out. I could have said goodbye and given an explanation. I could have prevented this gaping hole in my chest.

Dr. Towers sighs. It's quiet. More sad than frustrated, I think. "Do you want to go to State? Stay there all summer?" she asks.

I don't. I shake my head, throat thick with tears and a million overwhelming emotions. "I don't think I have a choice."

———

BEAN LIBRARY IS A DOWNTOWN SANCTUARY, a refuge in coffee and books. I'm at a table up front, three pages deep into my study guide for American Government. My phone buzzes inside my bag.

It's not my Mom, as I suspected. It's not Nathan or Deebie or Pa. It's a number I unblocked in Dr. Towers's office. A number that belongs to Van.

Van: Look. You can't ignore me forever. I need to talk to you

Would you answer your texts? I know this is your number

I'll keep messaging. You know I will

She will, and I could send her right back to Blocksville.

Van: Get your finger away from that block button, girl

I sink back into the booth, my eyes surveying my surroundings.

Van: *I found you. I'm looking at you right now.*

"What, sit here? With the lovely Mae Griffin? Thank you. Don't mind if I do."

I shriek and fumble my phone. Van saves it from hitting the floor. She looks the same, but not, an elegance about her now that on anybody else would be at odds with her behavior. On Evangeline Sutton, it works.

"What are you doing here?" I whisper-shout, snatching my phone from her. "You're supposed to be in Boone."

"Semester ended last week. I convinced Mason to make a stop." I stand, twisting around like a madwoman. "Settle down. He's in the truck."

I stare at the girl across the table. Her hair's tied in a blue bandana on the top of her head. She's in a sleeveless white top — vintage, I'm guessing — and a pair of high-waisted shorts.

"I've been texting you," she says. "To let you know we were coming." Her eyes glance down at my phone.

"I had an appointment," I say. I've missed her so much, and yet, she's one of the three people I've spent the most energy in my life avoiding. More energy, really, than Mom.

Van rolls her eyes. "An appointment."

I nod. I don't elaborate. She huffs and leans her hands on the table, standing over me. "I don't have a lot of time before Mason gets impatient, so I'm going to say my piece and get out. Lil's back. She wants to see you."

It takes a minute for Van's words to register. "Lil's back? Where did she go?"

"Houston. MD Anderson Cancer Center."

Cold fear snakes up my spine. "Cancer?" I say, the word barely a whisper. Van nods, her face solemn. "Moved pretty quickly, from what I hear."

"Wait. Hold on. Is she — is she dying?"

Van twists a napkin in her hands. "It's been rough. I've been up at school and Mama's been keeping me updated. Daddy's been in rehab the last couple of months."

I gasp. "*Rehab?*"

Van's lip curls. "You don't have to say it like it's something bad."

"No, that's — that's not what I meant. I was just thinking about your brother." Wishing I could hold his hand.

"Ezra's fine," she says. "He's dealt with it. He also said I couldn't talk about him with you."

I rub the ache in my chest, fully aware I deserve that. I should explain everything right now. But Pa might find out, and I worry about the consequences. Even with treatment in progress for Gill.

"Graduation's next week," I blurt out, wincing. "After that, I'm moving in at State. There's no time for me to go back, not this summer."

Van's mouth flattens out. Her nose wrinkles. "You haven't changed one bit."

I have! I want to scream, but I'm tongue-tied. I'm held down. Cornered. Trapped. So I do what I do best: fall back on old patterns. "What is that supposed to mean?" I ask.

"Nothing," Van says, standing. "Nothing, considering the contents of your family tree."

Fire fills my veins, and I lean in closer to her. "I am *not* crazy, Van."

Van throws her hands in the air, exasperated. "I'm not even *talking* about that right now. You build walls. Huge ones. And when something spooks you, you run. So your mom got sick. You aren't responsible for her actions. But you are responsible for a handful of broken hearts. And the worst part of it all? You're so caught up in yourself, you won't come home to see a dying oldwoman." She's breathing hard, her finger in my face and her knuckles white around the napkin. "I don't know, Mae. I gotta ask you. How's all this hiding working out?"

The clench in my jaw nearly breaks a molar. "Seems like it's worked out well."

"Alright," Van scoffs. "If that's the story you're selling.

But can I remind you of one quick thing? There's a bitter old man in our hometown who's spent his *life* clinging to his tragedy. You know the damage he's done, what it's meant for my family."

"Don't. Compare me. To my grandfather."

"Why not? You're doing the same thing."

My hands slam the table and I wince a little, reining my anger in. "You have no idea why I made this choice."

"I *don't* know because you won't tell me! You won't tell any of us!"

I wish I could explain that I can't.

Van drops the shredded napkin. She bends down, reaching for her bag. I hear the zipper open and close, and when she straightens back up, she clutches the old camcorder. The one I've left at her front door twice.

"Mason was right. This detour was stupid." She sets the device down and shoulders her bag. She doesn't look back at me as she leaves, but she does turn her head and throw her last words over her shoulder.

"Nice talking to you, Griffin. I'll give your regards to Lil."

THIRTY-THREE

Maliah stands at the door of our dorm room, holding a cardboard box. "I think this is the last of it," she says, and I pretend not to hear the hopeful note behind it. I wouldn't admit this to Dr. Towers, but I've built walls instead of boundaries. I don't think I can drop them. Not now.

But I'm not rude, and sharing a room with her was pleasant, so I stand and walk to the door. I offer a smile, a feeble token that doesn't make up for the last year of closed-off behavior. "Yale's lucky to have you. You'll do great."

Maliah studies me without pretense, her head tipped to the side like she's sussing something out. I raise my eyebrows, a challenging *yes?* in my demeanor. But Maliah doesn't budge.

She nods her head toward my last box on the dresser, the camcorder bag resting on top. "We don't know each other at all, even after an entire year of rooming together. And it's not like I didn't try. But you've been staring at that camera all week, moving it from place to place in some weird sort of....active avoidance. I don't know who gave it to you or what's on there, but it's obviously important. Maybe you should quit hiding from your life."

My stomach swoops in rebellion, Maliah's words pulling tight against my skin. I *have* stared at the bag all week. I've moved it around. Come *thisclose* to tossing it out the window. But I haven't tried to figure out why Van left it.

The weird, used-to-hallucinate part of me kind of hoped it would vanish.

Poof.

Clearly, that didn't happen, because the darn thing's staring at me from across the empty room. Maliah's gone now, the bare walls, fluorescent lights, and institutional gray carpet a spotlight on the camera. There's no place else to look.

Breath catching in my throat and hands trembling, I turn the camera around in my hands. It looks the same. Feels the same. I sink down on the bed, the bare mattress sagging under the weight of my anxiety. I press the button to turn it on.

The video's blurry at first, just a mishmash of shapes and colors. "Okay," I hear my Mom whisper, and I nearly drop the darn thing. Did she go in my room? Take it from me? She must have, because I never once brought it out.

"What am I doing wrong?" Mom mutters, and I get a clear view of scraggly Minnesott grass. Mom huffs a few times and the camera jolts a little, until, "Finally..."

The camera jolts again and the video clears.

Van and I are out on the river, riding the day's swells on floats we'd tied to the pier. I remember this. It was hot — so hot, you couldn't stand on the shore without your feet burning. We gave up on spreading blankets and lounge chairs and headed out into the surf.

Mom chuckles, and I catch movement to the right of the frame. Mason's creeping up behind Van, and I watch myself jolt upright as he flips her out. I know the next moment by heart: my leap into the water, Ezra's appearance as he grabs me around the waist. I blink the tears from my eyes as I watch the two of us sink laughing below the surface.

My heart hurts. I miss them so freaking much.

The recording has more footage, brief glimpses from the summer of my heart. Sparklers on a starlit night. Bonfires and beach karaoke. Stolen kisses, group hugs, soap and water and dirty Jeep hoods. I'm grinning in every frame.

I don't know how Mom found the camera. Right now, I really don't care. And maybe it's a little weird — she got all this on film and we never even noticed. But it's something she did for me.

A single tear drops to the screen and I swipe at it, leaving a rainbow streak behind. I turn the camera off with shaking hands. I blink a few more times, enough to see what I'm doing as I put it back into the case and zip it. I dig my phone out of my back pocket.

Me: Deebie, I've changed my mind

———

RALEIGH TO MINNESOTT is three hours. I spend the drive with my stomach in knots. Deebie's made attempts at conversation, mostly about the graduation ceremony. I've hummed and nodded at appropriate intervals, grateful she hasn't pressed for more.

Pinecliff's driveway is still bumpy. The magnolias along the side are in bloom. At the end of the drive stands the house in all her Griffin glory: white columns, red shutters. Two porches and a black front door.

Deebie parks off to the left under the shade of a pecan tree. I don't move to get out. Neither does Deebie, and the two of us just sit there, the wind from the river knocking trash from the trees onto the windshield. I focus on breathing. Grounding myself.

"Did you know we used to have livestock?"

I look up at her. "What?"

"Your mama was maybe five or six. She used to follow Pa on the rounds and help him with the animals. She grew particularly attached to the hens."

Deebie's hands drop down from the steering wheel, resting quietly in her lap. "The hens were egg-layers, mostly, but they don't lay forever, you know. So they had lots of really good days, and when they were done, Luther would take them out behind the shed and get them ready for a chicken dinner. Once your mama realized what was happening…well. Let's just say all hell broke loose."

Deebie chuckles to herself, remembering. "That child took to sleeping with those hens. Crawled in there with a blanket and stayed all night; made a ruckus any time Luther came near the hen house. Eventually, he lost patience and told her those chickens were set for slaughter. She stomped her little foot and said she would find each one a retirement home. And she did. Scoured the neighborhood looking for homes for geriatric chickens. By the end of the third day, we didn't have a single one left.

"We let go of the livestock shortly after that, but that behavior was your mother to a T. She loves deep. She loves fierce. And when her love grows roots, you can't pull them up with all the salt in the ocean. She thinks with her heart first, not her head, and it's the most admirable thing about her. It's also gotten her into a heap of trouble, not unlike her baby girl."

I flush, processing her compliment. Or was it a criticism? I don't know. She goes to open her door, smiling a bit as she turns back to me. "I have an inkling as to why you came with me, though of course, I don't know for sure. Don't worry about State. I had the moving crew put your things in storage. But will you promise me one thing?"

Bewildered, I nod. What is she asking? She's never been one to make demands. "Any decisions you make," she says, "don't just think with your heart. Use the brains you've got, also." She reaches out and pats my cheek, the touch of her hand oddly comforting. "You really are like your mama. Both your roots run pretty deep."

Deebie leaves me in the car and I sit there, too twisted up to move. It's not until someone knocks on the window that I jump, then climb my way out of the vehicle. Only to come face to face with Nathan.

My dad.

"Lima Bean," he says.

"I'm just visiting. I came to see Lil. Not staying long."

I don't know if he knows. I didn't say anything before I left, and my mom wasn't in a place to talk to him. I don't even know if he's seen her since.

I clasp my hands behind my back and rock forward, my insides screaming at me to move. But Nathan just smiles at me, a tentative quirk of the lips from behind his ball cap. His presence feels like home.

I throw my arms around his neck and hug him, try to telegraph my feelings through my embrace. And while his response is stiff at first, he eventually folds me in his arms and murmurs something soothing.

"Hello, daughter. It's good to have you home."

————

MY MOTHER TOLD him in the hospital three days after she'd woken up. He'd taken my grandparents by and was waiting in the hall when Deebie dragged Pa out of the room by the elbow.

"Luther, I think it's time we let them talk."

And so Nathan went in, and he listened, and he very nearly passed out on the tile floor. "We've been talking," Nathan says, smacking at a mosquito. We're on the front porch, him with a beer, me with a giant glass of tea. Condensation keeps dripping on my legs, but it's a steady enough distraction that I don't move it. I need something to keep me grounded. Apparently, water droplets do the trick.

"Does that mean you've been to see her?"

Nathan nods. "Been driving out about once a week.

Doctors think they've found the right combo of therapy and meds, so they're looking about outpatient."

Standard Dewitt Griffin operating procedure. "They always say that," I remind us both.

"I think it's different this time. Really. She's been in there, what. Ten months? Different program. Lots of art therapy. She, uh...she really misses you." I miss her, too. My bones ache with it.

But missing her isn't enough.

"I've got pictures of her artwork. I could show them to you if you want?" Nathan's phone is in his hand, his face so bright with hope I can't say no to him. The corner of his mouth tilts up.

We flip through a dozen or so photos. The last one catches my eye. "I've seen this before," I say, and Nathan taps the photo to make it larger. It's the painting she was working on the afternoon I found the credit cards.

There are two people on the shore, a tall man dressed in faded jeans and a t-shirt. The other, a little girl, looks up at him and holds his hand.

"This is…"

"It's us." He clears his throat. "Well, it's you and me, specifically. I don't mean to presume anything by calling this — he gestures between us — "an *us*."

I run my fingers over the screen. It *is* us. Father and daughter. A what-could-have-been, courtesy of my mom. I sniffle, fighting the press of moisture behind my eyelids. Nathan hands me a tissue. "Since when have you started carrying those?"

Nathan chuckles, wiping at his own eyes indiscreetly. "Don't know what it is about the air around here, lately, but I've been getting allergy attacks left and right."

I give him a playful shove and I'm rewarded with laughter, the kind that resonates in my soul. It takes root in my chest, crowding out the ache I've felt for just about forever, easing the fear of what comes next.

THIRTY-FOUR

Lil's hair is purple. It's also really short. From my spot at the edge of the pines, I watch her run a bony hand through it. She's thinner than I remember, her collarbone more pronounced.

"Go on," Nathan says, his hand on my shoulder. "Go talk to her. I'll be here, cleaning out the brush."

"I've done yard work with you for years, Cartwright. I can tell you've just cleaned this."

He winks at me. "I think I missed a few spots."

Nathan turns and pulls a pair of clippers from the golf cart and motions toward the house. "Y'all need to clear the air. Lil's got some things to say, and I imagine you've got your share to unload, also. I know you, and I know you left that dent in her trailer door."

I flatten my lips. "I was angry."

Nathan points to a pair of work gloves and I hand them to him. "Oh, believe me, kid. I know."

I look down at the ground, ashamed it was so obvious. "What if I don't know anything else?"

"Aside from being angry?" he asks me.

"And resentful, yeah."

Nathan uses a gloved hand to squeeze my shoulder. "You won't know unless you try."

I blink at my eyes' sudden blurriness. "My therapist would like you," I say.

"I'm a likable guy," he smiles, then tips his chin up at the farmhouse. "How long you gonna make her wait?"

A bead of sweat drips down my nose as I reach the front porch steps. "There you are," Lil sighs.

"Here I am." I lift my hands in a plaintive, *It's me!* gesture. "Your hair is purple."

She smiles. "Tried something new when it came back."

I swallow and look behind me. Nathan lifts the clippers in a salute. I take a deep breath and count the steps — one, two, three before Lil reaches for me, scooping me into her arms.

Hugging the old Lil was soft, like the center of a marshmallow. Hugging the new Lil's like getting cozy with a stick. "Sit down," she says, but I shake my head and lean against the railing. "I think I'd rather stand."

The expression on Lil's face freezes and I shuffle awkwardly from left to right. "It was a long drive," I say, desperate for something to ease the sting of my rejection. "My legs are kind of tired."

Lil gives a curt nod. I don't think she believes me, but I'm grateful she lets it go. "Well, I'm gonna sit," she says and sinks down into the closest rocker. "It's good to see you again, shug."

"It's good to see you, too," I say, because I'm supposed to. I haven't figured out if I mean it yet. The breeze picks up as conversation stalls. I don't know what to say. I don't know why I'm here, except that Van said Lil wanted to see me.

My eyes drift to the mail slot on the farmhouse door.

"The letter was a bad idea, wasn't it?" The corner of Lil's mouth tilts up.

"I mean…" I pull my lips to the side. The letter was a gut punch. "I would have preferred seeing you before you left."

"Of course, you would have. I'm sorry. I'm sorry for everything."

"It's…okay?" I say and stand there, not sure how I feel about this.

"Are you asking me a question? Or absolving me of all my sins?"

"I don't know," I answer honestly. "I'm just here because of Van."

Lil's chuckle is soft, like the breeze off the river. "At least I know where I stand. Grab the shoebox off the entry table and bring it out here, would you? I have some things you need to see."

The old box is right where she said it was, on the antique table by the front door. I come back out on the porch and set the box down on the side table next to Lil's rocker, expecting her to open it. Instead, Lil motions to the box with a sweep of her hand, her eyes fixed on me. "Open it up," she says, and I can't believe we're doing this. Every other time we've been here, Lil's chosen what I got to see.

"Why now?" I ask, genuinely curious. "If you'd been honest from the start —"

"I've never lied to you, Mae," her voice is firm. I give her a look — I've earned the right to be a skeptic. "Never," she affirms, holding a hand up like she's taking an oath. "I never lied to you. I just…tried an indirect approach."

Indirect approach. I purse my lips together and pry the lid off the box. I'm drawn to a yellowed piece of paper first, pulling it out and running my fingers along the sepia-toned edges.

The State of North Carolina hereby recognizes the marriage of Patrick Sutton and Effa Griffin…

They were married. I swallow hard.

"How do you — *why* do you have this?"

"Effa was my dearest friend."

"So she gave you her marriage certificate? And…" I keep digging through, "a book of poetry? A letter from Patrick." I skim the first lines — he's telling her about Asheville — something about a writer's group. "Why do you have this? It's personal stuff."

"Effa's life was difficult." Lil leans her head back in her chair. "Her mother Annie was sick. Josiah'd had a falling out with the Suttons and he worried about Patrick's influence. But Effa and Patrick were so in love. I stood up for Effa when they got married, against Josiah's wishes. And then when the baby came along —"

"She was *pregnant*?"

"She found out just before she died."

I turn the news over in my head, the reality of it a filter. Like I'm looking at my mother in a new way. Pieces fall into place: her decision to run and keep her pregnancy a secret. Was she worried about repeating Effa's history?

"Effa was a poet." Lil's voice plucks me from my thoughts. I'm confused at first until I look down at the book of poetry I'm holding. *The Collected Works of Effa Griffin*.

"They were moving to Asheville so she could join a writer's group."

Lil nods. "She was worried about it, mostly because of Luther. But I told her I thought she should go. It wasn't a permanent thing, the move, and the time away from Josiah would have been good for her. She gave me her letters, the book, her marriage certificate. Asked me to keep them safe."

"Were they on their way to Asheville the night of the accident?"

Lil nods. "First leg of the trip. Plan was to stop in New Bern for the night, but Josiah caught wind of it and went after them. And, well. You know the rest."

I sink down into a spare rocker, processing. "Why didn't you say something, Lil? I had all these crumbs from the blinks, and you just expected me to put everything together like I was freaking Nancy Drew."

She laughs and folds her hands together; rocks a little, back and forth. "Your mother came to see me, Mae, the night before her graduation."

"You argued."

Lil's eyes fill with understanding. "You saw it in a blink."

I nod. "The afternoon I found your letter."

She rolls her eyes a little. "Me and my brilliant ideas."

There's a long pause before she speaks again, and when she does, her voice is small. "I thought I was doing the right thing. That's all I've ever tried to do. Encourage you and your mama's gifts. Be a stand-in for sweet, brilliant Effa." Lil runs a knuckle under her eyes. "Anyway," she breathes, "when your mother came to me with a positive pregnancy test and a whole bushel of questions about Effa, I told her everything. It spooked her. A few weeks later, she was gone."

Frustration and guilt tug at my insides. Guilt because I've been so unfair to my mother; frustration because of Lil. "She stayed in touch with you, though. You knew I existed. You knew exactly where we were. Why didn't you say anything? To my grandparents? To Nathan?"

"Dewitt worried about what Luther would do. And I agreed, at least initially. I wasn't sure he would take it well."

"So you just...kept quiet."

"Not exactly, no. I mean, I did for a long time. But the more trouble your mama had, the more determined Luther was to be difficult, the more I knew I'd made a mess of things. And then you ended up here for middle school. I watched you blink on my front steps. I knew right then you were sensitive to this town, to its magic and the fabric of roots. Of family. You were the key, I thought, the opportunity for healing. If I told you everything at once, I worried it would be too much for you, like it was for your mother. I didn't want you to go running off."

A strong gust of wind pushes me backward, rocking me a

little in my chair. I look out in the yard, and there, at the top of the hill where the land slides down to the river, sit two young women, side by side. Effa's on the right—I'd know that dark hair anywhere. A blonde, long-haired beauty sits to her left. It's Lil, I'm sure, and the little hairs on my neck stand up to confirm it. I close my eyes for a second. When I open them, they're gone.

"It's not your fault, you know, what happened with your mother."

I nod toward the river. "It's not your fault either, Lil."

Lil chuckles, the sound a touch deeper than I'm used to. "Lima Bean. Ain't we a pair."

We sit on the porch in companionable silence. Lil reaches for my hand. I try not to think about how fragile she feels, the way her fingers are cold, like ice. I keep my focus on the now, instead, on Lil's wisdom and the weight of my family's history. And I think about the next steps I'm going to take.

THIRTY-FIVE

Weathered boards groan beneath my feet and I wobble, giving my sea legs a chance to kick in. I swallowed my pride and texted Van after I left Lil's, asking as nicely as I could if she'd seen Ezra. Her response was terse — *marina.* Followed by a stern warning that I should watch myself.

Her exact words were, "Hurt him and I'll cut you." *Duly noted,* I texted back. And yeah, she was direct. She was also a little violent. But I know Van, and she wouldn't have added that last little bit if she weren't thawing around the edges. Passionate, pushy Van is a good sign. Indifferent Van means you're toast.

The marina's deserted this early in the season. Despite what Van said, Ezra's not around. Physically and emotionally worn out, I plop down on the dock edge to put my feet in the water. I wince a little — it's cold. With nothing left to do but wait, I let the startled dance of a couple water skeeters entertain me. A huge part of me — the part still wary of my grand-father — wishes I could skate away like them.

About a dozen craft are moored at the marina: a couple of outboard motors, a Flying Scot, a keel. But a small pram catches my eye. No more than ten feet long, the solid-wood hull is a warm, honey color. An ache in my chest burns so deep, it's hard to breathe for a minute. That boat is Ezra Sutton's work.

The minutes pass and still no Ezra. I watch the sun dip lower in the sky. My skin's adjusted to the late-spring chill of the water but my toes have started to tingle.

Excellent.

My legs have fallen asleep.

Annoyed, I pry the backs of my legs from the decking and scoot back on my butt. I take a deep breath and stand just as some *thing* crashes into the water, the creek arcing up in a frigid blast. Startled, I wobble, and for a brief second, I think I've recovered my balance.

I haven't. I tumble straight over the edge.

I sputter my way back into the sunlight, long strands of creek grass plastered to my face.

"Crap. Mae. Hold on." I can't see for the hair in my eyes, but I'm pretty sure I know who that voice belongs to. Bouncing on my toes in the sticky creek bottom, I drag a hand across my face and blink at an outstretched hand, a lean, corded arm, a chiseled bicep and shoulder.

I'm ogling my ex-friend. Ex-*boyfriend*. My life is on repeat. Nice.

"Can you get to the ladder?" he asks me. I reach out and

grab his hand. His palm is warm. My foot connects with the bottom rung, and with a single tug, I'm propelled up and out of the water, face to face with Ezra Sutton. I shiver in my wet clothes.

Ezra wraps me in a threadbare towel, rubbing my arms and muttering under his breath. Something about *dumb chivalry* and *freaking Griffins*, interspered with an occasional curse.

"I'm fine," I say. "Thank you."

His hands still and his fingers go stiff. Our eyes meet: one heartbeat, two, then three before he blinks, shakes his head, and steps back, taking his heat with him. "Fine," he spits out, scowling. "Leave the towel in the marina laundry bin."

His back muscles flex as he heads for the boardwalk, his footfalls heavy with every step. I deserve his harsh tone, but that doesn't take the sting away. "Ezra!" I call out. "Wait!"

He stops. Like, physically stops moving. I thought for sure he'd ignore me and go. But he's standing still, his back turned, his fists clenched and turning white around the knuckles.

"Ezra, could you….could you please turn around?"

"I don't want to do this right now," he says, low and even. I panic at the pain in his voice. He starts walking again, his steady stride taking him down the slip to the pram and aboard the shiny oak beauty. I set off at a run, desperate. He releases the deck lines and pushes off.

Legs pumping and lungs heaving, I barely have time to think. I skid to a stop at the end of the slip and make a horribly rash decision. I back up, get a running start, and leap.

Time seems to slow as I propel myself forward, arms and legs windmilling the air. I don't know that I scream, but I definitely inhale about half a dozen mosquitos. Nathan will kill me if I break my neck.

"Ooof." I land hard in the middle of the sailboat, my stomach connecting with it first. It knocks the wind out of me — a great whoosh of air that leaves me breathless. My field of vision fills with stars.

In the moment it takes to regain use of my extremities, my lungs decide to reboot. I give a great, hacking cough and flip to my back, staring up at the sky as the static fades from my vision. A blurry figure looks down, eyes narrowed and full lips pulled to the side.

"What do they teach at that school you went to?"

Ezra. Ezra. Ezra. My heart pounds and I suck in a breath. "Government, philosophy, literature," I wheeze out. "The occasional grounding technique."

"Is that what that was?" he asks, still leaning over me.

"That came from a movie I watched."

Ezra barks a startled laugh but goes silent just as quickly. I giggle and it sounds like a gasp. Gingerly, I try to sit up, but I feel the press of Ezra's palm on my shoulder. "Hold on a second, Jason Bourne. I don't want you to pass out."

I get a quick triage for bumps and bruises before Ezra pulls me to my feet. We're mere inches apart, and I sway as the pram moves with the water. Ezra drops one hand to my waist, brushing the side of my face with the other one. I feel a new kind of tightness in my chest.

"Ezra, I—"

"Creek grass," he says, holding a slimy green ribbon. "You had creek grass on your ear." He flings it over the side, then turns his back to me and adjusts the tiller.

"Wait a second," I gasp, still winded. "Are you taking me back to the dock?"

He nods, but doesn't look at me. Renewed panic flares in my chest. "We should talk," I beg. "I have things I need to tell you."

He lifts a shoulder, his back still facing me. "Well, I've got nothing left to say."

I wince and rub at my breastbone. Honesty freaking hurts. So does slamming face-first into a boat, but I'll say it's worth it if he'll listen to me. "Please, Ezra. Just hear me out for a second. And then you can take me back to the dock. I'll get off the boat —" I pause to bite my lip — my chin is wobbling. "And you won't have to see me again."

Ugh, that last part kills me. I hope he still wants me in his life. Ezra stares me down, and I can tell by the set of his jaw that he's deliberating. "You got five minutes. Talk."

It's hard to get the words out initially, and it's not because I'm still catching my breath. It's the angry set of his jaw, the sneer contorting his features. The fear of what happens next.

"That night," I say, "in the hospital, my grandfather threatened me. I don't know how he found out, but he brought up your Dad's alcoholism. He threatened to write another letter. Spread it all over town."

Ezra's face is expressionless save for a slight tick in his jaw. I take a breath, reminding myself that honesty matters, even if the consequences hurt.

"Pa said I had two choices. I could go to Briarwood right then. If I went, he'd fix it all — write a glowing article about you. Retract those awful letters. If I didn't, he said he'd ruin your family for good. I didn't see another way out. He cornered me after Mom's attempt just to get what he wanted. That's when I knew you were right."

"About what?" he asks in a voice like gravel. I wrap my arms around myself. I'm cold — so cold — but Ezra doesn't move to comfort me. I shuffle to one of the boat's bench seats and sit.

"About Pa. About my family in general. We're like a cancer. Our evil just spreads. I couldn't keep doing that to you, putting you in situations where you'd get hurt because of my family."

The boat shifts as Ezra moves toward me. A light touch whispers my arm. He sits down, and it takes every bit of willpower I have not to lean into him. "Mae," he breathes, the ghost of his voice skating my earlobe. I'm afraid of what he's going to say.

I shake my head and angle away from him. He heaves a weary sigh. "Now it's my turn to ask. I need you to look at me."

"No." I want to but I can't.

I feel him stiffen beside me. "You're going to shut me out? After you chased me down. After you jumped onto *my boat* and blurted everything you just told me. You're going to crawl into your shell and hide from me, from what happened to us?"

I remember Van's words from Bean Library. "Isn't that what I do best?"

"Maybe, yeah, but I don't think it makes you happy."

I can't help the next words that spill out of me, even though they're petty. "Why do you care about that?"

Look," Ezra growls. "I'm mad and I'm hurting, but not for the reasons you think. I'm mad that I didn't get a say. I'm hurt that after everything, you didn't think you could tell me. I'm gutted that you didn't think I was someone you could trust."

His words hit me right in my center. That's exactly how I feel about my Mom. About Pa, too. About Lil, and all the truth they hid from me. "I should have trusted you. That behavior's a Griffin family flaw." I turn just in time to see Ezra's lips twitch, a tiny smile picking up the edge. "All the secrets we've kept and the hurt we've caused; it's the same thing over and over."

"Your grandfather, yeah. Your mom? Maybe. But you — you're different, Mae."

"Not hardly. It's exactly what I did to you."

He reaches out and takes my hand. "Okay, yeah. But what about right now? What are you doing?"

"Trying to apologize?"

Ezra smiles this time, a real one. "And how many grand apologies have the Griffins performed?"

"Zero," I scoff. "We're not a grand gesture family."

"Actually," he shifts my hand and holds it up, lifting my pointer finger. "I think I'm looking at the first."

My cheeks flush. I can feel it, from my neck to the top of my ears. Ezra lets our hands fall back to his lap. The last trace of anger on his face has melted. "I really hate missing you, Lila Mae."

"I hate missing you, too," I choke out, my throat tight and my insides raw. "I'm sorry I left. I'm sorry I didn't stand up to Pa. I'm sorry I was such a coward." I'm sorry, I'm sorry, I'm sorry.

Ezra drops my hand and leans forward, elbows resting on his knees. He drags a hand through his hair, and his eyes flash with frustration. I'm pretty sure that was my last chance. I promised that if he wanted me to go, I would get off this boat and walk away from him, permanently. I steel myself for the worst.

"It's okay," Ezra whispers.

I nearly fall out of my seat. "It's...it's okay?" I gasp, and the corner of his mouth curls up, the green of his eyes glittering in the afternoon sunlight. A literal horde of butterflies takes flight in my heavy chest.

"It's okay." He takes my hand again, turning my palm face up and tracing the lines of it. "Trust and forgiveness. That's love."

"You still love me," I blurt.

"I do..." he trails off.

"But?" I nudge him.

"But I'm still mad, and I'll probably be mad for a little while longer. Like, at least the next thirty minutes or so."

His dimple pops, the smirk on his face widening. I wrinkle my nose and shove him in the arm. "You...you..."

"Incredibly talented boat maker slash hottie?"

I'm smiling so big my face hurts. "You doofus!"

"That's a new one," he whispers, and he wraps me in his arms.

THIRTY-SIX

I shift gears for Ezra on the drive up to the trestle, his hand a solid weight on my knee. We jostle in our seats as he turns onto the access road, the movement mirroring the shaken nerves in my stomach. I breathe in for five, out for five. I give up and chew the inside of my lip.

"They know you're coming. I texted."

"Did you tell them what I told you?"

"No," he says, and his thumb moves back and forth against my kneecap as I downshift into neutral. He sets the parking brake. I let go of the stick, cringing at the sweat I've left behind on the knob. Ezra reaches across my seat and pulls a rag out of the glove box, capturing my hands with it. "You can do this," he says, squeezing my fingers.

"I hope you're right."

Van and Mason are in the creek below the trestle turning lazy circles in their inner tubes. Mason sees me first — his shoulders jump and he mutters something.

"Don't worry," Ezra says to me. "I got dweeb number two."

"Did you bring any water, Copley?" Ezra calls to Mason, his hand firmly wrapped around mine.

"Does hard seltzer count? Ow!" I don't have to look up to know Van just smacked him.

"The blue cooler has a bunch," she says.

My hands are shaking when Ezra cracks a bottle open, handing it to me with concern. "Take a sip," he says, and I have to admit the cool liquid does soothe my nerves a little. I start a litany of grounding exercises to try and enhance the trend.

Four things I see: Van and Mason in the water. Mason climbing out of his tube. Van grabbing his arm, expression pinched, teeth clenched as she whispers something to him. Mason shrugging her off.

Three things I hear: Their argument, like I'm under water. Van saying my name. The splashing as Mason trudges off, out of the creek and up toward the trestle.

Two things I smell: Earth. Water.

One thing I feel: Ezra's hand.

Van stands in front of me, her hand cocked on her hip. "You've decided to grace us with your presence."

Ezra breathes a warning. "Van."

She narrows her eyes at her brother, a twin stand-off that I've witnessed before. But then Van's smile breaks free and she shoves him in the arm, turning to me before speaking. "You know I'm just joshing. Had to put up a good front for the boyfriend so he thinks I'm on his side."

Van almost knocks me over with the force of her embrace. It's so effusive my water bottle goes flying. "Oops," she says. "Not sorry," and she clings to me. "It's so good to have you back."

"You're not...mad? At me?" I marvel.

"Oh, I'm beyond pissed off. But that doesn't mean I'm not gonna squeeze you 'till it hurts. We can talk it out. Hug first, yell later. I missed you something fierce."

"Same," I squeak under the pressure of her biceps.

"Vanny, let her breathe."

"Eh, she's fine. Right, Mae?"

"Not really," I manage.

"What? Oh! Sorry." She backs off a little and flexes. "Been lifting at the campus gym." She motions over her shoulder toward Mason, perched at the top of the trestle. "Let me get the brat."

Mason's the last to warm up to me, his hesitation gradually lessening as we sit on the mossy bank. I was expecting it to be hard, brutal, even, to be back here with them. It feels like I never left.

"You talk to your Pa yet about any of this?" Mason reaches for another beer. I rehashed everything that happened before I left, combined with all the new information Lil's given me.

"No. I haven't seen him yet."

"Don't wait too long," Ezra says, and I wonder if he's thinking about his father. "It only gets more difficult the longer you let things sit."

I consider Ezra's comment as we head back toward the

house. Van and Mason are in front, Van at the wheel of Mason's hatchback. Ezra and I are behind them, my brain turning with each shift of the gear.

I checked my phone before we left the trestle. Mom has called me twice. I hear Dr. Towers's voice in my head, a loop of walls versus boundaries. I sigh, frustrated. Ezra squeezes my knee.

"You want me to drop you at Pineciff?"

We're already at the edge of town. The Griffin Cemetery is just ahead on the right, set back from the road near a stand of pine trees. A dark blue Buick sedan sits on the soft shoulder.

It's my grandfather's car.

"No," I say, slowly. "Can you pull over here?"

I got an Ezra side-eye special, but he does as I ask. "The cemetery?"

I hop out of the Jeep and point to Pa's car behind me. "No time like the present, right?"

Recognition dawns on his features. He turns the Jeep off and unbuckles his belt. "I'm coming with you," he says, and my heart swells in time with my head's shake.

"Thank you, but I have to do this on my own."

I climb back up on the wheel well. He meets me halfway. "Text me if you need anything," he says before pressing a kiss to my forehead. I'm not nervous as I watch him go.

Stiff grass tickles my ankles as I cross the field in front of me. I don't see Pa, not until I'm close enough to see the headstones. He's sitting on the ground, knees bent and arms folded across his middle, leaning against his mother's grave.

Pa doesn't move as I sit in the grass beside him. I haven't seen him in months. He looks physically the same, but the confidence he had is missing. His shoulders sloop. He's weary. His face looks almost resigned.

He shifts against the stone and speaks to me. "That tree over there, by the creek."

I look ahead: there's a large live oak along the water. "Do you mean the big one along the bank?"

"Before my mother got sick, she had my father put a swing there. It was simple, just some rope and a two-by-four. We'd have picnics out here. Family time, or what have you. I loved it…" he trails off, lost in a memory. "Well. It was good until it wasn't."

I lean back on my arms. "What happened?" My cheeks color. There's so much I already know. What I don't know is what he'll say, whether or not he'll share the truth of it. I dig my nails into the earth beneath me. Anticipation zings up my arms.

"My mother had ideas. She'd get obsessed with them." Pa shifts his legs so they're straight out on the ground. "She'd get so wrapped up she wouldn't eat. Wouldn't sleep. I remember waking in the night and seeing a light on in the boathouse. And then one day she just—" he gives a sharp, quick whistle and smacks the palms of his hands. "Took off. Took Daddy's car up to New Bern. Never had a driving lesson — not one. She didn't make it to New Bern, of course. Put the dang car in a ditch off 55 close to where they built the Piggly Wiggly. Daddy was furious. Embarrassed. People started talking after that."

I pull my knees up to my chest and pick the dirt from my fingernails. I need something to do with my hands. "Talking about whom? Your mother?"

He nods, the set of his mouth giving way to a rueful smile. "We had that reputation to uphold. The Mighty Griffins. Daddy took her to a hospital up in Raleigh — one the Suttons had experience with for a cousin or something. We thought she'd be better when she got back."

In my mind, I see a listless Annie, ignoring Luther as she digs in the ground. "She wasn't better," I say, and he shakes his head, eyes shining. He holds the folder out.

The stiff paper smells like leather. I lift the front flap and set it in my lap. It's a thick stack of yellowed paper. "Medical records?"

"From her stay in the hospital."

Observation logs. Medication records. A diagnosis: manic depression. "She was bipolar," I say, the words barely a whisper.

"You've done your research, then."

There's a bit of pride in his voice, and I smile. "I took History of Psychology. I learned a lot, like the way they've changed the names of conditions. Treatment protocols they no longer use."

I keep flipping through — more logs; a doctor's evaluation.

"*They gave her a lobotomy?*"

The words come out like a whisper. There's no air left in my lungs. Annie wasn't better when she came home. She wasn't even Annie. They'd severed connections in the front part of her brain.

"Pa," I wheeze.

He takes the folder from me. "Nathan found these in a storage box."

"How long have you…"

"Last week. Asked him to clear out the shed. He brought the box up to the house. I looked through it." He points at the folder. "Her records were in that box."

I'm suffocating. Gasping. The final pieces click into place. · "That hospital. The Suttons recommended it."

"They didn't mean no harm."

My eyes go wide. Pa laughs a dry, rueful chuckle. "Surprised you, didn't I?"

I nod at him, mouth open. He smiles. "Started talking to a therapist. Ultimatum from DB. My Daddy needed someone to blame. Those doctors were far away, but the Suttons were right here, in Minnesott. He'd all but lost my mom, and then Effa as well. She was taking off with Patrick. I went with him the night of the accident because I didn't want her to go."

I close my eyes at the image of little Luther covered in his sister's blood. "You didn't see the deer."

"But you did. You're like your mama."

"Shrimp on a biscuit. You knew?"

He nods. "'Course I knew. You think I bought that *I tripped and fell off the pier* cover story? It's one of the reasons I pushed so hard for Briarwood. I thought…" he scratches at his chin, covered in coarse gray stubble. "I didn't know what I was doing. I thought someone at Briarwood could help."

"Help root it out?" My tone is snarky.

"No," he says. "Help you thrive. Every fight we had. Every choice I made, I thought I was doing the right thing for my family. My therapist is real good. Working with her, I see I was dragging us down in the name of appearances. I lost my daughter. My granddaughter. And for what? Fear and a misplaced grudge?"

I slide my hand over his. Squeeze it. It's stronger, more present than Lil's. "You haven't lost us," I insist. "I'd like to start over. Get to know you without the lies."

He smiles at me, the expression genuine. The warmth of it soothes my soul. "I reckon that will work," he says, "but on one condition. You've got to make things right with your Mom."

THIRTY-SEVEN

My mother's mental health facility, Haven, is not what I expected. Mason, apparently, agrees.

"This place is *nice*. They have trees. And gardens." He steps out into the sunlight through a red brick arch, the end of the covered walkway we've just passed through. "With Schrodinger as my witness — is that a cat?"

It is a cat. Three of them, actually, winding their way around the courtyard the way cats do.

"I'll concede the animal life is a little unexpected," Van says, wrinkling her nose at our feline welcome committee. "But otherwise," she grabs Mason by the arm before he can snag the tabby he's eyeing. "I'm impressed."

It is impressive for a residential facility. It looks more like a resort than a hospital. Plush carpeting inside. Spacious rooms that allow for independent living. Green spaces and parks and even a couple of fountains. I hope the treatment's been just as good.

Nervous, I lean into Ezra. He wraps a hand around mine. "What'd you think it would be like?" Ezra asks Mason.

"I don't know," Mason muses. "Something more…prison-ish?"

"A prison?" Van's shriek draws the attention of a nearby orderly. She gives him a friendly wave.

"Yeah, like a prison. You know, bars. Drab lighting. Residents who demand their pudding by rattling metal cups."

"This is not a Dickens novel," Van says, and she mouths a giant *I am so sorry* at me. I shake my head and smile at her. It's Mason. What does she expect?

I do have to admit, though — this group field trip wasn't the plan. Mom's being discharged today and I was supposed to drive up with Pa, Nathan, and Deebie. Except I chickened out.

Deebie found me in the back of my closet five minutes before we needed to leave. Rolling her eyes, she thrust my phone into my hand and said, "Text Evangeline." Then she tossed a pecan roll at me and left.

Sugar dusting my lips and crumbs clinging to my t-shirt, I announced the trip was off. *I'm going to hide here,* I said. *Forever and for all eternity.*

Make room for company, Van responded. Shortly after that, all four of us were headed west in the Jeep.

So we're here and only a half hour behind my grandparents and Nathan who are inside with the discharge nurse. We've been killing time outside, waiting for me to get used to the idea of seeing my mother. That hasn't happened yet.

Ezra pulls me to the edge of the walkway and cups my

cheeks with his gentle hands. "You don't have to see her, you know," he says, and I nod, watching the sunlight play in the flecks of his irises. "But if you want to, you got this. Don't let fear tell you otherwise."

Van sidles up next to us and puts her arm around me. "Sweet moment, but I've *got* to get Mason away from the cats."

Ezra looks around. "He getting clingy?"

"See for yourself," Van says.

We peer out into the sun in the middle of the courtyard. There's a cat around Mason's neck. He's got the other two, also, one in the crook of each arm.

"Oh dear," I say.

"Exactly." Van sneezes for emphasis. "No one wants to ride home with my snot."

"Let's go," I say, and I startle a little, surprised by the steadiness in my voice. Ezra's hand rests on the small of my back and I know his presence is part of it.

"Are you sure?" he asks.

"I'm going to see her at home," I say, shrugging. "Might as well get it over with."

It takes a few minutes to extricate Mason, but pretty soon we're approaching Deebie as she leans over the front desk. Her face lights up, and she shouts a warm, "Hey there, kiddos."

I cringe a little. "Seriously?"

"Hush." Van pokes me. "She can call us whatever she wants."

Deebie puts her hand on Van's head and pats it. "I've always liked you best."

Van preens while Deebie explains the discharge procedures. Then she looks at me and says, "Your Pa is just gathering some last-minute information. We've already been up to see Dewitt. Are you ready to go? I know she's looking forward to hugging you."

I stiffen in place, unable to speak until Ezra does it for me. "We'll walk up there together. Then she can decide what she wants to do."

I head for the bank of elevators, my best friends and my boyfriend on either side. "I think I might puke," I whisper, and Mason hands his hat to me. "Use this. I got an extra one in the Jeep."

"Five things you can see." Ezra leans into my ear and I melt into him, rattling off my answer to his request. We're down to one thing I can feel when we stop in front of Two Thirteen, Mom's residence. I stare at the front door. Someone's tacked her art to the wood, including the painting Nathan showed me with the man and the little girl on the shore. She's scribbled the name of the piece in the bottom right-hand corner:

Father and Daughter At Home

"I'm not sure I can do this," I say to no one in particular.

Van answers. "I'm sure you can."

"We're right here," Ezra says, "if you need us."

Heart in my throat, I knock.

"Come in."

My mother's apartment is light and airy, with western-facing windows along the outer wall. She's had afternoon sun, and the realization thaws my nerves a little. Afternoon light is her favorite.

"Mom?"

I don't see her. There's a spotless kitchen to my right. Packed boxes fill the living room straight ahead, and there's an open door leading to what looks like a bedroom.

"In here," her voice calls from the hallway. My knees buckle and I lean against the wall.

It's been a long nine months of terse, two-minute phone calls and texts I haven't answered at all. Being here feels strange, like I've opened myself up to a different dimension. My fists clench, and I dig my nails into my palms.

"You're here." Mom stands in the bedroom doorway. She's filled out. Her skin glows, waves of chestnut brown falling around her shoulders. When she smiles at me it's tentative, but her eyes are bright. Alive.

I stand there, a thousand unsaid words on my tongue. I manage to squeak out a "hi," and her smile grows as honest and true as it is brilliant. She crosses the room in four quick strides and gathers me in her arms.

"My baby girl," she whispers. "I've missed you." My breath catches in my throat. She steps back from the embrace, her cheeks heating a little as though she's embarrassed. "Sorry. I should have asked if a hug was okay."

"It's fine," I say. Mom's smile grows wistful.

"You were never good at lying to me."

I don't want it to be a lie. I want to mean it. But if I've

learned anything in my eighteen years as Dewitt Griffin's daughter, I don't always get what I want.

"Your apartment's nice," I say, fumbling.

Mom snaps to attention. "Oh, yeah, thanks. It's pretty empty now," she gestures around the space, her tone of voice apologetic. "But it's been cozy. A good space to heal."

"H-how are you feeling?" I cringe at my awkwardness.

"I feel good. Better than I've felt in a long time."

I press my lips together and nod, looking anywhere but at my mother. Her hand reaches out and rests on my arm.

"I've missed you," she says again, and I sniffle. Should I tell her I've missed her my whole life? I don't know how to say what I feel or regret, so I say nothing. I just nod and take a step back.

Mom's shoulders stiffen to match her smile. Guilt snakes its way around my heart. Desperate for a subject change, I clear my throat and motion to the boxes. "The twins and Mason are here, out in the hallway. We can help you carry this down."

"Right. Okay." Her eyes fill with disappointment. She wrings her hands together and looks around. "Let's start with these," she says, motioning to two cardboard boxes labeled *bedroom*.

"Got it." I grab the first one and head for the door.

Three ridiculously expectant faces stare back at me. I roll my eyes and shove the first box into Van's arms. "How's it going?" she whispers.

"Unbearably awkward."

"Because you're making it that way? Or is it her?"

"Van," Ezra warns.

"Don't 'Van' me, little brother. I may only be two minutes older than you, but I know what I'm doing. Step aside."

Ezra does the opposite and comes to stand beside me, his presence soothing my soul. "What my sister's *trying* to say," he rolls his eyes at her, "is that you and your mom can start over. You gave Mr. Luther a second chance. You went to see Lil even though you didn't want to. Don't let old habits keep you from opening up to your mom."

"Hey, kids."

I jump. My mom's at the doorway with a smile that doesn't reach her eyes.

"Ms. Dewitt!" Mason pulls her into a hug. "It's good to see you, Professional Artist Lady. We are here to escort you home."

Mom laughs, the sound of it filling the hallway. I need to get out of here, right now. "We should get the rest of your stuff," I say, then turn on my heel with Ezra's words on a loop and my stomach churning. I know I'm not being fair.

My friends make quick work of Mom's belongings, their meaningful glances driving me nuts. With the last box in her hands, Van turns at the threshold and levels a look at me and my mother. "Don't come downstairs until you've figured yourselves out."

I open my mouth to protest, but Van shushes me. "Lila Mae Griffin, you heard what I said. This reunion's been a long time coming and Miss Dewitt, I apologize for overstepping my boundaries. But the two of you are just so...

so….*stubborn*," she spits the word out. "The whole lot of y'all Griffins are."

The elevator dings at the end of the hallway. "Ezra Sutton, don't you dare make me take the stairs!" Van takes off down the hall, a pleasant wave and a "Take your time! No need to rush!" thrown over her shoulder.

And then my mother and I are alone.

"Well," she breathes. "I'll just get my purse, then." I watch her disappear through the door. I lean against the frame and blink back tears, my eyes catching on the portfolio resting on the kitchen counter. I don't know if Mom brought it out when I wasn't looking. Or maybe I just didn't see it before.

The leather's cool in my hands as I flip the folder open, a half-dozen pieces nestled inside. The first two are of the shore, followed by a handful of pieces she must have done here in the garden. I open the last slot and gasp, pulling the canvas out with shaking fingers.

"I did that one from memory."

I drop the painting. "Shoot, Mom. I'm sorry."

She tilts her head to the side. "About what?"

"About this," I say, gesturing to her portfolio. "I didn't ask if I could open it. I just…"

She puts a hand over mine and squeezes. "Lima Bean. It's fine." She points with her free hand to the canvas I dropped, her eyes soft as she reviews it. "What do you think? Do you like it? I wanted to capture the two of us last summer before…well. Before everything."

My mom's work tends toward realism. For the most part, she paints what she sees. And I guess there are elements of that here, from the clear central image of my mother and me laughing on the porch swing. I remember this day, last summer. She got it right, down to the outfits we both wore.

"You were spying on us all summer."

"I wouldn't call it, spying, per se." Mom leans over the canvas, her fingers trailing the more abstract, outer images. They're little glimpses of the life we had for those few solid weeks in Minnesott — moments she shared with her parents, or Gill and Rosie. Moments I shared with my friends.

Which reminds me. "You recorded us."

She pulls a face. "I did. I saw you with the camera that first night. And then you didn't bring it back out, not that I saw, anyway. You'd given up so much for me. That summer, you were living. I went into your room and found the camera. I didn't want you to forget."

I study the painting in my hands, lost in the fine details. There's a quiet mist that swirls around each vignette. And I know what it is without having to ask — she used her brush to capture my ability. The thing I fought so hard to hold at bay, to keep a secret.

She's made it beautiful. For me.

"I'm not going to push you to talk to me. Van's like her mother, I think. They both mean well, but sometimes...." Mom shakes her head. "I just want you to know that I love you. I've made a lot of mistakes, and I can't promise I won't make more of them. But I've been talking with Dad. Trying to patch things up with Nathan. I'd like to have the same chance with you."

My lip quivers and I bite it. Tears press against the back of my eyes. "I've made mistakes, too." I sniff. "A lot of them. I never should have shut you out."

Mom shrugs. "We do what we know, Mae Griffin. A common pattern in our family line."

"How do we break it?" My voice is soft — barely a whisper. She pulls me to her as a tear rolls down my cheek. I close my eyes and inhale the warm scent of her, linen, lavender, and turpentine.

"I don't know," she says in my ear, lovingly. "I don't know, but I want to try."

The truth is, I don't know either. My life's become one big *I don't know*. But maybe that's okay. Maybe I don't have to know anything yet, except that I am loved unconditionally. That fear doesn't have to rule my life. That the normal I've been chasing is just whatever I make of it.

"Okay, Mom," I whisper back to her. "I'm ready to give it a try."

EPILOGUE

TWO YEARS LATER

"Do not, under any circumstances, let Caleb light the candles. We all know what happened last time."

"I don't think he was there," I whisper to Mason, motioning to John, the drummer he hired.

"Really?" Mason asks.

"Really," I tell him.

Mason grimaces. "Whatever. Just don't give the guitarist a lighter. Or a cigarette. *Definitely* don't give that kid a joint."

John nods at Mason. "Nothing flammable. Got it." Then he turns on his heel and speed walks toward the reception like the hounds of hell are chasing him.

"Think you put the fear of God into him, then?"

He wipes the sweat off his brow. "I don't know about you, but I am *not* in the mood to put out fires. The Treetorns are here because your mom and Cartwright asked me. This is our one and only stop on this little reunion. We gotta get it right."

I squeeze his arm. "You're the best. Also, a weirdo."

He winks at me. "I aim to please."

"Well if that's the case, do me a solid? Grab me a glass of merlot." Van sidles up next to him, her 1940s-inspired engagement ring glinting in the sun. The baby blue of her vintage cocktail dress sets off the green of her eyes.

"As you wish, my lady." Mason snaps his suspenders and he's off.

"Those were a good call," I say, nodding at the pinstripe pant-and-suspender combo the men in the bridal party have on.

"You're just saying that because my brother looks hot."

He does. I'm not gonna lie about it. I about died this morning when he showed up at the church. With his sleeves rolled up. Sporting that ridiculous bowtie I thought would look awful.

I dragged him outside and around the back of the building for a fiery pre-wedding smooch.

"Speaking of your brother, where is he?" I smooth the chiffon layers of my dress. It's so long, Ezra had to help me hold the skirt while he walked us up the aisle. Van gave me the side-eye from her spot next to her mother, mouthing, "*You should have worn the heels.*"

Van pulls her phone from her dress pocket. As the unofficial wedding coordinator, she's excelled. "They should be here soon." Her eyes narrow a bit, and I get a little nervous. It's the same look she had before she threatened the organist.

"If they're not here in the next five minutes, I'll call him. Pictures shouldn't take this long."

"It's fine." I shrug. "Everybody looks happy."

Van looks up from her phone and gives the crowd a once over. "You know, I believe you're right."

About a hundred or so guests mill in front of Lil's farmhouse, drinking a signature cocktail called The Monet. Rob from The Silos made it up, and I was pleased that his choice of ale came from Anchor Brewing Company. He got both of my parents' interests in one libation swoop. Deebie and Pa are holding court on the porch steps, welcoming guests as they tour the house. Faint strains of music float from the back, where the twins, Mason, and I spent hours stringing fairy lights from the live oaks. I made the table centerpieces from seashells and Spanish moss.

Six months ago when Nathan asked Mom to marry him, I never imagined we would be here. Everything is perfect, from the things we can't control, like the weather, to the ethereal netting over the pecan roll bar. Even Miss Mary's here, in her Sunday suit and pillbox hat with the veil on the front of it.

The only thing missing is Lil.

I clear my throat, eyes misty, just as Ezra's turquoise Jeep pulls up. The guests in the yard break into applause as Nathan leaps from the car and opens the door for my mother. Her hair is down, the ivory skirt of her dress blowing in the wind along with it. They look over at me, eyes shining. I blow them a happy kiss.

"Go get your man," Van says to me. "I've got to get your parents sorted out." She runs off toward the Jeep, grabbing her wine from Mason's hand and taking a sip without spilling any of it. Mason just stands there, head shaking, a besotted smile on his lips.

"We'll be doing this again next year," Ezra whispers, and I shiver against his breath at my ear. I lean back into his arms, eternally grateful.

"You think they'll get married here?" I ask him.

"Twenty bucks says they elope."

"I don't know. I think we're making a Charleston to Boone road trip."

He squeezes me. "I'll take that bet." Then he turns me around in his arms, his eyes bouncing between mine, warm and searching. "I should head on back, see if your dad needs anything. You want to hang here a while still?"

I know what he's asking. After all the time we've spent together, he can feel it in the air. I nod at him, and he presses a quick kiss to my lips before shooing the remaining guests to the reception proper. He's the last one through the door, and the golden light of afternoon dances on his skin as he mouths the words "*I love you.*"

Leaving me in the yard with Lil.

She doesn't speak, but I know she sees me. That's one of two blink-related things that have changed. The first one is *who* I see — my ancestors have gone quiet. The second is *how* I see them.

Lil is aware of me.

She looks healthy here, her long hair back and in a braid over her shoulder. The color's returned to her cheeks. She nods at me once, then disappears — a fine mist that feels like sea spray.

And the sound, the sound of the wind and the waves and her voice carrying over the water is quiet. So quiet.

Go on, Mae. Take the leap.

THANKS FOR READING BLINK AND WE'LL MISS IT

Not quite ready to leave Minnesott Beach? No worries! You can download additional bonus scenes at www. ginnykochis.com.

AUTHOR'S NOTE

While I've changed some of the details to fit Mae's story, Minnesott Beach, North Carolina does, in fact, exist. It's a beautiful little town along the Neuse River, about forty miles from the Atlantic Ocean and the southern edge of the Outer Banks.

The indigenous Algonquin tribes called the area "TaTaku," the place where land and sky meet the water. It's true: you really can stand on the shores of the Neuse and have a hard time discerning one from the other. It's a place unlike any I've visited on earth.

I am privileged to have roots there, first planted in the late sixteenth century. My grandmother was born in 1904 in a still-standing white farmhouse in town. She and her sisters were a wild, creative bunch, each with her own quirk or difference. My great-aunt Lila Gray struggled the most out of all them. Her story became the inspiration for this book.

I thank God every day that mental health issues are no

longer as taboo as they once were. We've still got a long way to go, but as someone who comes from a long line of brilliant, differently-wired women, I can't help but be grateful for the change. We can talk about mental health now. Therapy doesn't have to be a secret. And being different isn't something we have to fear. We can be who we are, unique and unrepeatable — exactly as God designed us to be.

If you find yourself reflected in the pages of Mae's story, I hope it is a comfort to you. Please don't be afraid to reach out, to speak up, to ask for support or to be someone's support system. You are needed, you are loved, and you are valued. The world is brighter because you exist.

If you are struggling and need help, reach out to your loved ones or the following organizations:

- IASP worldwide at https://findahelpline.com/i/iasp
- National Suicide Prevention Hotline at https://988lifeline.org/

ACKNOWLEDGMENTS

Three years ago I got a text from my friend, Rob.

If I can write a book, anybody can do it. I think you should give it a try.

Rob had written four by this point, his *Avery and Angela* series. I kept telling him it was too hard. That creative nonfiction was my thing, that I was good at telling real stories. I didn't have the imagination to make up a world and its events and the people in it.

I was wrong.

Robert Kugler was right.

This story has been on my heart for two decades. It's miraculous to finally see it on the page. Thank you, Rob, for giving me the nudge that pushed me over and for providing generous, invaluable support as a friend, critique partner, beta reader, and editor. This book owes much to you.

To my editor, Erin Broestl. You are the absolute best.

Anyone who puts up with my em dash abuse and flagrant disregard for standard comma conventions should be nominated for sainthood. This is my official endorsement for you.

To my critique partners and beta readers: Sheila Doherty, Meggie Daley, Maryann Eberle, Bobbie DeLong, Leigh Ebberwein, Erin Lewis, Zephyr Thomas, Julia Miller, and Colleen Pressprich, just to name a few. After three complete rewrites and a million revisions, I think we finally got it right.

To Kirsten Oliphant and the Create If Community for invaluable insight and support.

To the Lit Chicks, Betsy, Jen, Julie, Maureen, and Ross. I am so grateful to have you ladies in my corner as readers, reviewers, and friends.

To Erica, who has seen more versions of this novel than I can count. Thank you for being you, friend. Even if it's just going to the Air and Space Museum, I'm proud of us for doing hard things.

To Dr. Hilary Towers. A million times over, thank you.

To my Dad. I miss you. Thank you for making me a reader.

To my Mom and my sister, the two most wonderful women in my life. Thank you for talking me down off the ledge and being my personal cheering section.

To my daughter, Gray, for the cover illustration; my daughter Brinson, for video editing advice; my son, Finley, for all the awesome hugs and unintentional insight into Mason's character. I love all three of you. I am lucky to be your Mom.

To my husband, Dan, for believing in me, especially when I couldn't believe in myself.

To God, for pretty much everything, really.

And finally to you, my reader. Thank you for giving this book a chance.

ABOUT THE AUTHOR

Ginny Kochis writes books for the unique and unrepeatable, for teens and adults who don't quite fit the mold. She tells stories about love, friendship, faith, and family starring differently-wired characters. While Ginny lives in Northern Virginia with her husband and three children, she's happiest on the shores of the Neuse River. All she needs is her family splashing around in the water and a good book in her hand. *Blink and We'll Miss It* is her fiction debut.

Have a question for Ginny? Want a glimpse of the real Minnesott Beach? Looking for solid reviews of books for teens and adults featuring differently-wired characters? Come see her on Instagram or at www.ginnykochis.com.

instagram.com/authorginnykochis

Printed in Great Britain
by Amazon